P9-BYU-146

THE RED THREAD

ALSO BY ANN HOOD

Comfort

The Knitting Circle

An Ornithologist's Guide to Life

Somewhere Off the Coast of Maine

Do Not Go Gentle

THE RED THREAD

a novel

ANN HOOD

W. W. NORTON & COMPANY
New York • London

Printed in the United States of America
First Edition

For information about special discounts for bulk purchases, please contact W. W. Norton Special Sales at specialsales@wwnorton.com or 800-233-4830

Manufacturing by The Courier Companies, Inc.
Book design by Chris Welch
Production manager: Andrew Marasia

Library of Congress Cataloging-in-Publication Data

Hood, Ann, 1956-
The red thread : a novel / Ann Hood. — 1st ed.
p. cm.
ISBN 978-0-393-07020-0 (hardcover)
1. Mother and infant—Fiction. 2. Loss (Psychology)—Fiction.
3. Adoption—Fiction. 4. Adoptive parents—Fiction.
5. Birthmothers—Fiction. I. Title.
PS3558.O537R43 2010
813'.54—dc22

2009042605

W. W. Norton & Company, Inc.
500 Fifth Avenue, New York, N.Y. 10110
www.wwnorton.com

W. W. Norton & Company Ltd.
Castle House, 75/76 Wells Street, London W1T 3QT

1 2 3 4 5 6 7 8 9 0

For Annabelle

There exists a silken red thread of destiny. It is said that this magical cord may tangle or stretch but never break. When a child is born, that invisible red thread connects the child's soul to all the people—past, present, and future—who will play a part in that child's life. Over time, that thread shortens and tightens, bringing closer and closer those people who are fated to be together.

ORIENTATION

A bird does not sing because it has an answer. It sings because it has a song.

1

MAYA

In her sleep, Maya dreamed of falling. But in her waking life, she was as solid as a tombstone. People relied on her. They trusted her for support and help and advice. That was why she sat in her friend Emily's kitchen listening to Emily complain about her marriage and her stepdaughter Chloe and her childless suburban life. The kitchen had been decorated to look like something in the French countryside, all exposed wood and large stones. The fact that Emily didn't cook made the kitchen even more ridiculous.

"Why are you grinning?" Emily asked.

Maya said, "You don't even like France and you have these big signs hanging here." Maya pointed to one with a huge pink pig and the word *cochon* written in white below it.

"I do like France," Emily said. "I just didn't like my so-called honeymoon there, driving around with Chloe in the backseat grumbling and getting carsick."

"I know," Maya said. She patted her friend's hand. "An eleven-year-old should not be on a honeymoon."

"We had to keep finding pay phones so she could call her mother and tell her how miserable she was. And those phone cards never worked." Emily sighed. "It has been downhill from there."

Maya looked out the window, to the terraced garden. The flowers there were arranged by color, all of the oranges together, then the yellows and pinks. Weren't flowers meant to commingle? she wondered. Hummingbird feeders hung above the flowers, swaying slightly in the late spring breeze.

"Do they come?" Maya asked.

"Hummingbirds?" Emily shook her head. "I seem to be able to keep everything small and fragile away."

Once, when she had lived in Hawaii, Maya had watched a variety of hummingbirds dart in and out of a feeder in her neighbor's yard. They were as tiny as bumblebees, those hummingbirds. Their heart beat, she knew, at a rate of 1,260 beats per minute. Like the racing heart of a fetus, she thought.

"Not like you," Emily was saying. "You give people life. You give them hope."

Maya Lange ran the Red Thread Adoption Agency. It placed babies from China with families in the United States. In the eight years since she'd opened the agency, she had heard about every fertility treatment available. She had seen more broken hearts than she could count. With over four hundred babies placed, a person might think that by giving these families their babies, her own heart would have healed. But hers still felt like someone had punched a hole in it.

"A woman in my Pilates class told me that I might be allergic to Michael's sperm," Emily continued. "There's a doctor in

Philadelphia who injects women with their husband's sperm to build up antibodies. She said that after ten treatments you can maintain a pregnancy instead of reject it."

Maya did not answer her friend. Long ago, she had buried her own secrets. They belonged only to her, and a man she no longer spoke to. Sometimes she wondered if he too remained haunted. Guilt did that to a person. It made you silent, afraid, alone. It made you listen to other people's pain but keep your own to yourself.

"You think that's weird," Emily said.

Maya shook her head. "Nothing is weird on the path to parenthood."

"You sound like your own brochure," Emily said.

"Do you know what I do find weird, though? The garden. Why are the flowers separated like that?"

"Like what?" Emily said, frowning.

"By color. One of the wonderful things about flowers is how orange looks good next to purple, and pink and red are beautiful together. If we dressed that way, we would look absurd. But flowers were meant to mix like that."

"The landscaper did it," Emily said. "It was all her idea."

The women were quiet, each gazing out at the sunlight-drenched garden, lost in their own thoughts. The expanse of the wooden farm table lay between them.

"Except the feeders," Emily said quietly. "I hung those. I wanted to bring hummingbirds here."

Maya thought again of those tiny hummingbirds in her neighbor's yard. "Once . . ." she began.

Emily looked at her expectantly.

Maya shrugged. "Just a hummingbird story," she said. "Not even a story, really."

The sound of the front door opening and the noisy arrival of Emily's husband Michael and his friend broke the somber mood. A familiar, uncomfortable feeling settled in Maya's stomach.

Emily leaned closer to Maya. "Your boyfriend's here."

Maya rolled her eyes. "Please," she said.

Emily had taken it as her mission to find a man for Maya, despite Maya's insistence that she had no desire for a relationship. Everyone needs human contact, Emily had argued. Even Maya Lange. That began a steady stream of mismatched dates that had gone on for too many months. On Friday nights, Maya drove from her house in Providence to Emily's home twenty minutes away in the suburb of Barrington. The town had curvy roads lined with stone walls, leafy trees, oversized houses set away from the road. The only parts of them visible were the turreted roofs and soft glowing lights.

Michael came into the kitchen, his necktie already loosened, the latest victim trailing behind him. When Michael bent to kiss Emily hello, Maya warily studied her date. All of the men seemed the same: balding, belly just beginning to stretch, nice suit and polished shoes. This one wore glasses, those narrow rectangular ones everyone wore to look hipper or smarter than they actually were.

"Jack," he said, extending his hand.

Maya shook it quickly.

"How about a Stella?" Michael called, opening one massive door of the stainless steel refrigerator.

"Sounds good," Jack said.

"Can you open a bottle of chardonnay for us?" Emily said.

Michael pulled out the beer and a bottle of wine and set about getting glasses for everyone.

"Why don't you have a seat?" Emily said to Jack, who stood awkwardly in the kitchen.

"Shouldn't we go into the living room?" Michael said. "Get comfortable?"

He placed drinks on the table, then returned to the refrigerator for hummus and dips, a platter of vegetables.

"Why don't you go on?" he said. "I just want to call Chloe and see how her game went."

"Lacrosse?" Jack asked, dipping a baby carrot into the hummus.

But Michael was already dialing the phone, and Emily had started to gather the food. Jack shrugged, and followed Emily out. For a moment, Maya stayed seated. She wanted to be in her own small house, safe from blind dates, the awkwardness of a goodbye kiss.

"How'd it go?" Michael gushed into the phone.

Sighing, Maya grabbed the wine bottle and her glass, and headed toward the living room.

THEY ALWAYS ATE at the same restaurant on these double dates, a dark, low-ceilinged place that claimed to have been there since the eighteenth century. The food was always off a bit, an onion jam that overpowered the meat, or a too-mustardy vinaigrette. But part of the charade was to pretend she loved the food, so Maya commented on how interesting it was, what a daring chef. She drank too much wine and talked too little.

While Emily and Michael discussed desserts, Jack caught Maya's eye and smiled. It was a warm smile, and it touched her, as if they might have something in common. Unexpected tears came to her eyes, and she focused on the dessert menu, with its complicated combinations of chocolate and brie, sage ice cream, and lavender crème brûlée. The oddities of the desserts, that strange need to mix sweet and savory, struck Maya as sad.

The image of her ex-husband struggling to make a perfect pie crust came to her. She had craved apple pie, and to please her he set about making one. A scientist, he had worried over the temperature of the butter, the proportion of lard to flour, the use of ice water. This is why I study jellyfish instead of culinary arts, he had said to her. Sweat made his hair stick to his forehead and he looked boyish in that small kitchen. Outside the window, a palm tree stood guard, and the smell of frangipani turned the air sweet. He had kissed her then, his hand lingering on her stomach.

"You okay?" Jack asked her. His voice was low and he leaned across the table toward her.

"I was just thinking of apple pie," she managed to say.

He smiled, revealing crinkles at the corners of his eyes. "Good old-fashioned apple pie," he said. "Yes."

Maya tried to return the smile.

"I know a place where we could get some," he said. "Leave these two to their sage and lavender."

For a moment, Maya allowed herself to imagine it, eating apple pie with this nice man, enjoying an intimacy, a kiss, the promise of another date.

But she shook her head. "The drive home," she said. "Thanks, though."

Briefly, she saw the disappointment in his face, as if he had failed somehow. She wanted to tell him that he had done nothing wrong, that it was her inability to get close to someone again, that she destroyed things she loved. But the look passed from his face and he turned his attention to Michael.

Emily tugged on Maya's sleeve. "Ladies' room?"

Maya followed her into the small bathroom intended for one person, pressing against the wall so Emily could close the door.

"He's nice," Maya said. "The nicest so far."

"But you won't go get apple pie with him?" Emily said. She

twisted strands of her chestnut hair around her finger so that it looked tousled. Then she carefully applied lipstick, and blotted it on a tissue. The women's eyes met in the mirror. "Of course I was eavesdropping."

"I might see him again," Maya said. "But the drive—"

"Uh-huh." Emily leaned toward Maya and smudged the lipstick on her lips. "Better," she announced.

"If he asks," Maya said, "I'll give him my number, okay?"

Emily shrugged, but Maya could tell she was pleased.

"Maya?" Emily said, when Maya turned to leave. "Maybe it's time for you to help us get a baby." Her green eyes were teary. "I mean, Philadelphia and sperm injections. Maybe it's time, you know?"

Maya touched Emily's arm. "There's an orientation Monday night. Why don't you and Michael come and get the information. No commitment."

Emily wiped the corners of her eyes and nodded.

Once again, she stopped Maya when she turned to leave.

"Have you ever thought about doing it?" she asked.

Maya frowned.

"Adopting a baby yourself?" Emily said. They had been friends for almost five years, ever since they'd met at a Lucinda Williams concert at Lupo's Heartbreak Hotel in Providence. Sitting beside each other that night, they'd laughed at how each of them sang along under their breath, how they'd both cried when she sang "Passionate Kisses." This was before Emily had married Michael, and the two women had grown close over dinners at New Rivers restaurant and Saturday afternoons sitting through two or three movies in a row. Still, Emily asked the question with hesitation.

The bathroom was so small that the women's bodies pressed

against each other lightly. Maya could smell the floral cleaning solution, and a faint whiff of hairspray. Emily was her closest friend, but Maya could not tell her how once, when she'd first opened the Red Thread Adoption Agency, she had filled out all the forms to adopt a baby herself only to balk when she imagined questions about her character. Somewhere, there were records about everything. She'd had a family get denied over a DUI in college, another over an adolescent shoplifting charge.

Maya shook her head.

Emily studied her face for a moment, as if she knew Maya was lying.

"Maybe someday," Emily said finally.

"I'm glad you're doing it," Maya said, relieved to turn the conversation away from herself.

Hunan, China

WANG CHUN

"Who will get this baby?" Wang Chun asks out loud. "Who will take her in and cherish her?"

She lifts her baby daughter to her breast and guides the nipple to the child's mouth. This baby is slow to suck, as if she knows her fate. Chun wills herself to keep such thoughts from her mind. It is all yuan, *destiny. To think of her daughter's fate will not change it. Hadn't her mother told her, "The sky does not make dead-end streets for people"? Hadn't her husband said when the first pains began just five days ago, "Remember, Chun, we can have many more babies if we must"? Hadn't he told her this morning as she set out from their home with this baby in the sling, bouncing gently against Chun's hip and still-swollen stomach, "Remember, Chun, a girl is like water you pour out"? And hadn't she nodded when he said this, as if she agreed with him, as if she too believed a daughter was just water that you poured out and let flow away?*

The child's sucking is lackluster and weak, and for an instant Chun's heart lifts. Perhaps this baby is sickly. Perhaps her weak sucking is a sign that she would not live long. Chun almost smiles at the idea. If she is going to lose her daughter anyway, wouldn't it be easier now at only five days old than later, at five months or even five years? But then, as if the baby reads Chun's thoughts, she latches onto the nipple hard and begins to suck noisily, voraciously. The baby lifts her eyes toward Chun, eyes that until this moment have not focused on anything at all. Instead, they have been cloudy and half shut, like a kitten's. Now the baby settles her solemn gaze right on Chun's face and sucks the milk from her breast hard as if to say, No, Mother! I am here to stay!

Chun wants to look away, but she cannot. Their eyes—mother's and daughter's—stay locked until the baby has her fill. She hiccups softly, then lets her jaw go slack without dropping the nipple completely. It seems she does not want to let go.

"You must," Chun says softly. "You must let go." She intends these words for her infant daughter. But somehow she seems to be speaking them to herself.

The sun is setting, turning the sky a beautiful lavender, the clouds violet and magenta and gray-blue. Chun has not allowed herself to call this baby anything. But now she leans forward to kiss the top of her daughter's head, and as she does so she whispers, "Xia"—colorful clouds.

Then Chun takes the now-sleeping baby and settles her into the basket. She places the cotton blanket over her snugly, being sure to tuck it in tight. The basket is of a type particular to her village. Someone who knows her village, who has traveled the seven hours down the back roads, past fields of kale, would recognize this basket. They would see this sleeping baby in this particular basket and know where she had come from. The blanket too might provide a clue. It is made of pieces of Chun's own clothing, with fabric bought in the village. The purple and navy blue cotton had been her own pants and tunic. She cut them carefully into squares and sewed those squares together the day after the baby was born, knowing what she would have to do. But a person who had visited her village might be able to say that this fabric came from there.

Chun chides herself for her sentimentality. It is a bad idea to leave clues. Her very own neighbor was recently caught leaving an infant daughter in this very city where Chun now stands staring down at Xia. This neighbor brought the baby right up to the door of the social institution, leaving her in a box that had held melons sold in the village market. She had placed the baby there at sunrise, then stood half hidden behind cars parked in the yard.

When the head of the institution arrived for work, she saw the woman there and said sternly, "You! What are you doing in this yard?"

Of course the neighbor tried to run, but either fear or guilt kept her there, frozen to that spot behind the cars, crouched and trembling.

"You do know that I am legally obliged to call the police if you have left something here?" the woman said. Her eyes darted to the doorway where the box sat with the baby inside.

"Is that yours?" the woman said, her voice kinder now. "I will turn around, and when I look in your direction again, you and your belongings should be gone."

The woman did just that. She turned around and waited several minutes.

Chun's neighbor ran to the door and took her daughter from the box that had held melons and fled that yard. When she returned home later that day, dusty and hungry, with the baby in her arms, her husband slapped her so hard that she fell to the floor.

What else could he do? Chun's husband asked her when she told him this story which the neighbor herself had told Chun. And Chun had answered, Nothing. There was nothing else he could do.

She did not tell her husband the rest of the story, how the neighbor's husband had taken the baby from her, and set off down the road that led out of the village himself. He left instructions for his parents to not let his wife back in the house until he returned. Luckily it was summer, and the woman slept in the garden and ate the radishes that grew there. Her breasts began to leak milk, and to grow hard and painful from the need to nurse her daughter. Inside, her older daughter peered from the window, curious about her mother sitting alone in the dirt with large wet circles spreading across her cotton dress. But the child was too young to ask questions or to help her mother, who began to wail as time passed and her breasts ached and overflowed and her husband did not return.

That night she slept outside in the dirt, and the next day she ate radishes for breakfast, and then, out of her mind from pain and grief, she unbuttoned her dress and squeezed the milk from her breasts even though she saw her mother-in-law staring at her. Her lip where her husband had hit her felt swollen and she could still taste the iron of her blood there. And she bled from her recent childbirth so that the inside of her legs felt sticky. Her breasts could not seem to empty of their milk and ached even more.

When her husband came home empty-handed that afternoon, he did not let her in. He did not even make eye contact with her. He simply ignored her. The sounds of her husband and their daughter and her in-laws making dinner and eating together, the smells of ginger and hot pepper, all of it assaulted her. She called to them to let her in, to give her food. But it wasn't until the next day that he appeared at the door and motioned her inside.

What have we learned from this? Chun's husband had asked her.

She shook her head.

Number one, he said: Leave the child when it is dark. Number two: Walk away. Number three: Do not go to the institution.

Number four, Chun said.

Number four? her husband asked, confused.

Number four, Chun said, do not love the child.

DARKNESS HAS FALLEN. *It is time.*

Chun lifts the basket carefully so as not to wake Xia. She emerges from the cluster of trees at the edge of the park and walks across the grass, past the abundant flowers, to the pavilion. Tomorrow is the first day of the Flower Festival and this now-empty park will be filled with people. Someone is sure to find this basket from the distant village with the baby girl inside it, and when they see the precious gift there that person will surely take Xia to the appropriate place.

She has been told not to wait to be certain this happens. Her husband has warned her to walk away. But the night is so dark and the basket looks so small, like a toy, that Chun finds she cannot leave. She stands in the dark, silent park, hesitating. Would it be so terrible to go back to that cluster of trees and wait there? From that place she can see the pavilion. She will be able to see a person emerge with the basket that holds Xia. She will not have to tell her husband that she has done this. She can simply say that the long walk made her weary and that she slept a long time before heading back home.

Satisfied with her plan, Chun walks back past the flowers, across the grass, to the cluster of trees. She takes the sling that had just a few hours ago held her newborn daughter and rolls it up like a pillow to put beneath her head. As she looks upward, the leaves make a pattern like lace against the sky. Chun stares at this pattern and thinks of how she does not want to make this journey again.

Last year she had a daughter whom she left at the police station of a different city. The year before she had a daughter whom her husband had agreed, reluctantly, to keep. She does not want her heart broken again. How many daughters can a woman lose and still love her husband? Still cook dinner and grow vegetables and smile at others? Her heart is broken into so many pieces already. One daughter who knows where? One daughter in a basket across the park waiting for someone to find her.

Yet even today, only five days after this child was born, her husband had smiled at her and said, Hurry back, and Chun had known he meant hurry back so that we can try again for a son.

But Chun feels certain that she was made to only have daughters. She stares up at the leaves and considers her dilemma. Can a woman turn her own husband away in bed? Can she deny him his needs, his longing, his son? Chun has no answers. She knows only this: She cannot abandon another baby.

Her eyelids grow heavy and her mind goes where she does not want it to go. Last year, when she left her three-day-old daughter on the steps of the police station, it was January and cold. What Chun fears is that despite the layers of clothing, despite the blankets she'd so carefully swaddled the baby in, despite her pleading with the heavens to protect her baby, the child did not get found in time and froze to death in the winter night.

The thought jolts her awake. Chun sits up, her heart beating hard. Even though it is not quite dawn, trucks are pulling into the park. Chun stumbles to her feet. Her mouth is dry and foul-tasting. Her breasts are heavy with milk. She puts her hand to her chest as if that small gesture can stop the pounding of her heart. Men in orange work clothes emerge from the trucks and begin unloading chairs, swaths of cloth, equipment of some kind. They move toward the pavilion, their figures slowly illuminated in the rising sun.

Then Chun hears the sound of excited voices. One of the men lifts her basket high, like he has won a prize, and hands it down to the men. Xia is lost in a blur of orange. Chun waits, unsure of what to do. Then she turns from the park and walks north, toward home, with quick determined steps.

"Who will get this baby?" Wang Chun asks out loud. "Who will take her in and cherish her?"

Of course, she has no answers. Only a mother can love a baby the right way. Only a mother truly cherishes her children. Something in her wants to go back and shout: That is my daughter! But Wang Chun keeps moving steadily away.

MAYA

Maya stood in her office surrounded by pictures of the children. Dark-haired girls grinned at the camera from under Christmas trees or inside spinning Disneyland pink teacups or sitting on green grass in front of tulips or rosebushes or in bedrooms so white and frilly they seemed to be made for princesses. The pictures told Maya that these children, once abandoned somewhere in China and brought to orphanages where they often slept two or three or four to a crib, these children were now happy. In fact, not just happy, but special. They had toys and vacations and pretty clothes. Look at me! the pictures seemed to say. Look at how happy and special I am.

On the morning before an orientation, Maya liked to come in early, before her secretary Samantha or her assistant Jane arrived, before documents appeared for her to scrutinize and phones began ringing. On these mornings, like this morning, Maya came in early with her Venti no-fat no-foam latte and looked at the pictures of the children. Since 2002, when she opened the Red Thread Adoption Agency in a one-room third-floor walk-up office in an old foundry, Maya had placed four hundred and fifty-one children from China.

At six o'clock tonight, prospective families would begin step one of the adoption process, an orientation in the office suite. The new offices on Wickenden Street were spacious, a maze of rooms with glowing computer screens and gleaming desks, conference rooms and coffeemakers, central air-conditioning, fax machines, copy machines, nameplates on the doors. And the pictures of those four hundred and fifty-one children everywhere. Maya never told anyone, but she knew each child's name—the Chinese ones the orphanages gave them and their new American ones. She knew which province they came from and where they lived now.

Once, she had heard Samantha and Jane gossiping about her.

"She knows them," Samantha had whispered. They were making a fresh pot of coffee, standing in the corner, heads bent together. "Every one of them."

"Even Maya Lange can't remember over four hundred names like that," Jane said.

Maya stood outside the doorway until the conversation switched to Samantha's date the night before. Samantha was a relentless dater, determined to meet the right man and to marry him and move out to East Greenwich or some other suburb where the houses had shutters and rolling lawns. Quietly, Maya slipped back to her office and sat at her desk wondering if they found knowing all those children by name a spectacular accomplishment or an embarrassing oddity. She knew that Samantha and Jane were both slightly afraid of her. She was a perfectionist who did not understand mistakes. In her business, they dealt with children, and families who wanted children desperately. There was no room for error. One misplaced form, one incorrect piece of information, and a family could lose their place in the queue. A child could have to wait months longer for a home. Or worse.

Sometimes Maya wondered what these women would think if they knew anything about her own life. If she told them, This is what happened to my first husband and me long ago, would it make them like her more? If she explained how that one terrible thing had allowed her to make bad decisions, would they feel closer to her? She didn't want or need them to like her or want to be her friend. But she did wonder if they saw her as more human how that would change everything.

On this morning before the orientation, Maya found herself wondering these things again. She sighed and turned her attention to organizing. Maya found comfort and escape in getting things ready for her families. Their path to a baby was a long one, she knew. The orientation tonight. Then all of the paperwork, gathering their birth certificates and tax forms, bank statements and letters of recommendation. They had to be fingerprinted and have a criminal check. A social worker had to do three home studies, making sure they had a safe house with a room for the baby. And then more paperwork: U.S. approval, and all of those documents sent to China. This took six months to complete, and at the end of that time there was nothing to do except wait for China to send a referral. Maya had seen that wait be as short as a year and as long as three years.

Maya sipped her coffee and grimaced. No matter how many times she asked for no foam, the girl—the barista! and thinking this she laughed—couldn't get it right. Still, the bitter espresso tasted good and Maya let herself pause a moment in her ritual to think about Jack and how he had indeed asked for her phone number, standing by her bright orange VW Bug in the restaurant parking lot. She had felt an almost-forgotten stirring that night when he leaned down and kissed her. Just one kiss, but it had oddly moved her. Maya smiled thinking about it, but then reprimanded herself. What was the point in romanticizing something that was never going to happen? She straightened her skirt, as if allowing even the tiniest bit of intimacy into her thoughts had mussed her up somehow. Maya took another sip of her coffee. Perhaps she would write a letter to the company about foam in lattes.

But not today. Today she would get ready to meet the new potential families. She went to the wall that held the earliest pictures and took a deep breath. Olivia. Ariane. Melissa. Her finger touched each photograph lightly as she said the girls' names. Kate. Caitlin. Michelle. Julie. Isabella. Rose. Morgan. Maya smiled. There they were. The first ten. All of them brought home from Sichuan Province in December 2002. She'd gone with the families that first time, making sure everything went perfectly. Julie's parents lost their passports and Maya had taken care of that. Olivia's parents didn't have their money for the orphanage donation in clean, unwrinkled bills, and Maya had taken care of that, finding a bank in the middle of nowhere that had over a thousand new American dollars and convincing them to take the slightly used ones in return. Then Jordan had developed a fever and Maya had taken her to the local hospital and stayed with her through the night until the fever subsided. Michelle's mother had forgotten to mention that she had a peanut allergy and went into anaphylactic shock during the farewell dinner. But Maya had remembered that Caitlin's mother was allergic to bees and had an epi pen which Maya retrieved and administered herself.

Every detail. Every problem. Every child, her responsibility. And despite the lost passports and the wrong money and the fever and the peanut allergy, everything was perfect. Here were these ten girls, all of them happy, special. Maya slid her finger down to the next row and repeated the same process. Ali. Elizabeth. Joy, she said, her finger lightly touching each shiny image until she had worked her way across this wall, and the bulletin board in the hallway and the other one in the orientation room and the one by the entrance door. Four hundred and fifty-one children. By the time she had finished, the front door swung open and Samantha walked in.

"You're here early," she said in the Rhode Island accent that grated ever so slightly on Maya's nerves. "Orientation tonight, huh?"

"Yes," Maya said. "I think I would like the Little Schoolboy cookies. The dark chocolate ones. And that Paul Newman lemonade."

"Pink? Or regular?" Samantha said.

Reg-u-lah. Maya shuddered. "Regular," she said precisely.

If Samantha noticed, or cared, she didn't let on. She slid into her seat behind her desk and placed the earphone behind her short dark hair, ready for the day to begin.

IN THE SUMMER of 2001, after Maya's divorce was final and she had left Honolulu and her life behind for a part-time job teaching marine biology at the University of Rhode Island, her parents took her to China with them for a monthlong vacation. She had not wanted to go. Instead, she wanted to sit in her apartment on Transit Street in Providence, and drink too much wine and watch bad TV movies, alone. But perhaps knowing this was what she would do, her mother insisted. She bought her a ticket even after Maya said she didn't want to go and sent her guidebooks with key attractions highlighted in bright green. The terra-cotta soldiers. The Great Wall. The Forbidden City.

Ever since Maya's parents retired, all they did was travel. Patagonia, Peru, Cambodia. Now China. They had both been marine biologists who taught at the University of California in Santa Cruz, and Maya grew up trying to get their attention. Her parents loved science more than anything. It was what they discussed at dinner. It was how they spent their weekends and vacations, in labs and peering into microscopes. Maya learned early that to be a part of this family, she too needed to love science. When she won the Northern California Science Fair's first prize in fourth grade for her project on the nervous system of jellyfish, her parents finally noticed her. Until she grew up and left them and they could go back to what they loved best: science and each other.

After her divorce and a move across the country to a cold climate, they noticed her again. Her mother had never been very good at parenting, relying on clichés to make her points. "One door opens and another closes," was one of her favorites. And "Tomorrow is another day." Maya could not imagine a month of clichés when her heart was so broken and her life so destroyed. But as each step of the trip clicked into place—visas obtained, tours booked, airplane seats selected—she found herself swept up in the idea of an exotic place where she could not understand the language, where nothing had the fingerprints of her old life on it.

When she stepped off the plane in Beijing and saw her parents waiting for her, she rushed into their arms. But in spite of the foreign locale, China was distorted by the stunned, wounded person Maya had become. You need help! her mother would shout at her when she found Maya drunk in the hotel lounge at night. You need therapy! Hot and hungover, Maya climbed the Great Wall and ate dim sum and listened to tour guides with their thick, almost undecipherable accents.

One morning, the guide met their small tour group in the lobby, excited.

"Big news! Good news!" she said. She wore a pale pink Gap T-shirt and stonewashed blue jeans. "We tour orphanage this morning! Very exciting."

"I'm not going," Maya whispered to her mother. "You know how I feel about babies." The word *babies* caught in her throat.

"Maybe it would be good for you," her mother said.

"Stop telling me what's good for me," Maya said, her voice louder.

"No baby!" the guide said. "All ages!"

She opened her ridiculous green umbrella, indicating it was time to follow her.

Maya let herself get swept out of the hotel, into the bus. "I'm not going in," she told her mother.

Yet she did. That was something Maya could never explain. She spent a good deal of her time avoiding babies, making up excuses for missing her colleagues' baby showers and christenings. But that hot August morning in Guanzhou, Maya followed that green umbrella into an orphanage and her life changed. All around her, everywhere she looked, she saw children. Babies and toddlers and preschoolers, even teenagers. Children everywhere. The head of the orphanage gave an uplifting talk about the children, and then they stood together and sang a patriotic song. The smallest ones ran forward and handed everyone a chrysanthemum. Then they filed out, their backs straight as rulers.

The tour guide opened her green umbrella and everyone except Maya began to leave. Maya ran up to the head of the orphanage.

"Yes?" the woman said sternly, her smudged glasses sliding down to the tip of her nose.

"I . . ." Maya said, but she could not find the words. Emotion cut into her chest.

The director pushed her glasses up and nodded. "You want child?" Back then, it was almost that simple: with a small amount of paperwork, Westerners could go to an orphanage and choose a child to adopt.

Maya shook her head. Through a window she saw the older children playing in a courtyard.

"No?" the director said, frowning at her.

"No," Maya managed finally. "I don't want one. I want all of them." She opened her arms wide. "Every one."

And so the Red Thread Adoption Agency was born. Fifteen families came to that first orientation, and within a year and a half, ten of them had their daughters. By then, the rules had changed. There was more paperwork, and the babies were matched with their adopting families by Chinese officials in an anonymous office. Families waited until a match was made and a photograph of their baby was sent to them.

In China, Maya wrote in her first brochure, *there is a belief that people who are destined to be together are connected by an invisible red thread. Who is at the end of your red thread?*

2

The Families

NELL

What Nell knew was that this time it would work. She was a person who accomplished her goals. Every morning she ran five miles through Waterplace Park along the river, came home, showered, read the *New York Times* and did the crossword puzzle—which she always completed, in ink—ate an English muffin with peanut butter and drank two cups of black coffee, then walked the ten blocks to work where the first thing she did was make a to-do list. The last thing she did before she turned off the light on her bedside table was to make sure every item had been checked off. In between, she worked as an investment banker, making deals with countries in Asia. She had mastered Chinese while still an undergraduate, Japanese by the time she graduated from Harvard with her M.B.A., and had just enrolled in a Thai class for fun.

Nell had no doubt that this time she would get pregnant. When her husband Benjamin had mentioned the possibility of adoption, Nell had pretended to consider it. But it was ridiculous. They would have their own babies, and soon. The shots of Pergonal that she gave herself every day had produced five eggs this month. Statistically, one of them would result in a baby. All she needed to do was have sex with Benjamin for the next three days, making sure to stay in bed afterward with a pillow under her butt and her legs elevated. She drank cough syrup every morning to keep her mucous thin. She switched to decaf coffee and gave up wine at dinner. If all of the things on her to-do lists were this easy, she would have no challenges at all.

Tonight, she put on the lacy nightgown Benjamin had given her for Valentine's Day, the one that made her feel self-conscious. Nell preferred sleeping in one of Benjamin's frayed Brooks Brothers shirts than sexy lingerie. But Benjamin had been grumbling about having to make love on a schedule, and she wanted him to be agreeable. She even spritzed on some of the Cartier perfume he liked so much. For her taste, its scent was too cloying. But she wanted everything to be just right. In two weeks, she would take a pregnancy test and it would be positive. These small concessions were worth that.

Nell glanced down at her list: Cartier, candles, chilled wine. She smiled at the row of checkmarks that filled the left-hand column of the paper.

"Nell?" Benjamin called from downstairs. "You up there?"

She heard his footsteps on the stairway. "Nell?"

"In here."

He appeared in the doorway of their bedroom, his suit jacket over his arm, his tie already loosened. She liked her husband's looks, the shock of sandy hair that always fell in his eyes, the tan he kept year-round from sailing, his square jaw and angled cheekbones, all of the things that had told her the first day of business school that he was from a certain kind of family. Back then, her to-do list had broader items on it. Harvard was one. Marrying a man like Benjamin was another.

"You okay?" he asked, not stepping into the room.

"Better than okay," Nell said. She poured him a glass of wine and held it out. "Five eggs," she said, and even though she thought his face fell slightly, she continued. "Five! We're on our way."

Benjamin came into the bedroom, tossing his jacket on the chaise and taking the wine from her. "So you intend on seducing me, then?" he said. He wanted to sound playful, but she heard the tightness in his voice.

"Absolutely," she said, climbing onto his lap.

Of course she had hoped for memorable sex. But Benjamin had been methodical, quick. She told herself not to show him how disappointed she was. After all, she needed him to cooperate for the next two days as well. So when he kissed her lightly on the lips and got out of bed, she forced a smile.

"Nice," she said.

"How about going to that new place for dinner?" he said, already moving toward the bathroom. "The French bistro? What's it called?"

"We have to wait an hour," she said. "Remember?" Nell wiggled her toes at him.

"Right," Benjamin said.

As he walked into the bathroom, Nell noticed the way his tan lines stopped midway across his forearms, how the rest of him was pale white. She looked away. When she heard the hard spray of the shower, Nell reached for her pad and placed a careful checkmark next to the last item. Then she closed her eyes and worked on relaxing.

THEO

"No secrets," Sophie whispered to Theo.

They were sitting in a little Thai restaurant, eating pad thai and chicken with basil. Sophie had been telling her husband about her day, the usual complaints and struggles of working for a nonprofit, and, it was true, he had zoned out. Her days often sounded exactly the same to him—broken copy machines, phone calls not returned, lazy volunteers, the problems of the world that Sophie intended to fix single-handedly.

Theo speared some meat with a chopstick.

"A bhat for your thoughts," Sophie said.

Theo shook his head. Ever since they had met in Thailand five years earlier, Sophie had offered him a bhat for his thoughts instead of the standard penny. She was there working at a refugee camp; Theo was backpacking through Asia and Australia, running away from his broken heart back in the States.

"What do you mean no?" Sophie laughed. "You think I'm not good for it?"

She reached into her silk and mirrored square purse bought at a Bangkok street market, rummaged through all the junk she toted around, and produced a bhat. Somehow, she had an endless supply of them. If she wasn't so moral and good, Theo would have suspected that she'd robbed a Thai vending machine before they'd come home. She put the bhat right beside his sweating bottle of Tiger beer and looked at him, amused.

"Well?" she said.

Theo sighed. Sophie wanted to know every thought he had, always, and sometimes it wore him out, this openness.

"It's boring," he lied.

"So?"

He held the bhat between his thumb and forefinger, worrying it. "I was thinking of the car I had in college. An old blue Mustang." He shrugged. "See? Not very interesting."

"But what about it?"

Sophie had soft curly brown hair and a round face. All of her was round and soft and open. Theo looked away from her and finished his beer.

"Nothing about it," he said. Then he added, "I loved that car," hoping that would satisfy her.

But she was frowning now. "What made you think about it?"

Exasperated, he said, "I don't know." He caught the waiter's attention and held up his empty bottle.

"Another beer?" Sophie said. "You've already had two."

"Jesus, Sophie, give me a break."

She chewed her bottom lip and for a moment Theo feared she might actually cry. She was like that, oversensitive, as likely to cry at a sharp tone as at stray cats on their fire escape.

Sophie took the bhat and held it up. "My turn, then," she said, and the forced cheer in her voice made Theo feel guilty.

He touched her curls. "Shoot," he said.

"I think we should go to one of those orientations. At the Red Thread?"

"The Red Thread?"

Now she looked exasperated. "The adoption agency. I brought home the brochures a few weeks ago."

Theo's chest tightened. So this was why Sophie had wanted to come to their favorite Thai restaurant, a place that was supposed to remind him of when they met and fell in love. Back then, he had told her how afraid he was of responsibility and commitment. He had said that right up front, even as they lay naked and sweaty together beneath a mosquito net. Don't push me, he'd said. He was a person who liked to coast through life, who avoided the hard stuff. She had found him romantic. *Oh,* she'd whispered, *one of those.*

She had let him do just that: coast. But now her increasing desire—no, her need—to have a baby was changing everything. Theo knew what he was capable of. He knew what he had done in the past when he was confronted with difficult choices, and he wasn't proud of those things. Lately, he had found himself noticing a stranger's long muscled legs when she walked past him on the street, or the particular shape of someone's mouth, and he could easily imagine those legs wrapped around him, those lips on his own.

The waiter put the beer on the table without removing the two empties, adding to Theo's guilt.

"What's the rush, Sophie?" he asked, trying to sound kind but not quite managing it.

"Rush?" she said. "We've been trying for almost four years."

To Sophie, trying meant not using birth control. But Theo knew couples who had really tried, using ovulation kits and fertility drugs, and more. That was a path he had no interest in. If they happened to get pregnant, well, fine. But if not, well, that was okay too.

"Besides," Sophie added, "we want to adopt too. So why not get started? When we get pregnant, we'll just have more kids, right?"

Somehow, Theo thought, decisions got made without him knowing it. When had he agreed to adopt and have biological kids? How many kids were they supposed to have anyway? Ever since he met Sophie, Theo had felt swept up in her world. And he wasn't always sure he liked it. Whenever he got this feeling, a strange mix of guilt and claustrophobia, Theo thought of Heather, the girl who broke his heart and set him off on that yearlong trip that ended in Bangkok and Sophie. Heather had been the opposite of Sophie in every way, a dancer who was all sharp angles where Sophie was round curves; all blond and straight where Sophie was dark and curly.

"Plus," Sophie was saying, "it takes longer now for Chinese adoptions. We might as well get started."

"Uh-huh," Theo said. Heather used to place herself flat against him. They were almost the same height, and when she pressed her body against his like that, it was as if she was really part of him, the other half. When she would try to roll away, he would make her stay. Don't go, he used to whisper into her hair.

"And maybe we should get one of those ovulation kits. Yvonne at work used one and got pregnant right away. I mean, the worst thing that happens is we end up with two kids right off."

He had zoned out again, he could tell by the way she was looking at him now, hurt, about to cry. So Theo grinned at her and kissed her hard on the mouth.

"Great," he said.

"Really?"

"Absolutely."

She threw her arms around his neck and gave him a dozen little kisses. "For a minute I thought—"

"Ssshhh," Theo said, kissing her again to quiet her. "Let's go home and practice."

EMILY

Emily stood at her bedroom window and watched her fourteen-year-old stepdaughter Chloe climb out of Michael's black Suburban. Even from here Emily could tell that the girl was sulking. The only one who enjoyed these visits was Michael. Chloe and Emily hated them. Although Emily could only guess at why they made Chloe so miserable, she knew too well why she dreaded them. Michael fawned on Chloe. He made Emily disappear. Or feel like she had disappeared. There was a difference, Emily reminded herself. That was what her therapist, Dr. Bundy, said.

Chloe had lost even more weight since her last visit. But when Emily had voiced concern over this, Michael had jumped at her. "She's eating healthier," he'd said. "That's all. Why do you always have to find something wrong with her?"

Now, Emily lit a cigarette, leaning close to the screen to let the smoke blow outside. "If my daughter lost so much weight," Emily had started to say, but then she saw the flicker of pain dart across Michael's eyes and she'd shut up. He wanted her to think of Chloe as her daughter. And she didn't. Couldn't. Emily would not have a child who was so uptight, who worried so much about labels on clothing and what to do to get into the right college.

Unconsciously, Emily's hand settled on her stomach. Its emptiness felt vast, endless to her. She knew that inside her intestines coiled and her liver filtered impurities and blood coursed. But it could not hold the thing that mattered. No, Emily corrected herself, she couldn't hold on to it. Three times she had gotten pregnant. And each time she had felt herself filling. It was glorious, that feeling. Her breasts grew full. Her belly. Her heart. At night she would close her eyes and imagine it, a baby taking form inside her. It looked like a seashell, milky and opaque. Oddly, her mouth tasted salty when she was pregnant, as if she'd just swum in the ocean. Each time, she knew she was in trouble when that taste turned metallic. She woke and tasted zinc instead of salt. Then the cramps began. Then the bleeding. And finally the emptiness. Three times.

"Hon?" Michael was calling up stairs. "Chloe's here!"

"Big deal," Emily muttered. She took a last long drag on her cigarette before grinding it out in the quahog shell she used for a secret ashtray.

When she turned away from the window, they were already standing in the doorway, frowning at her.

This was always awkward, the greeting. Michael expected Emily to rush over to Chloe and hug her. Emily thought Chloe should approach her. "That's how I was raised," she explained. "The child goes to the adult."

Instead, they all looked at each other uncomfortably.

"Cute haircut," Emily said, forcing a smile.

Chloe shrugged. Her skinny arms held on tight to herself. "Were you smoking?" she said.

"No," Emily said.

She watched Chloe's gaze move to the quahog shell and the thin trail of smoke that still drifted upward.

Michael cleared his throat. "So I was thinking that I would take Chloe for dinner. Maybe a movie." He elbowed Chloe lightly. "How does pizza sound?"

She wrinkled her nose. "I just had pizza last night," she said.

While Michael offered up other options—sushi? clam cakes and chowder? Johnny Rockets?—Emily remembered what she'd read on a website devoted to diagnosing your teenager's eating disorder. They have excuses. They've always just eaten, or want a different kind of food. They go vegetarian, or simply say they are eating healthier. They lie. Emily watched Chloe's face as she refused each of Michael's ideas.

"Hon," Emily interrupted finally, "we have that thing tonight, remember?"

"What thing?"

Emily looked from Michael to Chloe and back to Michael. "The orientation. For the adoption." She smiled, a real one this time. "Chloe should come," Emily said. "After all, this is going to be her sister."

"You're adopting a baby?" Chloe said to her father.

But it was Emily who answered. "Yes," she said. Something in her shifted, something small but significant. "Yes, we are."

CHARLIE

Charlie stood in the backyard hitting baseballs. He knew without looking what Brooke was doing. She was rubbing the pineapple ginger lotion he liked so much all over her arms and legs. She was blow-drying her hair, pulling it straight with a big fuzzy round brush and keeping it straight by spritzing some coconut hairspray on it. She was the Caribbean, Brooke was. When she was finished she would smell all tropical and fruity. Good enough to eat.

Thwock! Charlie smashed one fastball after another across the yard and onto the beach. From here, he could see nothing but the blue expanse of ocean and sky, and he liked to think that someday, if he hit hard enough, one of these balls would disappear into that blue. Some astronaut on the space shuttle would see it sail by. Some guy out crossing the Atlantic in his beautiful yacht. It was like shooting rubber bands at the stars, Charlie thought. Ridiculous. Impossible. But somehow it was all about hope. *Thwock!*

From behind him, Charlie heard Brooke coming down the stairs, the clop of her heels on the worn wood of the deck.

"Is it that bad?" she asked him.

He waited for the ball. Swung. Watched it fly.

Then he turned, grinning. He put one hand on his heart, as if to still its pounding. "Look at you," he said.

Brooke frowned at him. "You're out here hitting baseballs," she said.

He shrugged. "That's what I do."

"Yeah," she said, "what you do when you're miserable." She put two fingers under her tongue and let loose a whistle. She stood close enough that Charlie could smell her.

"My pineapple princess," he whispered, pulling her close. Then he could smell the ginger lime. He felt himself growing hard and pressed against her. Out of the corner of his eye he saw all three of their dogs come bounding up from the beach, hair stiff with salt water, baseballs in their mouths. They dropped the balls on the grass and went back for more.

"We've got the meeting," she whispered back to him. But she was letting his hand ease inside her blouse, the almost sheer seafoam green one with the tiny pearl buttons that he liked so much. She was letting him find her nipple inside her bra and rub. He heard her breathe in sharply and he knew if he slid his hand under her skirt, the pleated full ocean blue one, and into her panties he would find her wet. So he did. And she was.

The dogs were back, dropping the new round of balls. Charlie nudged Brooke back against the house.

"Here?" she said, not resisting.

"We have a meeting," he said.

She unzipped his shorts. "Right," she said.

"Don't want to be late." He liked how much bigger than her he was, how he could lift her so easily. He liked when she wrapped her legs around him. He heard her saying his name. The worn beach shingles on the house were rough against his arms. He liked that too. And the heat from the sun on his shirt, and the bigger heat from inside him burning. His head filled with her smells, pineapple and coconut and ginger and lime, and the salt from the ocean and the grass somebody was cutting somewhere down the street, and even the smell of wet dogs, all of it blending and making him intoxicated.

"It's okay," she said, laughing, giving him permission to come without her this time.

She tangled his curls in her fingers, pulling him closer still. After, he saw that his mustache had left red marks on her neck. He pressed his fingers there gently, then lowered her slowly.

"It's okay?" she said, squinting up at him.

"More than okay."

"Not that," she said. "I mean the meeting. The whole thing."

Charlie nodded. He didn't know if it was okay. But last night when she'd tried to explain how much having a baby meant to her, she broke his heart. Baseball used to be like that for him. But a baby?

"Charlie?" she said.

"Come on," he said, "let's go get us a baby."

SUSANNAH

Susannah's grandmother had taught her to knit when she was ten years old. Susannah had sat her on her lap, facing out, and her grandmother had placed the needles in her hands, wrapped her arms around her, and knit. Their hands, making the motions together, were like being on a sailboat, rhythmically rocking. That was the year her mother got sick, and Susannah was sent to Newport to live with her grandmother. During the day, she sailed a small skiff named *Clarabelle*, after her mother. She used to hope the sailing would bring her mother closer to her. But it didn't. Instead, she felt like a small girl on a big ocean, alone. At night, she slept in her mother's childhood bed with its white canopy and stiff sheets that smelled of strong soap. This too failed to make her feel her mother's presence. She felt like a little girl alone in a big house. "It's a mansion, you know," another girl who sailed told her one day. "We live in mansions. It's just tacky to say that."

But when Susannah sat on her grandmother's lap and knit, the old woman's soft hands on top of her own, moving the needles through the stitches, she could almost feel her mother. Maybe it was the perfume, an expensive French one that they both wore. Or maybe it was the hypnotic sound of the needles clacking together. Susannah wasn't sure. She just knew that it was the favorite part of her day, unless the day included a telephone call from her mother in the hospital in New York City.

She supposed that was why she had picked up her knitting needles now, when she needed to find comfort. She'd had to search hard for them, up in the attic where her grandmother's and her mother's things were packed away in trunks and cedar chests. Susannah never looked at them. Her neighbor had told her that the things were valuable, that on *Antiques Roadshow* a woman's grandmother's belongings had been estimated at eleven thousand dollars. And her grandmother, the neighbor had reminded Susannah, had been rich. "Bloody rich," the neighbor had said. That woman liked to use phrases like that: bloody this and bloody that, joie de vivre, ciao. It drove Susannah crazy. The whole neighborhood did, with its tennis-playing women taking power walks every morning, and the monthly book clubs, and the men mowing lawns and barbecuing every weekend.

Her husband Carter loved it. But to Susannah, it was just one more way she didn't fit in. Susannah thought this and paused in her knitting. She lay her knitting in her lap and let her eyes drift toward the window where her daughter Clara played with the babysitter, a college student from Salve Regina.

Whenever she glimpsed Clara like this, from a distance, her stomach dropped as if she were seeing her for the first time: the dull eyes, the awkwardness. The babysitter, Julie, seemed able to pull something more from the girl, something that Susannah could not. Even through the closed windows she could hear Clara's squeals of laughter. She wondered if she and Clara had actually ever had fun together? Her mind landed on the one sweet memory she had.

When Clara was about three, Susannah had taken her out for the day on one of the J-boats from Sail Newport. Sometimes she went out alone on one, sailing out beneath the Newport Bridge, the water the only place she knew where she could be away from the confusion of her house with Clara's tantrums and Carter's patience and her own mixed-up feelings about all of them. That day, something in her had wanted to connect with her daughter, almost desperately. That used to happen back then. Clara's diagnosis of Fragile X syndrome was still new enough that Susannah found herself disbelieving it, hoping that she could break through to her daughter.

She had buckled Clara into a bright orange life jacket and smeared her pretty face with sunscreen and the two of them had set sail. Susannah could still see Clara, her face tilted up as if to catch the wind herself, her fine blond hair blowing around her, and a smile—a real smile, of this Susannah was certain. Susannah had imagined that they would have many days like that. She had imagined that she had found the thing that would bring them together, keep them together. But the very next week, when she tried to put the life jacket on Clara, the girl had howled and torn at Susannah's hands. Susannah kept trying, speaking in the soft soothing tone that Carter used, but Clara would not put that life jacket on, and eventually Susannah gave up. It seemed to her now that all of her attempts to teach her daughter some simple thing always ended with frustration.

Carter's old Volvo pulled into the driveway. Susannah sighed. They would have to leave right away if they were going to make the orientation at the Red Thread. She watched Clara run toward Carter, her pale blond braids flying behind her. Carter bent and scooped Clara into his arms. The two of them standing in the late afternoon sun looked golden, special, blessed. Susannah bit hard on her bottom lip and looked away from the sight of them. She picked up her knitting, hoping to feel the weight of her grandmother's arms around her.

3

MAYA

The Little Schoolboy cookies were laid out artfully on a green plate from China. The lemonade looked cool and refreshing in a fat round pitcher. In front of it, Samantha had fanned out the paper napkins with the Chinese characters for love and family and good luck on them. Maya moved each thing an inch this way, shifted a corner that way, until she was satisfied. Samantha's accent aside, she did get the details right. Jane was not always as good about the small things. She had to be watched, even nagged a bit. But tonight, she had rolled down the big map of China with the colored pushpins indicating the provinces from which they had received children. The information booklets and the Red Thread's own information folders had been placed on the antique red lacquer table. Everything was ready.

Samantha walked in with fresh coffee in the silver urn. Already she had placed cubes of sugar with small silver tongs and a pitcher of half-and-half on the mahogany sidebar. After she put down the urn and counted the porcelain cups and saucers, Samantha cleared her throat.

Maya waited.

"This sounds crazy," Samantha said awkwardly. She was a plain woman who tried hard to overcome that plainness, with mixed results. Tonight she wore vintage cat glasses with rhinestones around the frames, and a flat red lipstick that made her mouth seem smeared somehow. "You know how you told me to put away the oldest files? To make room?"

"Yes?" Maya said. New families about to arrive any minute, and Samantha decides to discuss her office tasks. "Well?"

"Well, I saw your file."

Maya let the information settle. She tried to stay calm, but she felt her heart pick up speed.

"I didn't read it or anything," Samantha added quickly. Too quickly? Maya wondered. "I just . . . I was surprised that you almost adopted a baby yourself."

Maya met Samantha's gaze. "Is that all?" she said. "Are we going to get back to work now?"

Samantha blinked. Nodded.

Thankfully, the office door swung open and someone called a hesitant "Hello?"

"Our families," Maya said, relieved. "They're here."

MAYA WATCHED THE people come in. Over thirty of them, all nervous. Even Emily and Michael looked terrified. She smiled at them, but Michael avoided her eye contact and Emily's face seemed as if it might crack if she dared to smile back. Why was everyone who walked in here so afraid? So tense? When you are about to begin the journey of getting a baby, it should be a precious time. For an instant, a memory came to the surface.

But she shoved it back, and focused on the couples. Samantha greeted them all warmly, poured them lemonade, offered cookies. She showed them the table with the information, brochures and reading lists, the photo album of happy new families holding their beautiful babies.

At precisely 7:00 p.m., Maya stood in the front of the room, beside the large map of China. She cleared her throat and waited for the people to quiet. She observed which couples held hands, which sat without touching. None of that mattered, of course. Yet Maya noticed everything, and she remembered it all.

"My name is Maya Lange," she began in her lilting voice.

She purposely spoke softly so they would have to stay quiet. Some of them even leaned forward in their chairs to hear her better.

"I opened the Red Thread Adoption Agency in 2002. That year I placed ten children, all from the province of Sichuan." She pointed to Sichuan on the map.

One of the women scribbled in a notebook, frowning. She had expensively dyed blond hair, this woman, with highlights and lowlights and streaks meant to look like the sun had kissed her. Her husband, with his loosened tie and shiny cuff links, did not want to be here, Maya noted.

"Last year," Maya continued, "I placed one hundred and ninety-seven children from eleven different provinces."

She liked the woman who gasped a little and nodded eagerly. She was plump with curly hair and a round open face. Maya wondered why her husband looked so frightened, why he jumped slightly when his wife placed her hand on his knee.

"This year," Maya said, "who knows?"

The group laughed politely.

Except the woman with the straight pale hair that was too long for her age. She was too close to crying to laugh, even a little. She didn't hold her husband's hand so much as clutch it, tight.

"Perhaps one of the babies this year will be yours," Maya said.

They had been through something. All of them had. People who came here to adopt had been through infertility failures, arguments, lost hopes and expectations. They were vulnerable, her families. She knew this.

"I have so much to tell you," Maya said, pressing the palms of her hands together. "So much information. So many details."

On cue, Samantha handed out the red folders with everything spelled out for them. Costs, deadlines, procedures.

"But don't feel nervous," Maya said. "You have already accomplished step one on the list: orientation."

Again, polite laughter.

Maya's gaze settled on the couple in the back. The man, with his walrus mustache and light brown curls, looked familiar. Had they been here before and changed their minds? No. The woman, a pixie with short dark hair and a sunburned nose, did not seem at all familiar. Maybe they lived near her and she had seen the man on the street or in the grocery store.

"Before we go through so much information," Maya said, "let's introduce ourselves. If all of you leave here deciding you will indeed adopt a baby from China, then it is very likely that you will be in the same DTC group."

"DTC?" the notetaker said without looking up.

"Documents to China. The day they arrive becomes the day your wait begins," Maya explained. "It is very likely, then, that you will all travel together to China, that your babies will come from the same province, the same orphanage. It is very likely that some of you will become lifelong friends. Best friends, perhaps."

The round-faced woman grinned broadly. Maya met the woman's eye and smiled back at her.

"Why don't you and your husband begin?" Maya said to her. "Just tell us who you are, where you live, why you are here."

The woman nodded enthusiastically, pleased, even eager to introduce herself. "I'm Sophie and this is my husband Theo. We live in the Armory District now but we met in Thailand."

Theo shifted uncomfortably, but she continued. "We traveled extensively through Asia. Vietnam and Laos and Cambodia."

Sophie glanced at Theo as if he might join in, but he didn't. "We decided we would have biological and adopted children, and it just seemed natural for us to adopt from Asia. You know," she said.

Maya waited, but that seemed to be the end of Sophie's introduction.

"And do you?" Maya asked.

Sophie frowned.

"Have biological children already?" Maya said.

It was Theo who answered. "No," he said. "We don't."

"Not yet anyway," Sophie said cheerfully.

But Maya could see that her husband, this Theo, was not cheerful.

Before Maya could prod, the notetaker put down her pen and turned to face everyone.

"I'm Nell Walker-Adams. I'm a lawyer here in town. We live on the East Side, over on Freeman Parkway. And we're here just for information tonight. Still undecided. We're still undergoing fertility treatments, but we've decided against IVF. So, who knows?"

"I'm Mr. Nell Walker-Adams," her husband said. "With such an efficient wife, who needs anything else?"

Maya ignored his sarcasm and instead said, "Many people come to the orientation undecided. One thing I like to tell everyone is that adoption is a sure way to getting a baby. If you start both processes, in a year you will definitely have at least one child."

"So the wait is a year?" Nell Walker-Adams asked, pen in hand. "From tonight?"

Others seemed to become more alert too. They were eager and anxious, Maya knew that.

"Approximately," she said. "We will give you all of that information. It's also in your packet."

Nell frowned, and began to flip through the pages in her folder. She wanted facts, this one.

"Is it my turn?" the man in the back with the walrus mustache said.

"Wait," Nell said. "I have another question. How do we get the child?"

"That's what you're here to learn about," Maya said. "The process."

"No," Nell said, shaking her head. "I mean, who decides which child we actually get? Do we get to choose one ourselves?"

"When China first opened to foreign adoptions," Maya said, trying to stay patient, "that is what happened. But now the process has become much more formalized. The Chinese government assigns you your child. There's actually a matching room where photographs of babies are matched with portfolios of prospective families."

"Randomly?" Sophie asked.

Maya smiled. This was actually one of her favorite parts of the adoptions, an almost magical occurrence. But she had to be careful how she phrased it. Talk about magic in the first ten minutes and she might scare people off.

"Technically, yes, it is random," Maya said. "But without exception, the matches are uncanny. For example, in my last group, a woman's father died right before the referral. He had been so looking forward to this grandchild. He knew the suffering his daughter had been through, the loss of pregnancies, the heartache. But when they got the referral, the baby's birth date was October 9. The grandfather's exact birthday."

Many in the group smiled, but Nell was jotting in her notebook again. "So no consideration or requests to things like IQ? Or likes and dislikes?"

"No," Maya said. "Nothing like that. But the matches are indeed magical."

"So I can't ask for a kid who's a swing hitter? Or one who can throw a knuckleball?" the guy with the walrus mustache said.

His wife, the pixie, slapped his arm playfully. "Behave," she said. "He likes to be center stage," she said, not apologetically but proudly, Maya thought.

"Then, yes," Maya said, "it's your turn."

"I'm Charlie Foster—" the man began, but he was immediately interrupted.

"I knew it!" Mr. Nell Walker-Adams said, leaning to shake Charlie's hand. "I was there. The grand slam in the playoffs. Holy shit. Charlie Foster."

Others nodded and grinned, also reaching across each other to shake his hand.

"Aha!" Maya said. "That's why you want that knuckleball."

"It was a long time ago," Charlie said.

"Not that long ago," his wife said. "I was there, and I'm not that old."

Charlie shrugged, but it was clear that he liked the attention.

"I'm the great one's wife, Brooke," she continued. "I keep him modest."

"Charlie Foster," Nell Walker-Adams's husband said, shaking his head. "Holy shit."

Nell glared at him, and he quickly apologized.

"A famous man," Maya said. "Perhaps some lucky baby in China will be the daughter of this famous man."

The smile faded from Charlie's face, Maya noticed, just the tiniest bit. So it was the wife who wanted to do this, she thought. Not the famous baseball player.

"I'm Susannah," the woman with the pale blond hair said. "Carter and I have a daughter Clara who's six. She . . ." Susannah paused. "She's six," she said again.

"We're looking into adoption," Carter said, "because she has some issues, some problems."

Maya nodded. "Yes, of course. Many families do this. You'll see. It's very typical."

She let her eyes settle on the next couple. And they told a little of their story. Then the next couple spoke, and the next. One woman was single and had come with her sister. One woman was alone because her husband was not yet ready to adopt. To Maya, the stories were both familiar and unique. The older man who had grown children from an earlier marriage, who'd had a vasectomy and now found himself with a young wife ready for her own babies. The weary couples who'd tried IVF and failed. The confused ones who still couldn't believe they were unable to get pregnant. The family that, after three boys, wanted a daughter. What they all had in common was this lust, this inexplicable need for a baby. Their desires were palpable in the warm room, as if these people had carried something real inside—hopelessness and hope, love and desperation—and offered it to Maya.

Maya looked out at her families and her heart leaped. She could help them. Every one of them.

"I guess that leaves you," Maya said to Emily. She smiled

warmly at her friend, wanting her to relax. "Full disclosure," Maya told the group. "Emily and Michael are friends of mine. I've been trying to get them to come to an orientation for some time now. And here they are."

"I'm so happy to be here," Emily said. "I have been ready to have a baby for such a long time. We've had problems having our own."

"Well, we do have one daughter," Michael said. "Chloe. She's fourteen."

Maya saw Emily swallow hard.

"Wonderful," Maya said. "So here we all are."

"It's his daughter," Emily said quietly. "From a previous marriage."

"That's wonderful," Maya said, hating that she had used that word twice in a row. She looked at these families, taking them in. Their names. Their stories.

"Let me tell you the Chinese legend of the red thread," Maya said.

AFTER THEY HAD all gone home and Maya and Samantha had cleaned up, Maya went into her office and reached into the bottom drawer. From it, she took the soft pink yarn that hung from two long knitting needles.

She had begun this ritual back in Honolulu, on that awful night almost ten years ago, the night that began with a hailstorm and ended by almost ruining her. That night was why her marriage broke up, why she went to China with her parents and decided to start an adoption agency. On that awful night, Maya had retrieved yarn and needles from her purse and she knit until she became exhausted. When she woke up the next morning, that night was at least behind her. Somehow, knitting became her talisman. She never made anything. Not scarves or hats or mittens. She never learned to purl or to read a pattern. She just knit.

After her first orientation, when the families had left and Maya was alone in her office, she felt suddenly burdened. Not just by their futures, but by the futures of those babies waiting in China. The weight made her literally so heavy that she could not stand. She dropped into a chair and tried to calm herself. But all she could think was that a baby's life was her responsibility. No! Not one baby. Many babies. Almost frantic, Maya picked up her knitting and knit row after row until her heart calmed.

All of those families got beautiful happy babies. But the weight remained. So Maya knit after each orientation, a ritual that she hoped would bring babies to these people. A ritual that let her believe, even briefly, that she could have the life of a child in her hands, and do everything exactly right.

Hunan, China

LI GUAN

"Ssshhh," Li Guan whispered to her daughter. "The mayor is poking his nose where it doesn't belong."

Li Guan and the baby stayed hidden in the small room off the kitchen where the pickles and potatoes were kept for the winter. In the kitchen, Li Guan heard the murmur of voices. Her husband's and the mayor's. She tried to make out their words, but couldn't. The baby whimpered and Li Guan pressed her closer.

"Ssshhh," she whispered again.

Just yesterday, Sheng, the nosy old woman who raised pigs and sold them for too much money, had come to Li Guan in the market.

"The last time I saw you," the old woman said, "you were with child. Where is that child?"

Li Guan had forced a laugh. "Me? With child? My daughter is almost nine years old now. Surely I've seen you in nine years."

The old woman frowned. "I saw you in the spring and you were round and your cheeks glowed."

"Thank you," Li Guan said, bowing her head slightly as she backed away from the woman. "You compliment me."

When this daughter was born, she had looked her husband in the eye and said one word: "No."

That small word held more meaning than Li Guan could begin to express. No, I will not give this child away. No, I will not let you do it. No, no, no. She is mine.

"How long do you think you can keep a child a secret?" her husband had asked her. "A baby, perhaps. But a toddler? A five-year-old?"

"No," Li Guan said.

She did not have a plan, except that she would have this daughter and keep her and love her, just like she did her first child.

Now Li Guan heard the door open and close. The mayor had left. Still, she waited in the pantry with her baby.

Her husband walked in, stooping so as not to hit his head on the doorframe.

"There is suspicion," he said.

When she didn't respond, he said, "If we are caught, we cannot pay such a large fine. My mother is not well. We can't afford to lose health care."

Still Li Guan remained silent.

"A daughter is not worth losing everything," her husband said.

"This daughter is," Li Guan said.

"Why is she so special?"

"Because she is my child," Li Guan answered.

HER FATHER-IN-LAW *glared at her as he ate. Li Guan stood at his elbow, ready to refill his bowl. She hated the old man. She was sorry his wife was so ill, but she hated her too. Li Guan had friends who had kind in-laws and friends who had tedious ones. But hers were cruel. Ever since she came to live with them, they mocked her. They thought she was too skinny, her voice too shrill. "Why did my son choose such a wife?" her mother-in-law asked every day.*

When her first daughter was born, they shook their heads in disgust. "Of course you could not give us a grandson. You are worthless."

Li Guan's friend had a book that said it was the man who determined the sex of a baby. The friend's cousin was a doctor who had studied in Beijing. In his medical book, many complicated things were explained. Li Guan and her friend read the book the way some women read cheap romance stories. They could not wait for the next chapter. They read about how food was digested, how blood flowed, how babies were made. True, they giggled at many of the descriptions. Sometimes they found what they read hard to believe. A man really produced millions of sperm at a time? And those sperm swam up a woman? They had a private joke: If one of their husbands wanted sex, they would tell the other she had to go fishing. "I am so tired," her friend might say. "I had to go fishing all night last night."

Before her mother-in-law got sick, Li Guan fought with her, as usual. They fought about everything: how Li Guan cooked. Li Guan's daughter—spoiled! her mother-in-law said. Lazy! Li Guan's disrespect.

"What a worthless daughter-in-law I have," her mother-in-law said.

"Ha!" Li Guan said. "It is your son who is worthless. It's the man

who decides the sex of a baby. He makes millions of sperm and they carry a special code—"

"Shut your mouth! Are you the devil? Is this nonsense witchcraft?"

"Yes, I'm a witch," Li Guan said.

The next day, her mother-in-law complained of a pain in her stomach. She could not get out of bed. Over the next few weeks, her symptoms worsened. Li Guan and her friend studied the thick medical book of the friend's cousin.

"Ovarian cancer," Li Guan decided.

"Or pancreatic cancer," her friend said.

Neither had a good prognosis.

"You need to see a doctor," Li Guan told her mother-in-law. The woman's skin was a sickly gray and her face seemed to have aged years in a matter of weeks.

"You put a spell on me," the woman said. "Only you can cure me."

Li Guan's husband tried to talk sense to his parents. "Li Guan has been reading a medical book. That's where she gets her information."

His mother winced in pain. "Make her take the spell off me. I know I made her suffer, but I will do whatever she wants if she will make me better."

As the mother grew worse, Li Guan's father-in-law grew more desperate. Until finally he agreed to take his wife to the hospital in Loudi, two hours away. Li Guan's husband arranged for a car to come and get them, and they carried his mother to it and laid her across the backseat. She had never ridden in a car, and even in her pain she grew frightened.

"The doctor will help you," Li Guan said, kneeling by the open door. Her mother-in-law had started to smell like rotten peaches, and Li Guan turned her face away from her slightly so as not to show her disgust.

"I curse you," the woman said, suddenly sitting upright and pointing at Li Guan. "You will suffer for the rest of your life for what you've done to me."

Despite the warm air, Li Guan shivered. "I swear to you, I've done nothing."

Her mother-in-law seemed frozen for a moment, her bony body stiff, her finger pointing and trembling. Then, just as quickly, she crumpled into a small heap, moaning.

Li Guan watched her husband and father-in-law squeeze into the front seat with the driver. She watched the small boxy car disappear in a puff of stinking black exhaust.

THEY RETURNED FOUR *days later with her mother-in-law and a cardboard box of pills.*

"If this medicine doesn't work . . ." her husband said. He shrugged, but didn't finish his sentence.

"Is it ovarian cancer?" Li Guan asked him.

"You are not a doctor," he said. "You are just a person who read a book."

That night in bed, Li Guan whispered to him. "One of your millions of sperm has found its way to my egg and fertilized it."

"What egg?" he asked gruffly. "Li Guan, I am tired from the days at the hospital."

"Women have eggs in their fallopian tubes—"

Her husband sighed and rolled away from her.

"In other words," Li Guan said, "I'm pregnant."

"How can this be?" he asked her.

"Fishing without a net," she said, giggling.

"What now?"

"Your sperm look like tiny fish. They swim up my cervix—"

"Enough," he said wearily.

Li Guan said, "Reproduction is an amazing thing."

HER MOTHER-IN-LAW refused to die. Every month her husband hired a car and driver and took her to the hospital, returning with another box full of pills. She grew thinner and thinner as Li Guan grew heavier with the new baby. She ate less while Li Guan ate more. She stayed awake, moaning and writhing in pain, while Li Guan slept happily and solidly all night.

When Li Guan gave birth, quickly in the kitchen as she cleaned long beans, her mother-in-law looked at the baby girl and smiled.

"Here is the suffering I wished on you," she said.

Again, like that warm day when her mother-in-law had cursed her, Li Guan went cold.

"Your mother is the witch," she told her husband. "Not me."

She would prove her mother-in-law wrong. She would keep this baby and give her more love than any baby had ever had before. She would teach her things, and one day perhaps her daughter would go to Beijing and become a doctor, like her friend's cousin.

Every night, Li Guan slept with her baby tucked beside her. During the day, she kept her close in the sling, pressed against her. She saw her father-in-law always watching her with his beady eyes.

"Make him stop," she told her husband.

"If we get found out, we will lose everything."

"No," Li Guan said. "If I lose her, I will lose everything."

One day a neighbor knocked on the door. "I heard a baby crying," she said, peering inside.

"It is my mother-in-law," Li Guan lied. "Poor thing. The pain is too much to bear."

Then the old woman in the market made accusations. And the mayor showed up.

"I can't keep this secret any longer," Li Guan's husband said that night in bed. "Perhaps I can make a case to the mayor."

"A case to break the law?" Li Guan said. "After you already lied to him today?"

Her husband sighed. Li Guan realized he sighed a lot. She hugged the baby close, and listened to the baby sounds she made.

LI GUAN'S MOTHER-IN-LAW began to shrivel until she resembled a shrimp, bent and curved.

A woman appeared at the garden fence and said, "How is your mother-in-law?"

Li Guan was on her hands and knees in the dirt, planting carrots. She pulled her jacket around her, to better hide the baby.

"She is very sick," Li Guan said.

"What do you have under your jacket?" the woman said.

"A bag of vegetables."

Li Guan did not look up, but she could feel the woman watching her.

"How old is your daughter?" the woman asked.

Li Guan swallowed hard. "She is nine."

After a few moments of quiet, Li Guan glanced at the fence. The woman was gone.

That night, as she slept holding her baby close, her father-in-law pounded on the bedroom door.

"Come quickly! Help!" he shouted.

Li Guan moved to nudge her husband awake, but her hands landed on empty space where he should be.

"Help!" her father in law yelled, pounding on the door.

Slowly, Li Guan got out of bed. She opened the door a crack.

"What is it?" she asked.

Her father-in-law yanked the door open all the way and pulled her out of the room.

"Hurry!" he said.

Li Guan glanced back at the baby, asleep in bed.

"Wait," she said, pushing him away. "I need to get the baby."

Her father-in-law grabbed her arm hard. "Hurry!" he said.

At the door to his room, he shoved her inside. The room was dark and smelled foul, like feces and sickness. On the bed, her mother-in-law lay curled like a shrimp, a strange sound escaping her throat.

"What is it?" Li Guan asked. But her father-in-law had disappeared.

Li Guan went to the bed, the smell worsening as she neared.

"Can you hear me?" she whispered.

No answer except that guttural sound.

Closer now, Li Guan saw that her mother-in-law had soiled the bed. Her head was arched back at a strange angle and her eyes appeared to be half opened.

Li Guan took a deep breath and rolled her mother-in-law off the sheet. Hastily, she removed the linens, lifting the woman to pull them off. With a cloth, she cleaned the woman as best she could. Strange how cleaning a baby was almost a sweet thing and cleaning a sick person was so awful. Still, Li Guan did it, murmuring assurances to her mother-in-law the whole time.

Finally, there were clean linens on the bed, and a clean nightgown on her mother-in-law. Li Guan opened the window to let some fresh air in. She leaned on the sill, exhausted, and took deep breaths of the cool night air. Under the full moon, she watched a man walking quickly down the road with a bundle. Where could he be going in the middle of the night? Li Guan wondered. Something about his duck-like walk seemed familiar. Li Guan watched a moment longer.

"Stop!" she yelled suddenly.

She ran from the window and out of the room to her own room. When she flung open the door, she saw immediately that the bed was empty. Still, she climbed on it, her hands searching the blankets for what she already knew was gone. Just like that, her secret was gone.

HOME STUDY

A bit of fragrance clings to the hand
that gives flowers.

4

MAYA

The couple standing before Maya in her office doorway had a problem. She could see that by the way the woman's shoulders slumped forward, as if she were folding herself into a cocoon. The man's jaw was set, his eyes bloodshot. He hadn't shaved either, which made Maya wonder if he'd been up all night.

"We were at the orientation last week?" the man said. "We wondered if we could have a minute of your time?"

"Of course," Maya said, even though she did not have a free minute in her day.

She had to review portfolios for the group scheduled to travel to China next week to pick up their babies. She worried that something would go wrong. Sometimes, a couple got to China and changed their minds. Sometimes, the baby was ill or different or developmentally worrisome. At the last minute, Maya had had to make a change somehow, or wait for faxed medical reports to run over to Hasbro Children's Hospital.

The entire ten days her families were away from her in China,

Maya worried. These babies, their photographs spread out before her, all looked fine, healthy. This orphanage posed them in front of large plastic fruit: bananas and pineapples and melon towered over the children, who sat looking confused in bright red silk jackets. But Maya knew better than to trust the photographs.

The couple walked into the office when Maya gestured toward the chairs in front of her desk. The sight of all those babies in those photographs spread out there made the woman start to cry.

Maya swept the photographs into a neat pile and turned them facedown beside her. Then she held out the box of tissues that she kept on her desk. People cried in this office. They cried from the nervousness of waiting for their referral. They cried when that referral came and they could see a picture of their baby for the first time. And they cried when Maya had to tell them their application was rejected.

The woman nodded and took a tissue. But she didn't blow her nose or wipe her tears. She just crumpled it into her hand.

"We looked over the information," the man said. "We even started to fill out the forms."

"How carefully do they investigate your background?" the woman blurted, sitting upright.

The man was chewing his bottom lip.

"It's pretty thorough," Maya said, knowing this was not the answer they wanted. "I had a couple just last month," she continued, "the husband had an arrest years ago, in college, for marijuana possession. A small thing really. But the couple chose to hide it, and when they were discovered, their application was rejected."

"But if they'd told the truth?" the woman asked. She had stopped crying and her mascara left dark smudges under her eyes.

Maya shrugged. "I can't say for certain. But it is possible that because it was so long ago, and he was so young when it happened—"

"It's Gary," the woman said without looking at her husband. "Back when he was in high school, he was on the hockey team, you know? And after a game one night they all went drinking and there was an accident."

She stopped.

Maya waited, but the woman just slumped back in her chair.

"Two of my buddies died," Gary said quietly. "I was drunk and I was driving and they died." He shook his head, as if what he said still didn't make sense. "This was over twenty years ago," he added.

"We have tried everything," the woman said. "For the past five years I have been poked and X-rayed and inseminated and anything else you can imagine. We've spent over thirty thousand dollars trying to get pregnant and then my neighbor shows up one day with this beautiful baby from China. And she tells me she adopted her because of you. She came here and a year later she was standing in my living room with her daughter. After we were here the other night, I could actually imagine it might happen. Finally. I was so excited I started to fill out the papers, you know? And then I get to the part about criminal records and background checks and fingerprinting and I realize we aren't getting a baby from you."

"It was twenty years ago," her husband said again.

"I know a woman," Maya said, "who also was responsible for someone's death. For her own child's death. And her guilt is so large that she doesn't want anyone to know. So she won't file the papers, because then she will have to answer questions about what happened and maybe be told that what happened was so terrible that she doesn't deserve a second chance."

"But why shouldn't I be able to get my baby just because of what he did?" the woman said, crying again.

"I'm saying that you should tell them what happened and perhaps you will get a baby. Not like this woman I know, who is too afraid to lose something again," Maya said.

They sat in silence for a moment.

Then the woman said, "I don't know if I have the stamina to go through it and not get a baby."

Maya nodded. "I'm just saying that you should consider going forward."

As they walked out of her office, the husband put his hand on the small of his wife's back and Maya saw the woman flinch at his touch. She wished they would fill out those forms and not hide from their past. Carefully, she spread the photographs of the babies across her desk again. The sight of the open faces of the babies calmed her.

When the phone rang, she was able to answer it without any sign of what had gone on in her office with the couple.

"Maya? It's Jack Sullivan."

That same feeling surfaced again, just as it had when he'd kissed her so briefly after dinner.

"I'm going to be in Providence next weekend and I thought I might be able to buy you a piece of pie."

"I don't know," Maya said. She tried to think of excuses to tell him, but her mind was blank.

"Maybe just grab a cup of coffee?" Jack was saying.

What harm could coffee do? Maya asked herself. "All right," she said.

"Don't sound so excited," Jack laughed.

"I'm sorry," she said, "I'm just busy here."

They made arrangements to meet, and Maya got off the phone as quickly as she could.

What was it about this particular man that was making her act this way? she wondered. He really was not so very different from the other men Emily had set her up with. She did not find him especially attractive. That stomach! And so little hair. But it had been years since she'd been with a man really, and perhaps that kiss had reminded her of all she had given up. In that moment, she had caught his scent, soap and lime. A few years ago, in an effort to try to connect with someone, she'd had some misguided brief relationships. But the sex had been unsatisfying and her inability to open up had ended things quickly.

Now here was this Jack Sullivan. A nice enough man. She tried to imagine him naked, but the thought made her laugh. Her husband had been a big guy, but solid. Thinking of him now, she could clearly picture how the muscles in his arms moved when he moved the oars in their kayak, how his large hands touching her hair, her breasts, the dip of her stomach between her hipbones, made her feel.

Maya swiveled her chair toward her computer with its screensaver of colorful tropical fish swimming and clicked on Google.

Adam Xavier, she typed. Her fingers trembled on the keyboard. He used to call her Madame X sometimes and it would make her feel safe somehow. Ridiculous how easily a person can fool herself into believing nothing bad can happen, that she is safe from catastrophe.

The computer blinked. Then Adam's name appeared before her, over and over.

He had many publications, she could see that even through the tears that filled her eyes. Maybe he was bald and soft now, like Jack Sullivan. A lot can happen in a decade. She glanced down the list, hit Next, and watched as his name appeared again. Maya clicked an entry with Santa Barbara in it. He had left Hawaii too, and had joined the faculty of UC Santa Barbara eight years ago. That was when she'd started the Red Thread.

Maya clicked again. "Adam Xavier and his wife Carly welcomed a daughter, Rain, on June 6."

Maya swallowed hard and read it again, as if this time there would be no wife, no daughter.

Rain.

He didn't like names like that. Hadn't he laughed when a colleague of theirs named her daughter Summer? The entry was from the University of Hawaii alumni magazine. 2006. Adam had a wife and a two-year-old daughter.

She tried to picture him other than how he had been when he was her husband. She thought of his determination and confusion when he baked her that pie. She thought of how grief ravaged his face that night in the hospital emergency room, the sound of hailstones as big as golf balls banging the windows, denting cars in the parking lot.

That hail had dented their car in such a way that when that long night was over and they were finally going home, Maya couldn't open the passenger door. Instead, she had to go in on his side and climb over the stick shift, knocking over his cold coffee that he'd left in the cup holder. She thought of how his blue eyes grew cloudy with accusation in the months before she realized she should leave him, leave Honolulu.

Maya clicked the Next button again, and still more entries appeared.

But she felt weary and sad. She didn't need to read anything more.

A firm knock on the door startled her. Maya looked up and there stood Nell Walker-Adams. Could her day get any worse, she wondered as she motioned Nell in.

"Nell Walker-Adams—" the woman began.

"Yes," Maya interrupted. "Please. Have a seat."

Maya could smell the leather of Nell's briefcase, the citrus of her expensive perfume.

"I apologize," Maya said. "I haven't had a chance to read your letter. We have families preparing to go to China and that is always a busy time here."

"It's just a thank-you note," Nell said, her eyes focusing now on the photographs.

"A thank-you note?" Maya said.

"For the other night. The orientation."

"Ah," Maya said.

This woman led her life by very particular rules. Maya could not remember receiving a formal thank-you note since the invention of email.

Nell's gaze settled on one of the photographs and she picked it up. "These babies," she said. "They're placed with families?"

"Yes."

"And those families waited how long?"

Maya fought the urge to make her return the picture to its place.

"Fourteen months," she answered.

Nell studied the picture, then looked directly at Maya. "I don't want to wait that long."

Maya managed to make a sympathetic sound. "The process," she explained. "The paperwork and home study—"

"Do you know that John Adams' house is in Quincy?" Nell said.

Maya frowned. "Yes."

"There is a staircase there. The main staircase. No one is allowed to go up or down it, except once a year, on the Fourth of July. On that day, only the descendants of John Adams enter the house and walk up that staircase."

"How interesting," Maya said. She wished Nell would put the photograph down. She wished she would leave.

Nell smiled—smugly, Maya thought. "My husband is one of those descendants. Of John Adams. Every Fourth of July we go to the Adams party and he walks up that staircase."

"A very distinguished lineage," Maya said politely.

"What would it take to move to the head of this queue?" Nell said, her voice firm, her gaze unwavering.

"It doesn't work like that," Maya said.

"Everything works like that."

"Everything except the Chinese government," Maya said.

"Surely one of these orphanages would be pleased to receive a generous donation—"

"These children are not being sold, Ms. Walker-Adams," Maya said. She struggled to keep the harshness out of her voice.

Nell studied Maya's face. "Of course they're not," she said finally.

She looked again at the photograph she had been holding, a nine-month-old girl with a funny tuft of black hair and a quizzical expression. Then she placed the picture back on the desk, right where it had been, and stood.

"Thank you for stopping by," Maya said. "If you have any other questions, please feel free."

As Nell collected her briefcase and adjusted her fitted jacket, Maya added, "Enjoy your staircase."

"Excuse me?"

"The Fourth of July," Maya said, forcing a smile. "It's in a few weeks and your husband will again climb the staircase."

Maya expected Nell's face to betray nothing, or perhaps a flash of anger or indignation. But instead her façade softened ever so slightly.

"I want a baby," she said quietly.

If Maya were a different sort of person, she might have comforted her in some way. But she simply nodded and took her seat again, turning her attention back to the portfolios on her desk even before Nell was out of the office.

5

The Families

NELL

Nell leaned against the building, and cried. For that moment, she did not think about her Thai lesson that she was going to be late for. She did not think about the people who passed her, averting their eyes. She did not think about her mascara, which had surely started to run. All she thought about was that baby she wanted, that vague round image that had lodged deep in her mind and that Maya Lange was keeping from her.

In Nell's world, a twenty-dollar bill slipped discreetly into a maître d's palm got a preferred table ahead of people with reservations. A dropped name got seats to Red Sox playoffs, sold-out Bruce Springsteen concerts, smash plays. Nell was used to getting what she wanted. So how could a baby, something so ordinary and commonplace, elude her like this? Even now, as she pressed her back against the cold stone wall, women with babies in strollers and Snuglis walked by, Russian nannies walked elementary school children down the street, distracted mothers held on to their toddlers' hands.

Everyone, Nell thought as she watched them, everyone had a child. Except her.

The Pergonal made her hormones go berserk. She knew that. Perhaps that was why Maya's firm refusal of her offer had set her off like this. Perhaps those hormones were responsible for this feeling she had now of being left out of a club, the only woman in Providence, in the entire world, who didn't—couldn't—have a baby. Right now, all Nell knew for certain was that she hated Maya Lange. And that somehow she would get herself a baby.

She took a deep yoga breath to collect herself. Take air in. Hold. Release. Again. After three breaths, she had stopped crying. She took out her BlackBerry and sent an email to that woman at work who had adopted not one but two babies from Guatemala. As soon as Nell hit the Send button, she felt back to normal. In control.

She dotted her cheeks with her handkerchief, careful not to rub off whatever foundation and blush were still there. She reapplied her lipstick. She smoothed her hair. She walked briskly, confidently, forward.

THEO

Theo hated teaching Thai to overachieving businessmen looking for an advantage in the Asian market. They were rude, smug, aggressive. Looking at them lined up in front of him, Theo tried not to think of how more and more lately he hated more things in his life than he liked. He tried to think of the island off the coast of Thailand where he had spent six blissful months working as a dive instructor. How being 14,000 feet under the sea had eased his broken heart.

He thought of the German and British tourists who stayed at the resort, a stretch of beach scattered with thatched-roofed huts, an open-air bar, and hammocks. Each week, a different girl fell in love with him, and he found himself drinking Tiger beer and making love all night, their flesh salty warm from the sun.

"Is my company paying for you to stare at us?" a student said. "Or to teach us Thai?"

The guy, in an expensive gray suit with a stomach out to here and a ruddy face, was sneering.

Theo fought his desire to sneer back. Think Tiger beer, he told himself. Think pretty blond German woman in your arms.

Theo smiled. He introduced himself and passed out the books, *Thai for the Businessperson.* Inside were phrases like, "I do not accept the terms of your contract," and "Shall we meet in your conference room at 9:00 a.m.?"

Will you sleep with me? Theo thought as the men took their books. That wasn't in there, though every class someone asked him how to say: "Can you find me a woman for the night?" and all of the men carefully wrote it down. Someone always came up to him after class and asked how to request particular sexual favors, which Theo dutifully wrote down for them phonetically.

"Lesson one," Theo said, and the men all opened their books.

He wondered what it would be like to be so obedient, so focused. For one thing, he supposed, he would have some money and not be forced to teach fat businessmen through a night school program. "Greetings."

The door flew open, startling everyone. The men all seemed to frown and swing their heads in unison to watch a tall, lean woman stride in. She wore narrow jeans, a white button-down shirt, and a blazer. All business with a bit of sexiness thrown in: the shirt was unbuttoned just enough so that Theo could see the lace of her bra. And she wore high heels. Despite himself, he grew aroused. Thinking of those German women in Thailand, and now this, after the mandatory sex with Sophie to get pregnant. Theo shifted.

Without an explanation, the woman took a seat right in the front row. She leaned over—that lace again!—and took a book, opening it immediately before looking at him expectantly.

"Lesson one," Theo repeated. "Greetings."

Halfway through the class, the same guy as before blurted, "Is it true that it's taboo to make jokes about the king in Thailand?"

Theo saw the woman roll her eyes.

He tried to make eye contact with her, to let her know he was on her side. The guy was obnoxious. But when she saw him looking at her, she frowned and looked away.

Why had that aroused him? Was he going to spend the next ten Tuesday nights trying to hide his hard-on? The woman wasn't even that attractive. Too much makeup. Her hair cut in a bob, his least favorite look on a woman with its severe edge, neither long nor short. Worse, she had on a headband. Theo hated headbands on grown women. His attraction to her was further proof that all of this adoption business and Sophie's single-minded pursuit of a baby were pushing him into places he did not want to go.

For the next twenty minutes, Theo talked about Thailand. He told them the story of Ramakian, how a young couple in love were banished to the forest and Sita, the bride, got kidnapped by the evil king. When he reached the end where Sita and Rama are reunited, Theo felt himself get choked up, the way he always did when he told this story. One man fell asleep, releasing small squawky snores every now and then, his chin resting on his chest. But everyone else seemed to come to life. Even the woman. Their books lay open in front of them, but they all listened to Theo. As he described Bangkok and its Grand Palace and Wat Phra Kaew, even the obnoxious guy took notes.

"We didn't get as far as we should have," Theo apologized when the noisy hour hand on the clock swept forward and clicked onto nine.

He gave them their homework assignment and shook hands with them as they left. Businessmen were handshakers, a habit that made him slightly uncomfortable. He noticed that the woman was lingering, pretending to fuss with some papers, rearranging something in her briefcase, until she was the only one left.

Theo willed himself to not get an erection, but when she finally stopped fussing and looked at him, he couldn't control it.

"Look," she said, her voice so commanding that he found himself standing up straighter, "I want to learn Thai and I don't want this to get in my way."

Theo nodded, even as he wondered what she was talking about. His hard-on? His history lesson?

"I assume you can stay professional?" she said, narrowing her eyes.

"Well, sure," Theo said, shrugging.

"There aren't a lot of Thai classes in Providence and I don't have the time to drive over an hour to Boston," she said. "So it's important. We'll no doubt run into each other at the Red Thread and I don't want that connection to interfere—"

"The adoption place?" Theo said.

"We were at the orientation last week. Your wife has the curly hair? You met in Thailand? You want a dozen multicultural children?"

Theo grinned and took a step toward her.

"I don't know if I want any children," he said in a low voice, as if Sophie might hear him.

The woman cocked her head. "Really?"

He shrugged again. "It is entirely possible I will never see you at that place again. I can simply be your Thai instructor and our paths will not cross."

She was studying him closely. "I'm Nell, by the way."

"I didn't listen to anything anyone said," Theo told her. "I was miserable and I wanted to get the hell out of there."

Nell laughed. "Then you don't remember how my husband embarrassed me by introducing himself as Mr. Nell Walker-Adams."

"Nope," Theo lied. He had heard that, of course. He just hadn't paid attention to who said it.

"Good," she said.

Now Theo studied her. She wasn't bad-looking. Why did she wear all that makeup? Why did she have her hair cut like that? Briefly, he imagined sliding that headband off her, and licking away all that lipstick.

"What?" she said.

"I was thinking about Tiger beer," he said, lying again. "A big cold one. Interested?"

Nell wrinkled her nose. "I don't like beer."

Big surprise, Theo thought. He began to move toward the door.

"I'm sure they have chardonnay too," he said over his shoulder.

He heard her high heels moving toward him.

"How did you know that's what I drink?" she said.

Theo held the door open for her.

When she walked past him, he caught a whiff of a heavy expensive perfume. He didn't like perfume either. So why was he getting a hard-on again? Why was he hurrying to catch up to her? What the hell was he doing?

THEO WAS IMPRESSED by how such a skinny woman could hold her liquor. Four glasses of chardonnay and she had only grown softer, not drunken. The lipstick had worn off, and he liked that her smile was slightly crooked.

Nell pointed a finger at him. "You're a romantic," she said.

"That's a bad thing?"

She shrugged.

"Why do you think I'm a romantic?" he asked her.

"You almost cried when you told us that love story."

Theo laughed. "Guilty as charged," he said. "It gets to me every time. True love triumphs."

"Like you and your wife?" Nell said. "True love?"

"Where's your husband tonight?" he asked her, ignoring her question.

She waved her hand dismissively. "Probably at a meeting. We don't have to have sex tonight so he scheduled something late."

Theo laughed again. The beers had made him light-headed and silly. He pointed his bottle at her. "That sounds very romantic."

Nell rolled her eyes.

She was an eye-roller, he thought. He liked that too.

"This baby thing," she said.

Theo waited, but she didn't go on. She just sipped her wine.

"Let's have one more," he said. "What do you say?"

"Are you trying to get me drunk, Teach?" she said.

"I just don't want to go home yet," he said, motioning to the bartender.

"That sounds very romantic," Nell said.

The bartender brought two more drinks, and Theo took a big swallow from his beer.

"My wife," he began. "Sophie. She wants to save the world."

"Ugh," Nell said. "I can't stand do-gooders. I'm a capitalist. I want nice things. I want to make gobs of money. And I want a baby. One goddamned baby. That's all."

Theo was shredding his cocktail napkins into long, even strips. She put her hand over his to make him stop.

"Sorry," he said. "Bad habit. I shred things."

She didn't move her hand right away, and when she did, he found himself wishing she hadn't.

"Why don't you want a baby?" she whispered, leaning closer to him.

Theo swallowed hard. He almost could say it to her in this dark bar, her crooked smile so close, that stupid headband keeping her hair in perfect place. But he didn't want to say it out loud. Instead, he leaned in closer still and kissed her, softly, right on the mouth. He could taste the waxy lipstick, the chardonnay, and something softer beneath. She didn't exactly kiss him back, but she didn't move away either. When the kiss stopped, their lips stayed close enough for more. He could feel her breath on his face.

"Isn't there a policy about teachers and students?" she whispered, trying to make a joke.

"No," he said. "There's not."

"A LATE NIGHT," Sophie said when he walked into the bedroom.

He was drunker than he'd thought back at the bar. That happened sometimes. You seemed fine, just a little buzzed, then you stood up and wham! All those beers hit at once.

"I guess," he said, trying not to stumble. He sat on the edge of the bed to pull off his T-shirt so she wouldn't notice him off-balance.

"You didn't call," she said.

Theo noticed she had on her batik nightgown. He hated that thing, with its faux cultural references. She'd bought it at a fancy lingerie store in Manhattan when she went there for a conference.

"Lost track of time," he said.

"I'm ovulating," she said, and when he didn't answer she added, "I left you three messages on your cell phone."

"Battery's dead," he said, which was true. It drove Sophie crazy how he always forgot to recharge his phone.

She let out a small, exasperated sigh. "I put on your favorite nightgown," she said hopefully.

Theo looked at her, surprised. Had he told her he liked that thing? Sometimes he worked so hard to please her that he couldn't even keep track of what he'd done or said.

"You've had a lot to drink," she said.

He kept looking at her until he realized what she was getting at. They had to have sex. Now.

Tears were coming down her cheeks. "I feel good about going forward with the adoption," she was saying. "I do. But I still want my own baby. I want to feel what it's like to have something growing inside me. I want to be able to put my hand on my stomach and press and feel that baby press back. To hear its heartbeat. To give birth and then hold this human being that we've made together." She was full out crying now. "I know it makes me seem like a bad person. I mean, there are so many children without homes in the world, but then I think about how we'll give them a home, we will. I just want one, one of my very own."

"Take it off," Theo said. "The nightgown. Take it off."

Her hands trembled as she lifted the batik nightgown over her head. Her breasts were large and full. Theo thought of Nell, the lace of her bra. He thought of how her lips had felt on his. He thought of how his hand had felt on the small of her back as he guided her out of the bar and waited with her until she found a taxi.

Thinking of these things, he knew he could do this. He pulled his pants off, his boxer shorts. He was already hard.

Sophie did not stop crying, even as he entered her. "Give me this one thing," she kept whispering to him.

He finished too fast, and rolled off her with his head swimming.

He had just closed his eyes when she said, "Maya Lange called tonight."

"Uh-huh," he muttered.

"She runs the Red Thread Adoption Agency?" Sophie was saying. "She asked us to host a little get-together for the families from our orientation group."

Theo opened his eyes, struggled to make sense of what she was saying.

"Isn't that flattering?" Sophie said. She sniffled, her crying finally done. She let out a little noise that she always made just as she drifted off to sleep.

But now Theo was wide awake.

"Isn't our place kind of small for so many people?" he said. He nudged her gently. "Sophie?"

Nothing, except the slow, even breath of her asleep.

"NELL," THEO SAID, his voice low. "It's me. Uh, Theo."

He was surprised how difficult it had been to reach her. First she'd been in a meeting. "Would you like her voice mail?" the secretary had asked. He would not. Then she'd stepped out. Then she'd been in another meeting. Then lunch. Then another meeting. Then she was on a call. It was almost five o'clock now, and finally Nell's voice, controlled and highly annunciated, had said, "Nell Walker-Adams," into Theo's ear.

"Yes?" she said, as if he had not kissed her last night.

"Uh," he said, aware that he sounded about as opposite of

her as a person could. "I thought we should talk about what happened."

"Yes?" she said again.

"Did you hear about the thing? The get-together at our house? It's for the—"

"I know what it's for," she said impatiently.

"Well, it might be awkward. I thought we should clear the air."

He waited, but she said nothing. He thought he could hear her clicking away on a computer keyboard.

"Look," he said. "It never happened. Okay?"

"Thank you for calling," she said.

"So that's okay?" Theo said, but she had already hung up.

Sometimes he wished he could just go back to Thailand and disappear there for a few months, or a few years, or a lifetime. He imagined himself on a beach there, the hot sun beating down on him, a buzz on from several beers, and nothing on his mind at all. Nothing.

Theo glanced at the clock. He had to teach his English class tonight. Thai businessmen who wanted to improve their English. He enjoyed this class so much more than the other one. The Thai men were relaxed, funny. He liked to reminisce with them about his time there, to hear stories about Bangkok or Chang Mai. Sometimes he even joined them for dinner afterward, savoring the hot curry they ordered. Sophie didn't like spicy food and they always had to get the mildest dishes.

Sophie. Theo thought of how this morning she'd so happily begun to plan for this brunch. She took everything so seriously. By the time he'd had his first cup of coffee, she'd already found a place to get dim sum and decided to buy red napkins and a red tablecloth. "The traditional color of celebration in China," she'd explained. He should admire her enthusiasm for everything. He should marvel at her willingness to please everybody. But more and more, it all annoyed him.

Sighing, Theo grabbed his backpack and headed out. He would stop at that little store in East Providence and get some silly decorations as a surprise for Sophie. Maybe some foil dragons. Or the fortune cookies with happy fortunes inside. He would try to do something that would make her smile.

But when he got off the highway, he headed downtown where Nell worked. It was ridiculous. He knew that. What was he going to do? Stand in front of her building with its shining glass and metal, and hope she walked past him? Even if he did that, what were the chances she would walk past him? Still, Theo paced in front of the building, looking expectantly each time the revolving door spit out a new group of people.

He wasn't even sure why he'd come. Too much to drink. Blurting how he didn't really want children, how Sophie needed to save the world. Theo shuddered at what this woman must think of him. Was he here to apologize? Or to see her again? A new group emerged, all men in expensive suits. Abruptly, Theo walked away. He got in his car and drove onto Route 195 East, to East Providence.

Inside the cramped, crowded store, he grabbed paper lanterns, a too-big foil dragon, shiny cutouts of the animals from Chinese astrology. He selected packets of chopsticks, chocolate fortune cookies. If Sophie were a different woman, she would recognize these gifts as the act of a guilty man. Especially this last one, Theo thought as he added a tiny pair of pink silk slippers to his basket. Perfect for a baby girl.

CHARLIE

Charlie stood on the beach in the drizzling rain and hit baseballs. Long ago, growing up in a house with parents who drank too much and fought too hard, he had found solace in his ability to make a baseball soar. When his parents started yelling, he would go outside into the Florida humidity and hit balls. The crack of the bat comforted him. Watching a baseball fly through the waves of heat and land far from him gave Charlie what he was not getting inside the turquoise bungalow where his mother's shrieks and his father's loud, angry yells escaped. Sometimes, there would be blood and bruises when Charlie finally came back inside. Sometimes one or the other of them would be gone. He never knew what to expect when he walked under the carport and pushed open the kitchen door. But out in the backyard, when he swung that bat, he knew what would happen.

Sixteen years married to Brooke, it was impossible to hide anything.

"It's raining, Charlie," she said, hugging herself.

Thwack!

"You are standing in the rain hitting baseballs," she said.

"Force of habit," Charlie said, keeping his eye on the ball as it sailed toward him.

Brooke grabbed his arm and he missed the ball.

"Charlie," she said, "tell me you don't want to do this. Say it."

Charlie lowered his bat. "You want a baby more than anything. That's what you said."

"I see pregnant women and I want to cry," Brooke said. The rain flattened her hair against her face. She shivered. "It's this thing," she said. "Like an ache. Here"—she patted her chest—"in my heart."

"You want a baby and I'm going to get you one. Even if it means—" He stopped.

"Means what?"

"Going all the way to China," he said, hoping this time she couldn't read his mind. He didn't want her to see what was there. He didn't want her to read his fear. Fear that a baby would take her away from him.

Brooke studied his face. She knew there was something he wasn't telling her.

"Don't get my hopes up and change your mind," she said. "Okay?"

He grinned at her. "You made me promise that one other time and I didn't let you down, did I?"

They had met in college, when he was the star baseball player, already getting recruited by the major leagues. When I land a contract and make it to the show, I'm going to marry you, he'd told her. That's when she'd said it the first time: Don't get my hopes up and change your mind. Okay? Three years later he played his first game at Fenway Park. That night, even though the Sox had lost, Charlie had walked into Brooke's apartment with a bottle of champagne and a diamond ring. I told you, he'd whispered to her. I'm a man of my word.

"That's not a yes, Charlie," Brooke said now.

"You're going to get sick out here in the rain," he said. He took off his jacket and wrapped it around her shoulders.

She stared at him, hard.

"Darling," he said, "I'm a man of my word. We are getting a baby. We are driving to Providence and going to this party and making friends with all these people who are going to China with us."

She started to walk away.

"Brooke?"

"I'm making my miniature quiches," she said without turning around. "It's a potluck."

Charlie watched her walk down the beach, up the crooked path that led to their yard, until she disappeared. When he couldn't see her, panic rose in him. He took a deep breath. This was what it would feel like if he lost her. But standing there in the rain, Charlie couldn't imagine how he could keep her. If they didn't adopt a baby, he would lose her. And when that baby arrived and she fell in love with it, he might too.

"Brooke!" he called, even though he knew she couldn't hear him from the kitchen where she stood, probably smiling, probably humming in her off-key way, unaware that he was out here, missing her already.

EMILY

"Don't do it." That was what Emily's friends told her when she started dating Michael. "Don't get involved with someone who already has a child."

They'd listed the reasons: He will always put her before you. He will always feel guilty that he doesn't live with her full-time. She'll resent your role in her father's life. When you have your own kids, he'll already have experienced all the things associated with that and you'll feel alone. You will never ever win.

She'd laughed at them. Maybe that was true for some people, like her old roommate Maureen who had married a man with four kids and spent most of her time fighting with them, or her husband, or his ex-wife. In the flush of love, Emily had never imagined that any of that would be true. Not for her and Michael. She'd married him and left her little house in Fox Point that she'd spent almost two years renovating and moved out here to the suburbs, into a rambling new house that still smelled of wood and paint.

Plenty of rooms for all the children they would have, she thought when they moved in. She left her job too, as a librarian at Brown University. Here, she volunteered part-time at the town library, where she sat, bored, three afternoons a week. But once the babies came, she would be happy for the diversion the library brought.

"Don't do it," her friends said, about getting married, about moving, about leaving her job.

But she had done it. All of it. And now, three years later, she was childless and he did put Chloe ahead of her and she was bored and fifteen pounds heavier than when she'd married him. The house was empty. Her days were empty. Her womb was empty. But that was about to change.

Emily and Michael had their first home study visit on Friday. Maya had told her not to worry. "Just be yourself," she'd said, as if that was the easiest thing in the world. But lately, Emily wasn't sure who she was anymore. Before she'd married Michael, she'd stripped floors and polished fireplace tiles with a toothbrush in her house. She strode across the Brown green like a woman who knew where she was going. She used to go to sleep at night happy, with her two cats purring at the foot of her bed. Sometimes she had men in that bed, and she knew how to have them satisfy her. She knew she liked peaty single malt whiskey and oaky chardonnay. She'd perfected three dinner party meals.

So how had she landed here, uncertain of almost everything in her life? Her husband loved his daughter more than he loved her, possibly even more than he loved anything. Around Chloe, Emily felt off-balance. She was neither her mother nor her friend. If she criticized her, Michael got angry. She couldn't comfortably discipline her or ask her about herself. The house was too big, and Emily could not find her place in it even after three years.

She couldn't find her place as a wife either. It had been months since she'd had a dinner party and made her beef daube or turkey in mole sauce or the ragù that took all day to get just right. Even books did not comfort her anymore the way they used to. She could remember hours lost in the bowels of the library, books piling up beside her.

Each time she got pregnant, Emily had believed she was finding herself again, making something of her increasingly senseless days. She could almost catch a glimpse of herself happy again, a baby in her arms, then toddling across the wide planks of the kitchen floor, running through the garden. She would hang a swing there, and sit the baby in her lap and pump her legs so that she and her child could soar. But with each miscarriage, another piece of herself vanished. "Be yourself," Maya had told her, squeezing her hand for courage and confidence. But who exactly was this person who still called herself Emily and lived in her body?

The social worker had smiled and nodded as they answered questions and showed her around their house. When she left, Emily had felt happier than she'd been in months, ever since the last pregnancy test had come out positive. After that miscarriage, she'd started to see Dr. Bundy. But now, with this first visit behind them, Emily could almost believe that she would actually have a baby of her own before long.

Today they were going to a get-together with their travel group at someone's apartment over in the Armory District, on the appropriately celebratory named Parade Street. Another step toward China and a baby. Emily didn't like potlucks. She liked things to go together. But Sophie had emailed everyone a dish to bring, so maybe this one wouldn't be too bad.

Emily had worried over her assignment: Something Sweet! She wasn't much of a baker, but maybe she should make cupcakes? Coffee cake? Or perhaps she should just go to the Italian bakery and buy something fancy and rich, like cannoli or zeppoli? She even considered calling the people who had Something Fruity as their assignment and ask if they would switch with her. That was easy. Fruit salad. Cut up some apples and oranges and pineapple. Throw in raspberries and everybody's happy.

She stood looking at the two platters of cookies she'd spent all morning baking, chocolate chunk and oatmeal raisin. Everybody liked cookies. She heard Michael and Chloe talking in Chloe's room, above her, and smiled. So confident was she of this new direction her life was taking, she'd even urged Michael to invite Chloe to the party. Today, finally, Emily could almost feel her own baby in her arms.

MICHAEL

Sometimes Michael felt as if he was in one of those rooms with the walls that squeezed in on you until they completely crushed you. One wall was Chloe and one wall was his ex-wife Rachel and one wall was Emily, the woman he loved. His wife. They crushed him with their jealousy and their neediness and their suspicions about each other. All he wanted was to live a happy life. He wanted to make love to his wife and to be a good father to his daughter and to avoid fighting with his ex-wife. He wanted to give Emily babies. He wanted to do the right things so that Chloe would grow up secure and confident. But somehow, he did everything wrong.

Like today. Didn't Rachel always tell him that Chloe felt excluded from his life with Emily? So he had told her cheerfully, hopefully, that they were all going to a brunch with the other families adopting babies from China.

Chloe looked at him and said, "No way."

"But it will be fun," he'd said.

"Are you kidding? A bunch of grown-ups eating bad food and talking about babies?"

When she put it that way, Michael supposed it didn't sound like fun for her. "Well," he'd said, "how about coming and keeping me company?"

She snorted. "Isn't that why you have Emily?"

He wanted to tell her that he had Emily because he loved her. Adored her, in fact. But that would make Chloe think he loved Emily more than he loved her. Hadn't Rachel told him that it made Chloe uncomfortable if he kissed Emily in front of her?

Michael tried again. "It would be good for you to get to know these folks," he said, "for when we're in China."

Chloe frowned. "China? I'm not going to China."

She thinks you're replacing her, Rachel had said. Even though Michael told her that was ridiculous, Rachel had insisted.

"Chloe," Michael said, "I love you. This baby is going to be your sister and I'm not going to love you any less."

"Okay, Dad," Chloe said. "Whatever."

Then she began to pack her little overnight bag, the purple one she'd had since she was a little girl and began the weekly journey back and forth between her parents.

"What are you doing?" Michael asked her.

"I'm not going to stay here while you and Emily go to a party," she said. "Mom can pick me up and I'll go to the mall with Arden and Kayla."

There were those walls squeezing in on him. The party and Emily and their baby waiting in China. Rachel shaking her head in disapproval. Chloe caught in the middle of it all. And Michael just wanting a day with his wife and his daughter with him.

He watched as Rachel's Passat drove up the driveway.

Chloe bounded down the steps, almost happily.

"We'll get you new luggage for China," Michael said, taking

that sad, worn little bag from her. "Three pieces. Grown-up luggage."

Emily came out from the kitchen. "What's going on?"

"My mom's here," Chloe said. "I'm going home."

The word *home* pierced Michael. This was supposed to be her home too. Did Emily look happy that Chloe was leaving early? Why couldn't she see how disappointed he was?

He followed Chloe to the car.

Rachel shook her head when she saw him. She rolled down the window. "Have fun at your party," she said.

"It's not that kind of party," Michael began to explain.

But Chloe had already settled into the passenger seat and Rachel was rolling up her window and backing up.

Behind him, he could feel Emily standing on the steps, waiting for him. Michael's heart felt heavy.

"Michael?" Emily said.

He turned toward her, but she was moving back inside, away from him.

SUSANNAH

"But she said children were welcome," Carter told Susannah, baffled.

"I just thought it would be easier to leave her with Julie," Susannah said. She busied herself with the huge bowl of fruit salad she'd made. Enough for twice the number of people.

Clara reached one dirty hand into the bowl of cut-up fruit and picked out raspberries, filling her hand with them.

"Stop her!" Susannah said. All of her work cutting up fruit and layering in the delicate berries ruined now. Clara had been outside playing in the dirt, and that dirt was in the fruit salad.

"You like raspberries best, don't you, Boo?" Carter said, gently lifting Clara off the chair she'd climbed and away from the food.

"I love raspberries," Clara said, her face red from them.

"See what I mean?" Susannah said. "What if she does something like that at the party? Sticks her dirty hands into the eggs or whatever?"

Carter shook his head. "I can't believe you," he muttered, scooping Clara into his arms and pretending to make her fly. Carter imitated the sound of an airplane as he dipped and soared his daughter past Susannah and out of the kitchen. Clara's giggles made Susannah even more tense.

She had imagined that she would give a daughter the things her mother had given her before she'd died. Hand-knit blankets for her dolls. Ice skates so that they could hold hands and skate across a frozen pond together. Glittery pink nail polish. Books to read together in bed.

But Susannah did not know what to do with this daughter. It seemed that since Clara was born, Susannah had known something was wrong with her. At first, she'd been afraid to say anything, even to Carter. But at the mommy group she joined, and in the park with other mothers and babies, it became more and more apparent that Clara wasn't right.

Susannah remembered sitting on someone's family room floor, watching the other babies laugh and roll and play, and the word *retarded* came to her mind. Clara was retarded. She had watched her daughter intently, the realization that this was why Clara was so dull-eyed, so slow to do anything other babies her age did, why she was so sensitive to noise and bright lights.

"Fragile X syndrome," the pediatrician told them. "An inherited form of mental retardation. The symptoms vary widely."

They varied widely and Clara had them all: Learning disabilities. Emotional disabilities. Socialization problems. An IQ of about 75.

Susannah remembered her grandmother telling her of another child she'd had whom they'd had to put away. So sad, her grandmother had said. But what could we do? Nowadays, though, people didn't institutionalize their children. They kept them. Information on Special Olympics and centers for disabled children always appeared in their mailbox. Well-meaning friends sent them books on children like Clara who had changed their parents' lives for the better. Selfish people had turned generous, judgmental people had grown magnanimous.

But Susannah remained selfish. She wanted a different child. No matter how many articles and books she read about the joy these children brought other families, Clara brought her only disappointment and shame. More and more she called Julie to come in the afternoon and take care of Clara. Although she made up excuses, usually Susannah just went into the bedroom, closed the door, and knit.

Then one day in the grocery store she ran into an old friend of hers. Lizzie had two daughters from China, both of them beautiful and smart. They had talked with Susannah, introducing themselves and telling her about school and their new puppy. The girls were bright-eyed, alert. The opposite of Clara. That night she had told Carter she wanted to adopt a baby from China. Maybe she would have that daughter she'd so desperately wanted after all.

At first Carter was reluctant. You can hardly deal with one child, he'd said, as if Clara wasn't a handful with her tantrums and her problems. But she'd invited Lizzie and her daughters over for dinner one night, and he'd seen it too. What normal children could give them. How they might actually talk to a daughter, and laugh with her, and let her eat at the table with them and snuggle on their laps.

Julie walked into the kitchen now, just as Susannah finished removing the berries Clara had squashed from the fruit salad.

"You're a lifesaver," Susannah said, wrapping plastic wrap over the top.

"She likes parties," Julie offered. "If you've changed your mind—"

"She's with Carter," Susannah said. "We've got to get going."

"Okay," Julie said.

Susannah carefully folded her knitting and put it in her bag. She would knit on the ride to Providence. Then they would arrive and they would walk into this group of strangers and Clara would be far away, out of sight, in her bedroom that Susannah had so hopefully painted with scenes from all of the books she'd imagined they would read together. *The Wind in the Willows* and *Peter Rabbit* and *Winnie-the-Pooh*. Clara could hardly sit still through something as simple as *Goodnight Moon*. Those murals made Susannah sad whenever she sat on her daughter's bed and read, "Goodnight nobody."

But these people today would be with her in China, getting their healthy babies. A family of sorts.

Carter came into the kitchen and Susannah headed out the door.

"Aren't you going to say goodbye to Clara?" he said.

"It will only upset her," Susannah lied. "I don't want to make Julie's job any harder than it already is."

She stepped out into the light summer rain and inhaled. It smelled fresh, new.

6

MAYA

Maya always made an appearance at these first get-togethers. She knew that if she stayed too long the group wouldn't relax. But her presence for a little while helped get things going. Sophie and Theo lived on the second floor of a green triple-decker. When Maya climbed the stairs, she heard the sound of voices already spilling from the open door. The apartment was all hardwood and color. They had painted the trim in each room white, but the walls were purple or red or yellow. Masks and textiles hung everywhere. Prayer flags draped across the kitchen.

"Look who's here!" Sophie said when she saw Maya standing in the doorway.

Everyone turned at once, and moved toward her, smiling.

Except Nell, Maya noticed. She hung back, an empty wine-glass in one hand. Maya nodded at her, and that was when she noticed Theo also stayed behind the others. He stood close to Nell, as if they had something in common. Maya frowned. Those two had nothing in common. Nothing at all. Why, here was Nell in some crinkly silk jacket and black cigarette pants, high heels, perfect hair and makeup. And there stood Theo all crumpled and unshaven. Maya had read all of their paperwork before she came and she knew that Theo worked part-time, teaching language lessons through adult education and translating business reports. That Nell Walker-Adams was a high-powered investment banker. Yet their heads were bent ever so slightly toward each other, as if they had a secret.

Sophie was handing Maya a plate of food. "Steamed dumplings and scallion pancakes and crab Rangoon," she was saying.

Every group did the same thing: a hodgepodge of Chinese dishes and potluck standards. But Maya thanked her and took the plate and the chopsticks she offered. As she nibbled on the food, the couples drifted up to her and told her nervously about their first home study visit, if they'd had one, and about the reading they'd done on China or the Yahoo adoption groups they'd joined. She commented on each piece of news with the same good cheer. These people believed she held their future in her hands. When she left, they would interpret each word she'd said, each expression, to see if they had moved up in line somehow, or committed a small infraction. Knowing this, she kept her voice measured, her smile pleasant. She encouraged each new step they took down this path to parenthood.

Then Nell Walker-Adams stepped away from her place by the red wall and said in her assertive voice, "Is it true they mark the children?"

"I've heard that too," the baseball player's wife said. She looked at Maya, worried.

"Some people believe—" Maya began, but that Nell interrupted her.

"I've heard they cut them here or here"—she indicated

between her fingers, around her ankles. "Or they burn them with a cigarette."

"A mother wouldn't harm her own child like that," Susannah said.

"Is it so they can find them someday?" Emily asked. "I can imagine a mother doing that."

"I heard it was so that the baby has a piece of the mother forever, because they won't be able to find each other," Brooke said.

"Some people do believe this," Maya said carefully. "But the marks on babies could be from so many places. Small injuries. These girls have no histories that we know." She shrugged. "There are many mysteries around them."

"I read on the Yahoo group about a woman whose baby had slashes around both ankles," Nell said. "More than a small injury."

"But the child was healthy?" Maya said.

"Otherwise, yes," Nell said.

"And she is happy now?"

"I guess."

Maya put her plate down on the counter. "What more do we want, then? Any of us?"

The talking began again, this topic abandoned for now.

Maya went from person to person to say goodbye. "You'll be hearing from us as soon as your home studies are completed," she told each one, shaking their hands firmly and with warmth.

Outside, the rain had stopped. It was a beautiful evening. Maya got in her car and headed back to the East Side, where Jack Sullivan was waiting to have a drink with her. She tried not to think about that. Instead, she put on her Moldy Peaches CD, almost silly in its optimism. She thought about the families she had spent the afternoon with. That Nell.

Maya forced that out of her mind too, and thought instead of Susannah, how she had looked almost frightened when they talked about the mothers marking the babies. She thought about Emily and Michael, and then that baseball player with his loud southern voice and big mustache, and then Sophie and how eager and hopeful she was about everything, and before she knew it, Maya was back on Wickenden Street and parking in front of Z Bar.

Jack was at the bar already. He was wearing a Hawaiian shirt, red with bright yellow and blue birds on it, and green palm trees. In front of him sat a half-empty mixed drink, something clear with a slice of lime.

When he saw her he stood, and kissed her lightly on the cheek.

She ordered a glass of wine, and drank it too fast in her nervousness.

"I'm a terrible dater," she admitted after he tried to make small talk, asking her about her work, about Providence, about her childhood. Each topic seemed daunting to her. "I don't know how to do it," she said.

"Then I'll talk," he said, and he told her about growing up in South Boston. He made her laugh with his stories of going to Catholic schools and how he lost his virginity in college in a car without any heat in the middle of January in Vermont. When he suggested they get a table and have dinner, she agreed readily.

Maya tried to remember what she and Adam used to talk about. Their work, of course. Politics. Somehow she had gotten to know all of these parts of his life, his family and his sexual adventures and his travel stories.

"Have you been married?" Maya asked Jack.

"Eleven years. We grew apart. It's so clichéd." He pried open a mussel and dredged it in broth. "You?"

"Yes. Clichéd too. He's remarried, has a child." She said these things like she knew them firsthand. Like it was all right.

After dinner, he suggested they go for a walk. But Maya surprised herself by asking him to come to her place instead. As she watched the headlights of his silver BMW follow her through the streets of her neighborhood, she felt that tug again, that yearning for something she once knew. That was when she realized she would sleep with him. If Adam could move on and get married and even have another baby, goddamn him, surely she could make love to someone. Surely she could spend the night in a man's arms, and wake up beside him and not feel terrified.

When they were inside her house, Maya opened a bottle of wine and poured them each a glass. But they only took a sip or two before it began.

As she unbuttoned his silly shirt, she whispered, "I lived in Hawaii. For years and years."

"That's why you seem so exotic, then," he said, shrugging out of the shirt.

She opened her mouth to say something else, but he silenced her with his tongue.

Somehow they managed to wait until they got to the bedroom, but then there was no more waiting. Maya opened herself to this man, this stranger, and for a few moments there was no Adam, no ambulance ride through palm-tree-lined streets, no hailstorm, nothing. There was just this: sex with a man she hardly knew.

But when it was done, and she settled into that familiar position of the woman's head on the man's shoulder, as her fingers played with the silver hair on his chest, Maya spoke.

"Something terrible happened," she said.

He seemed to hold his breath.

"I have never told anyone the truth," Maya said. "At night,

when I try to sleep, my mind takes me back to that day instead, even then I lie. I invent a slippery floor, a ray of blinding sunlight, a heroic attempt to stop the inevitable. But there was no water from her bath dripped onto the tiles. The sun, though bright in that way of tropical places, did not stab through the window. And I, the mother, her mother, stood and watched her fall. I tell myself that I reached out, groping, grasping, my hands almost, almost catching her, my fingers grazing the air."

Neither of them moved. Maya tried to stop herself, but it was too late. Now he would ask questions, jump to conclusions, run away.

"The startling horrible truth is this," Maya said, surprised by how calmly she spoke. "I gave her a bath, my daughter, my love. I filled the tub with Winnie-the-Pooh bath bubbles. I made sure the water was just right. Not too cold, not too hot. I splashed my fingers in it, sending bubbles into the air. That always made her laugh. Is there anything as beautiful as a baby's toothless smile? I remember watching her in that moment and my chest tightened with love. We think that love is an open thing, like open arms, but my love for her was close and tight, as if there was room for just the two of us in it, like a hug.

"She cried when I took her out of the bath. Cried hard. But I could smell the chicken I had put in the oven, almost done. I used to make it with lemons and garlic and rosemary. My specialty. There was laundry on the kitchen table waiting to be folded and my husband about to come home and who likes a dry chicken? And after dinner he would take the baby so I could finish my own work. I saw a cartoon once with a bride and a groom and the minister is asking: 'I now pronounce you tired.' That is motherhood too, exhaustion from playing and not sleeping and loving so hard. And roasting chickens and folding laundry and papers to grade and a husband.

"Even when I wrapped her in her fluffy towel, the one spotted like a Dalmation with a hood that had little ears that stood up and a small tail in the back that hung down, she cried. She wiggled and cried. The smell of roasting chicken filled the hot air, mingled with the sweet scent of bubble bath and my own sour sweat. I hadn't even showered yet. I cooed and hummed and did the things that calmed her. But nothing worked. Holding her against my hip in one arm, I reached for a diaper and the onesie that I liked so much, a soft pink one with that famous pencil drawing of John Lennon on it and the word IMAGINE. I sang 'Puff the Magic Dragon' softly.

"I reached. She cried. She threw her head back and squirmed, and then she was gone. Out of my arms, backwards, like a high diver, an acrobat, an angel."

Hunan, China

NI FAN

Ni Fan loved Xhao Hui. She had loved him ever since she first saw him on a hot summer day when she walked down the dirt road toward the market. She had a pole across her shoulders, and from that pole hung two baskets, one on each side, and in one of those baskets sat two sweet potatoes.

That was what she would sell in the market today. Ni Fan would get the yuan for the sweet potatoes and buy tea and rice with it and then she would walk back down this road to her family's house where her mother would be waiting, frowning and waiting because Ni Fan never brought home enough.

"Then you go to the market and sell nothing," Ni Fan had told her

yesterday. "Because that is all you give me to sell. Nothing. You expect me to get precious things for what I make selling a few sweet potatoes."

Her mother had yanked Ni Fan's hair. This was what people did when they were hungry. They yanked their daughter's hair. They beat their chests. They kicked at the soil that only yielded a few sweet potatoes instead of basketsful. Ni Fan understood this. But still, when her mother yanked her hair like that, Ni Fan thought: I hate you! She was fifteen years old, the age when girls hate their mothers and dream of a different life.

That hot summer day when Ni Fan saw Xhao Hui, he was standing in a field of kale and he had a funny hat on his head. She stopped walking to get a better look. He was very tall, and he wore a pale blue shirt and that hat. There was writing on the hat. Ni Fan squinted, trying to make it out.

"Girl!" he called. "What are you staring at? Have you never seen a man before?"

Ni Fan laughed at this. He wasn't a man at all. He was a boy her age, maybe a little older.

"Is there a man in that field with you?" she called back to him.

Sometimes when she remembered this, the hot sun beating down on her, the taste of her sweat on her lips, the smell of dry dirt, the weight of the sweet potatoes, all of it, she believed that by the time she finished that sentence she was already in love. She took a few steps closer toward him, and tried to read his hat.

"In some places, it is considered rude to stare," he said, grinning at her.

She was close enough now to see that one of his front teeth was cracked.

"In what places?" she asked him.

"England," he answered quickly, surprising her.

Ni Fan wondered where England was. Probably in the United States, where there were many odd customs. Her father had heard of these years ago when a student from America had traveled through the village. That boy had told the villagers about ground meat sold out of windows to people in automobiles, and machines that washed dishes and clothes, and a special machine used just to heat up cold food. "Americans," her father had told her, "are spoiled and lazy." Sometimes, when Ni Fan boiled water to clean the clothes, and carried the heavy cast-iron pot, she thought a machine that did this for her might be a marvelous thing.

"You are a daydreamer," the boy was shouting at her. He pointed a finger and grinned.

Ni Fan frowned at him, even though her heart soared. "Yes," she admitted. "I dream about machines that wash clothes."

The boy laughed. "Do you mean robots?"

"Yes," she said. She had no idea what robots were.

"Will your robot help me in the fields?"

"Yes," she said again.

Yes was what Ni Fan said to him a few days later when she passed him on her way to the market and he asked her if she wanted to meet him that night in the park. Yes was what she said when he asked if he could kiss her a few nights after that. And when he pressed himself against her, she heard herself whispering, "Yes, yes, yes." After that night, Ni Fan saw everything differently.

Had her mother, with her sour face and wrinkled forehead, once felt this desire? This throbbing low in the gut? This feeling that if she didn't see a boy and have him kiss her immediately, have him touch her there and there, have him enter her and move inside her and sigh in her ear, then she might die? Had her father, whose back was now bent awkwardly from work, once been so strong that he could lift her mother onto him? Had he known to probe her in such a way that she had felt as if she was falling from a very high roof?

"What's wrong with you?" her mother asked her as Ni Fan held her bowl of rice without eating it. "What are you staring at?"

Ni Fan shrugged. In two hours it would be dark and she would sneak away. She would feel the warm night air on her bare skin. She would feel her lover inside of her. She would fall from rooftops, from hilltops, from mountains.

Her mother smacked her on the side of the head. "Be useful," she said. "Stop dreaming."

Ni Fan stood and collected the empty rice bowls from her parents and her grandparents.

"Wouldn't it be nice if we had robots to clean our dishes?" she said.

Her father laughed. "Lots of dreams can occur over a long night," he said.

Angry, Ni Fan turned her back on her family. She threw the dirty dishes into the bucket of tepid water and began to scrub. She hated the way rice clung to everything, how difficult it was to remove.

Outside, darkness fell. This calmed her. Soon, she would be in Xhao Hui's arms, spinning dreams. Sometimes he whispered about the two of them leaving here and going to Beijing. There were jobs there, and shiny buildings made of glass and metal. People rode in automobiles. "Do they have robots in Beijing?" Ni Fan had whispered, imagining robots that washed clothes and dishes and even her own body. "Perhaps," he had whispered back.

Her stomach did that tugging that she recognized as desire. Hurriedly, she made fresh tea and served her parents and her grandparents. In her haste, Ni Fan splattered her grandmother's hand and the old woman swatted at her as if she were no more than a fly, a nuisance. How tenderly Xhao Hui brought her close to him, she thought.

"Be careful!" her mother reprimanded.

Hot tears sprang to Ni Fan's eyes, burning for the whispers of Xhao Hui.

Finally, after sweeping and wiping and serving, Ni Fan slipped away. She wished she had wings to get her to Xhao Hui faster.

When at last she saw his figure in the dark, lit by the glow of his cigarette, she threw herself at him, covering him with kisses. His hat with the odd writing fell off his head, and laughing, he threw her onto the ground, straddling her.

"You are like a tiger," he whispered.

Ni Fan smiled in the darkness, pulling down her pants, reaching for him.

"So eager, my tiger," he said.

Then he pushed into her. Their bodies moved together.

"Yes, yes, yes," Ni Fan whispered.

"MARRY ME," Ni Fan said one night after they made love.

Xhao Hui lay beside her, smoking a cigarette.

"Marry me and we can do this all the time. In the morning when we wake together. In the afternoon when we are taking a break from work."

When he didn't answer, she said, "Marry me and we can go to Beijing."

"Don't you know that matrimony is the grave of romance?" Xhao Hui said. "Look at your parents. And mine. They are bitter and repressed."

"But we won't become that way!"

He turned to her and kissed her. "Of course we won't because we won't get married. We'll just make love until we grow old and die."

His kissing grew more insistent and his fingers moved along her body.

"Three months we've been meeting like this," Ni Fan said, even as her back arched to meet his probing fingers. "I want to be with you in the daylight. I want everyone to see our happiness."

"Does this make you happy, my tiger?" he whispered, moving his fingers in just the right way.

Ni Fan tried to stay focused. She wanted to make her point.

"Does it?" he was saying, his fingers on that spot, so soft and persistent. "Does it?"

"If we marry . . ." she began.

She was on that rooftop, that hilltop. She heard her ragged breath.

"If we . . ." she began. But she did not finish. She was falling off a mountain, falling, falling, falling.

WHY DIDN'T *Ni Fan think it was terrible? Why didn't she realize the shame of it? Why did she run down the road, empty-handed, bursting with joy? Xhao Hui looked up when he heard her calling his name. For some reason, that day he wore his hat with the overlapping symbols* N *and* Y *backwards on his head. Later, Ni Fan would think of it as the day everything turned around. But that morning, she ran through the fields and shouted Xhao Hui's name. Her breasts ached as she ran and the aching made her smile even more.*

"I'm pregnant!" she blurted. As she had walked here to tell him, she had imagined all the ways to give him the news. But once she stood there before him, they all dissolved and there was just the news itself.

"It's true!" she said, opening her arms to him. She unbuttoned her shirt at the breast so that he could see the fullness, the darkened nipples. Then she unbuttoned more buttons to show him the swell of her stomach. "Look," she said proudly.

Xhao Hui clutched her shirt closed. "Dress yourself," he said harshly, and Ni Fan stepped back as if she had been slapped.

"Let me think," he said as she buttoned her shirt with her trembling fingers.

Xhao Hui paced in a small, tight circle, staring at the hard earth.

But when he looked up at her finally, he nodded. "I know this," he said, relieved. "In the next village there is an old woman who can get rid of the baby. Yes," he said, nodding. "You can act as if you are going to the market and instead you will walk to the next village. She will do what needs to be done, and you will be home by nightfall. You can think of a story for why you are late returning from the market.

You have such a good imagination, you will think of something. See how simple?"

Ni Fan shook her head as if to clear away cobwebs there. "Why would we do that?" she said finally.

Xhao Hui patted her arm. "Because it's best, Ni Fan. We aren't married. The humiliation will ruin your family." He lowered his voice. "It will ruin you," he said. "What man will marry you if you have a baby out of wedlock?"

"What man?" she repeated. Her mouth suddenly went very dry. Then she tasted bile rising from deep in her stomach, into her throat, and she began to retch. Ni Fan turned from him. She kneeled in the dirt, vomiting.

Xhao Hui stroked her back. "There, there. You'll feel better once the woman gets it out of you. Why, you'll be back to your old self almost right away. That's what I've heard. It's all very easy."

At last, the vomiting stopped. But Ni Fan was too weak to stand. She imagined this was what it felt like to be tossed about at sea. Everything shifted and spun.

"Why, you can even go tomorrow!" Xhao Hui was saying.

Ni Fan shook her head.

"Yes," he said, "tomorrow is as good a day as the next. Better to get it done."

"No," Ni Fan said.

"What?"

She thought she might be sick again. She dug her fingers into the dirt to hold on to something. Ni Fan looked at the boy she loved. "No," she said again.

ON THE MORNING *that she left her baby in the park, Ni Fan took the only sweet potato that grew in her family's barren field. That sweet potato would buy them enough rice for that night's dinner. The rice coffer was empty, and just the night before her grandmother had complained of hunger pains. Ni Fan tucked the sweet potato into the hem of her pants and wrapped her infant daughter in a strip of fabric that she slung across her shoulder.*

It was not quite dawn, the time of morning when she used to sneak back into the house after meeting Xhao Hui. The sky above her was still dark, but in the distance light shone, slowly making its way toward her. Ni Fan walked down the dirt road toward the park. No one had prepared her for the soreness left after childbirth—her breasts ached, and the very place that had brought her such delight now felt raw and wounded. When the pains had come two nights ago, Ni Fan had gotten through the labor by believing that once it was over she would be back to normal. But everything hurt her, inside and out.

As she passed Xhao Hui's field, she looked over hopefully. But it was dark and empty. The baby whimpered, and Ni Fan resisted the urge to comfort her daughter. Instead, she tried to walk faster, despite the pain everywhere. She wanted nothing more than to lie down and sleep. But first she must do this.

Ni Fan went exactly to the spot where she and Xhao Hui met and made love and dreamed of robots and Beijing. She laid the baby in the fabric, swaddling her in it now, and rested her on the grass. Then she took the sweet potato and tucked it in, resting it close beside the girl.

Ni Fan took a few steps away. She looked down at her daughter. Pain swelled in her, from her gut to her heart. Would whoever found this child know from that one sweet potato how valuable she was? Would they understand that this was a precious baby?

Slower now, she walked back along the dirt road, her hand pressing first her belly, then her chest, as if she could keep the pain away. But it stayed and grew. The sun was bright overhead now. Xhao Hui's field was still empty. Ni Fan bent her head, and walked.

DOCUMENTS TO CHINA

A child is like a piece of paper on which every person leaves a mark.

7
MAYA

That night, Maya fell. From skyscrapers, treetops, roofs, and winding stairs. She fell and she fell, but her body never hit the pavement or soft grass or hardwood floor below. Instead, she remained caught in the moment when she realized there was nothing beneath her except air. Her legs pumped and flayed, seeking something solid. Her arms reached out toward the ledges and branches and walls that she flew past, her hands gripped at the emptiness as if they might be able to grab onto something, anything, to stop her fall. But nothing could stop her. Maya just kept falling. She did not land. She spun and twisted. She held her breath.

"I am a solid guy," Jack told her the next morning as they drank coffee at her small round table, an ice cream shop castoff.

The chairs were too small to make sitting on them comfortable, and they forced Jack's and Maya's knees to bang together, their bodies to lean toward each other.

"You'll see that about me," he continued. "I can fix anything. Leaks, dryers that won't dry, and dishwashers that won't wash."

Jack looked rested, even with the stubble on his face. His eyes shone back at her, blue and alert. But Maya knew she had the dark circles under her eyes and the drawn face of a woman who has not slept. Even after her confession last night, Jack had been able to soothe her, to murmur the things that were meant to comfort, and then to press himself against her spoon-like as if they had slept together dozens of times before. Soon his breathing became the slow, even breaths of a sleeping man. But Maya, when she slept, kept falling.

"Are you listening?" Jack was asking her.

Maya nodded. "You can fix things."

"Except this," he said. "I can't fix what happened to you."

"I don't expect—"

He placed his hand over hers to quiet her. "I know you don't," he said. "But until it is fixed, I don't think you have room for me. For anyone."

Maya wanted to tell him that this was one broken thing that was unfixable. But why explain? He was telling her thank you, for the sex, for the coffee. He was telling her he would not be back. This filled her with relief and disappointment both.

Afraid she might cry, Maya stood quickly, banging her knee hard against his, and then against the hard round edge of the table.

"I need to get to work," she said. "So many people depend on me."

"And you never let them down, I bet," Jack said.

Maya turned toward him, angry. "That's right. I fix things too. I fix families. I fix their heartache and their loneliness."

Jack stood too, carefully. "What about your heartache?" he said.

"Oh, please," Maya said, gathering their cups and spoons. "What is this? A Hallmark card?"

She didn't like that he followed her into the kitchen, that he put the cream in the refrigerator, the sugar bowl in its spot on the shelf. What she wanted was for him to go. A big man, he filled her small kitchen. Not just with his bulk, but with his smell of soap and man, with his too-heavy footsteps. Maya gulped for air.

"Look," Jack said, standing in the middle of the kitchen, his arms opened beside him, "I like you."

"Oh, please," Maya said again. "Let's not do this. We had a good time, and then I completely lost it." She shook her head. What had possessed her to tell this stranger the very thing she had kept locked away for so long? "And now I need to get to work."

"No," he said. "I mean, I like you. When you are ready for a relationship, for something more, I want it to be with me."

"Okay. I'll call you when that happens."

Jesus, Maya thought, turning on the water and letting it run too hot, is this how people gave the brush-off these days? Angrily, she washed the cups and spoons, the wineglasses from last night. These remnants of their evening embarrassed her. The water stung her hands, but she did not temper it.

Jack placed his hands on her shoulders and forced her around to face him. Then he leaned down and kissed her on the lips. On any other morning, it would have been a lovely kiss. It would have been a kiss that held promise.

Maya wished he had not done what he did next. He took his hand and placed it so tenderly on her cheek that she did not know if she might cry, or slap it away. Before she could decide, Jack dropped his hand and walked out.

Maya stood still, right there in the middle of her kitchen with its cheerful mango walls and gleaming countertops, listening to those heavy footsteps walk across the living room. The door opened and closed with certainty. Still, Maya stood, not moving, until in the distance she heard his car start up and drive away. Only then could she make herself focus on what lay ahead.

Get dressed, she said to herself. Go to work. Do not think about any of this. Instead, Maya thought of all the babies waiting for parents. She thought of empty cribs, empty arms, being filled.

"WELL?" EMILY SAID as soon as Maya answered her cell phone.

"He's nice," Maya said. This was not a lie.

"Did you kiss him? Will you see him again?"

Maya jingled the keys to the Red Thread in her hand. She was standing at the door, ready for her real life to begin, and cursing herself for answering the phone.

"You devil!" Emily teased.

"Oh, Emily," Maya said, playing with the tricky lock. The key had to go in just right or it wouldn't open. "I shouldn't have."

The door wouldn't open. Maya put down her briefcase and leaned against it. Wickenden Street still looked sleepy. Soon enough, college students and mothers returning from dropping kids at school would fill it. But right now, it was quiet. The junk shops and futon store still closed, the Japanese and Indian restaurants also closed but leaving the stale smells of curry and fish in the air. But strongest was the coffee roasting down the street, an acrid, seductive smell that Maya liked. She took a deep breath.

"No, no," Emily was saying, "we're grown-ups here. People sleep together on the first date."

When Maya didn't respond, Emily added, "They sleep together and sometimes don't go out again. It's okay."

Maya sighed. How could she tell Emily that it wasn't the sex she regretted, but the intimacy that followed.

"The sex was actually nice," Maya said.

"Nice isn't what we want at our age from sex."

Maya chuckled. "It was good. Is that better?"

"Yes," Emily said. She paused, and when Maya didn't fill the silence, she said, "But why shouldn't you have?"

"It's the after part," Maya said, choosing her words carefully. "The cuddling. The spilling of histories."

She wished she could tell Emily what she had told Jack. Perhaps that would lighten her burden. But look at how she felt now, having told the story just once in all these years. Maya shook her head. No. Only she and Adam had the right to this story.

"You're rusty! That's what you do in relationships," Emily said. "You cuddle. You tell each other your awful middle names and who you went to the prom with and you show every scar you have and tell how you got it. Did you get to the scar part?"

"Yes," Maya said. Her throat felt tight and closed. "I've got to go. A couple is coming in—"

"Okay," Emily said. "But call me later?"

Maya promised she would and hung up hurriedly. All she wanted was to get inside her office and begin her day. This time, the key cooperated on the first try. Relieved, Maya went inside. The green lights flashing on all the telephones, the hum of the fax machine receiving documents, the pictures of all those baby girls, soothed Maya.

As she walked toward her office, her fingers swept gently over the photographs.

Good morning, beautiful children, she thought.

By the time she settled at her desk and turned on her computer, last night and the awkwardness of the morning had faded.

She solved problems with missing documents, with the Chinese government, with background checks and old criminal records and people desperate for this one thing: a baby. She consoled and listened and soothed and solved. So that when the small ding announcing a new email sounded, Maya was back to usual.

The unfamiliar email address, john74, threw her off. Families waiting for babies, wanting babies, or just wanting information emailed her every day. She should have looked more closely at the subject line: ABOUT THIS MORNING. Jack. Of course. Jack was often a nickname for John. She read the email quickly. He wanted to see her, to talk. Could they just be friends for now? Could he help her figure this out?

Maya's finger hovered over the Delete button. She didn't owe him anything.

But then she typed a reply quickly: *It's fine. No need to get together. Despite my breakdown, it was nice.*

She hit Send.

Nice. That was the word Emily had said adults shouldn't use to describe sex. But it did describe the evening. Or most of it.

Another ding. Another email from john74.

Maya considered not opening it. But she did.

Nice???????

She smiled, in spite of herself. Then typed: *Okay. Better than nice.*

When his next response came, she laughed. *Phew!!!!* he wrote.

Then another email immediately from john74. *I really do want to see you again.*

Maya kept that email open as she went about her morning. Almost an hour on the phone sorting out visas for the next travel group. She updated the website, adding pictures of families getting their babies on this last trip. The babies were from Guanzhou, and the pictures of the babies in new clothes, with bows in their hair, held by beaming mothers and fathers under the broad trees on the promenades, pleased Maya. SALLY BURTON WITH HER NEW FAMILY, she typed. SABRINA METZ WITH HER NEW FAMILY. ABBY RANDOLPH. GILDA MASERATI. PATRICIA KENNEDY. Each name like a promise.

When she finished, Maya clicked onto Jack's email, still there waiting for her.

Let me take care of some things first. Then we can get together again. She sent it, her heart banging.

From her bottom drawer, Maya took out a clean piece of paper. It had the Red Thread Adoption Agency logo on the top in red, with a long red line swirling off that final *y*.

Dear Adam, Maya wrote, *It has been many years since . . .*

She stared at the paper on her desk. What was there to say here? Since I ruined our lives? Since I killed our daughter? Since I left you sitting on the lanai with rain falling around you, your head held in your hands, your back heaving with sobs? Do you remember, Adam, how loud my suitcase sounded as I dragged it across the crushed shells that made the path that led away from the door? Do you remember how when you called my name, I did not answer you? Your voice sounded broken. You don't know that I dared to watch you in the rearview mirror as I drove away. You stood in the rain in front of our little pink house and called my name and I stepped harder on the accelerator, fleeing from you, from what I had done.

Dear, dear Adam.

Maya crumpled the paper and tossed it into the wastebasket beside her desk.

Last night, Jack Sullivan had held her while she talked. He had said, "How does a person go on after something like that?"

"They open an adoption agency and believe that by bringing children to desperate people, they are absolved somehow," she told him.

At first, when she opened the Red Thread Adoption Agency, Maya had believed that. If she could give enough babies good homes, if she could make enough women mothers, then she could forgive herself.

But now she realized that wasn't enough. She closed her eyes. Those moments replayed themselves again. The smell of roasted chicken. The warm sunlight. The feel of her daughter in her arms.

If she could just go back to that afternoon, she would not hurry. She would quiet the noises in her mind: Dinner! Work! Husband! She would just sit and soothe her child.

But just as it did every time that afternoon came back to her, Maya felt the weight of her baby, and then the emptiness as she fell backwards, out of her arms. The sound, a dull sound really, did not even frighten Maya. "She just fell wrong," one doctor told them later, in the emergency room. As if it were a simple mistake. Nothing more.

For weeks, Maya could not erase the image of how her daughter looked right after the fall, the way her eyelashes fluttered, the bubble of spit that formed on her lips and then turned pink with blood.

Dear Adam, Maya thought, the pen trembling in her hands. But nothing more came to her.

Outside the office, she heard voices. Maya glanced at the clock. Brooke Foster, wife of the famous baseball player, was early for her appointment. A soft knock on the door before it eased open.

"I know it's a little early," Samantha said.

"That's all right," Maya said, relieved at the interruption.

The door opened all the way and Brooke walked in. Her short cropped hair and turned-up nose reminded Maya of magical beings: elves and sprites and pixies. She wore a see-through white blouse with a white camisole underneath and a full cotton skirt in pale blue. Flip-flops. From a distance, she might be a teenager, but up close Maya could clearly see the lines at the corners of her eyes and mouth.

"You have questions?" Maya said after the usual pleasantries. "About the paperwork?"

There were always questions about the paperwork, Maya knew. But Brooke was shaking her head no.

Maya waited.

"My husband," Brooke said, but then she grew quiet.

"The famous baseball player," Maya said.

Brooke smiled. "Yes. The famous baseball player."

She took a breath, played with the hem of her skirt. "He loves me so much," she said without looking up.

Then she did look up, her eyes a bright blue against her tanned face. "Too much," she said. "He loves me too much."

"Ah," Maya said.

"His love can suffocate me," Brooke continued. "My friends are always telling me how lucky I am. He makes me coconut shrimp and margaritas. He plants tulips every fall. He buys the bulbs and times the planting to just before the first frost and then he digs these shallow holes and places them in such a way that when they bloom come spring there is no space at all between the flowers. It's like a blanket of tulips." Brooke shook her head as if even she could not believe it. "They're my favorite flowers," she said. "Tulips."

"I can see why your friends are jealous," Maya said.

"He brings me coffee in bed every morning," Brooke said. "He paints my toenails for me."

"Brooke?" Maya said.

"I know. Why am I here, then? Right?"

"I understand why you're here," Maya said.

"You do?"

"If he loves you so much, how can he make room for a baby?" Maya said.

"Loving Charlie isn't enough for me," she said softly. "But I'm afraid that I'm enough for him."

"It is surprising how much room there is in a heart," Maya said.

"We met the first day of college. He was relentless in his pursuit of two things: playing major league baseball, and winning me. Our senior year, when he was getting scouted by all the teams, I got pregnant. I was young enough or foolish enough to believe he would be as happy as I was. But he told me flat out that he could not have a baby yet. He was just getting started, he needed to concentrate on tryouts, on hitting that ball. We would get married someday and have as many babies as I wanted. I didn't know what to do. I was twenty-two years old and in love with my boyfriend and pregnant. Before I did anything, I woke up in the middle of the night with this pain, this excruciating pain."

Brooke's hand touched her stomach lightly, unconsciously. "It turned out it was an ectopic pregnancy. And my tubes ruptured that night. I could have died. In a way, I did die, I think. Because I couldn't get pregnant again after that. Charlie," she said, shrugging, "he was so grateful I made it. But I lost my only chance at being a mom."

"Until now," Maya said.

Brooke smiled. "Yes! Until now. I walk in here and I see all those pictures of children and I think: My child will be up there someday, smiling at some woman waiting in line."

"How can I help?" Maya asked.

"I don't even know. I'm just terrified Charlie will back out. I sent our documents to China and all I can think about is how we will get a phone call telling us we have a daughter and he will say he can't go through with it."

Maya had seen this very thing happen. Sometimes they muttered their decision quickly over the telephone. Sometimes they came to the office and looked at that photograph and said they had changed their minds.

Still, she said to Brooke, "He won't. When he sees your baby, everything will change."

"I want this more than anything," Brooke said. "I want a baby." She did not hide her crying. She cried hard and openly.

"There is a red thread connecting you to the child you were meant to have," Maya said.

"Do you believe that?" Brooke said. "Really?"

Maya wanted to tell her that she believed it so strongly she sometimes thought she saw them, those thin red threads zigzagging the sky, tethering babies to their mothers.

But she said, simply, "I do."

Brooke wiped at her cheeks with the backs of her hands, and nodded. "Thank you."

When Brooke left, Maya turned on her computer and typed in: *University of California, Santa Barbara*. She clicked until Adam's name and office phone number appeared on the screen. Without pausing—because if she paused she would not do it—she dialed the number.

The phone rang three times. Maya counted each ring like it was a heartbeat. Then an answering machine picked up.

"Hello, you have reached Dr. Adam Xavier. Please leave a message at the sound of the beep."

Adam's voice. It sounded so strong, so unlike the broken one that had called her name as she drove away from him.

The beep ended.

Maya swallowed hard, then said, "Adam. It's Maya. I was hoping we could talk?"

She started to hang up, but then realized she hadn't left her phone number.

Quickly, she said it. "Thanks," she added.

Her computer showed she had twenty-seven new messages. But Maya stood, put on her jacket, and walked out of the office. It was eleven-thirty in the morning. Eight-thirty in California. Of course Adam wasn't at work yet. Maya could not sit in her office and wait for a call that might never come.

The sun was bright, but there was fall in the air. Maya buttoned her jacket as if she were going somewhere. But she stayed still, digging her toes into the bottoms of her shoes, trying to root herself. She tilted her face upward, waiting.

8

The Families

SUSANNAH

Susannah held up the pink baby blanket for Carter to see. "Feel how soft it is," she said. "And washable." The blanket made her almost giddy. "I might add little rosettes," she said. "Scatter them around. White ones, I think."

Carter was looking at her, not the blanket.

"What?" she said.

But he just shook his head. He was in the living room, on the sofa that faced the window that looked out at the ocean. When they'd first bought this house, it had been full of small square windows. The first thing they'd done was to put in large ones, so that when they entered a room, the view assaulted them.

Susannah didn't like to think of back then, when they'd moved here and she was newly pregnant and hopeful. She had imagined many children, filling the house with them. She had imagined walking across the street, pails and shovels swinging, the air thick with salt, sticky hands in her smooth ones.

She laid the blanket beside Carter, hoping he would touch it.

Of course he wouldn't marvel at the evenness of her gauge, the neat regularity of her stitches. But couldn't he see that she had knit this for a new baby? That Susannah finally, after six years, felt something like joy creeping into their lives?

"Carter?" she said.

He pointed toward the ocean. "I think a storm's coming," he said.

Gray clouds huddled in the distance. She studied them briefly, then studied her husband's face. She used to think it was the kindest face she'd known. But now Susannah couldn't even recall the last time she had really looked at him. His hair was thinning, she realized. And he had a sunburn on his nose and cheeks. Cautiously, she traced a line from his temple to his chin. He looked at her, surprised.

"Is she asleep?" Susannah whispered.

Carter nodded.

Years ago, before Clara was born, they would stop the car on long drives just to make love. They would huddle in the backseat, his long legs stretched out and Susannah sitting on top of him. They would even slip into restaurant bathrooms, as if they could not wait to finish their dinner, their need for each other was that great.

But now, as Susannah unbuttoned her white shirt, she could not even remember the last time. It had been so long ago that it had disappeared from her memory. Usually, Carter was late from work, or trying unsuccessfully to get Clara to sleep. Usually, Susannah wanted instead to be alone, to knit, to pretend that she was living the life she'd imagined.

Tonight, though, her body trembled with wanting him. She didn't even care that he sat, watching her but not reaching for her. She slipped off her shirt and unhooked her bra and heard his small gasp at the sight of her breasts. Then it was almost like before, how he grabbed her. How he yanked her zipper down and pulled off her jeans. How he brought her onto his lap, frantic.

Outside, the storm arrived. It was a magnificent one, with sharp, bright lightning and rolling thunder. When the rain started, it hit the windows like bullets. Somehow the storm added to Susannah's excitement, and when she came it was as if she was swept away in all that wind and rain.

"Whoa," Carter said when it was over. "What got into you?" He grinned at her and held her shoulders so that she wouldn't leave his lap.

But Susannah didn't answer him. Her desire had turned into something else, a dark, creeping sense of dread.

"Not that I'm complaining," he said, and Susannah remembered now how chatty he always got after sex. "It's been too long," he said. "Since what? Christmas?"

Susannah wanted to say something, but if she said it out loud it might make it true, so she just sat, feeling him growing softer inside her.

"Or maybe even longer," Carter was saying.

The baby blanket had fallen into a pink heap on the floor. Susannah wanted to pick it up, but Carter held her in place. She began doing the math. She counted backwards and, afraid of where she landed, counted again. Carter kept talking about things that didn't matter and Susannah kept counting backwards until finally she knew that no matter how many times she did it she would land in the same place. Her last period was exactly two weeks ago. Unlike all the other women at that brunch, the one who couldn't carry a baby and the one who couldn't get pregnant for some mysterious reason and the one who had scarred fallopian tubes, Susannah could get pregnant. She just didn't want to.

"Mama?" Clara's voice cut through the air.

Susannah saw her daughter standing in the doorway, her hair

tangled, the front of her nightgown caught in her pull-up, the shadows of headlights passing on the beach road crossing her face.

"Why are you on Daddy's lap?" Clara said.

Carter chuckled. "Why are you on Daddy's lap?" he whispered.

Susannah's stomach churned. "What are you doing out of bed?" she asked.

"The thunder," Clara said. "It scared me. Is it angels bowling, Mama?"

"Yes," Susannah said, sighing. "It's angels."

Susannah moved, but Carter whispered, "Stay. It has been so long since I have had you like this."

She didn't stay. Instead, she stood and wiggled back into her jeans. In the rain-soaked light, Clara's face seemed almost serene as she watched her mother move toward her.

"I'll do it," Carter said.

"No," Susannah told him.

She remembered how the night she got pregnant with Clara she had actually felt the moment of conception. A strange fluttering like the way her stomach felt just before a roller-coaster took a plunge. Carter had laughed at her when she'd told him. But Susannah had been certain. She'd placed her hand on her stomach as if to let her baby know she was there. "You wait," she'd told him. "We are pregnant."

Now, as she moved toward that child, her stomach did that same flutter. Tears sprang to her eyes. She could not have another Clara. If this made her a bad person, a terrible mother, then that was what she was. The faded memory of her own mother gripped her. Before her mother got sick, she had been Susannah's constant companion, knitting clothes for her dolls and teaching her to sail and ice-skate. All these years later, Susannah could easily picture her mother spinning on the ice, her white skates and pale blue coat a blur. Or at the tiller of their Catalina, the wind blowing her straw-colored hair in her face, the tip of her nose pink from sun.

Susannah took Clara's hand and held on tight.

"Ouch!" Clara said, yanking free.

Clara stamped her foot and howled, all remnants of serenity gone. When Susannah told her to stop, Clara stamped her foot again, hard enough to make the floor shake, then ran down the hall.

Susannah watched her go. She knew she should run after her. She knew all of the steps it would take to get her daughter back to bed. But she stood, her hand on her stomach, this time trying to stop the fluttering there. Thousands of miles away, she thought, there was a baby for her. Maybe that baby was already born. Maybe she was right now sleeping peacefully in a crib, her whole bright future waiting for her.

"Susannah?" Carter was saying. "Get her. You know she could hurt herself. Susannah!"

She heard him zipping his pants, getting to his feet.

"Jesus," he muttered. As he passed her, he glared.

"Carter," Susannah said softly.

He was already halfway down the hall, but he spun around to face her.

"We didn't use anything," she said.

He frowned.

Behind him, in Clara's room, drawers slammed to the floor and trinkets and toys smashed.

"What if I'm pregnant?" she said, the words large and unwieldy in her mouth.

Hadn't the doctor told them the chances of another child with Fragile X were high?

"I don't have time for your histrionics," he said, waving her off.

Quickly, he padded down the hall. "I'm coming, Clara!" he called.

At the sound of his voice, the noises grew louder.

Carter's voice, calm and certain, filled the air.

Eventually, Susannah knew, Clara's screaming would turn to whimpering and she would fall asleep with her head in her father's lap.

Perhaps that flutter was only fear. Perhaps it was something like desire, like yearning. Susannah tried to picture China. But she only had some old movie images of pointed straw hats, bamboo baskets, streets crowded with bicycles. She would go to the library tomorrow and take out books. History and sociology. Cookbooks and economics. She would begin her preparations for that baby.

NELL

She was supposed to be reciting the conversation with the class.

"Hello. My name is Nell. How are you this morning? Bangkok is a beautiful city. I am honored to be here."

Nell said the strange Thai words fluidly. But she could not stop thinking about kissing Theo. Years ago, when she was in high school, all of her friends had a crush on the lifeguard at the country club pool. He was a star swimmer at the public school, a rangy boy with a mop of golden curls and an upper lip set in a perpetual sneer. The boys they dated all went to the private boys' school. At night, while their parents ate in the dining room, the boys stole gin from the country club bar and made too-strong gin and tonics on the beach. Nell and her friends met them there, drinking with them, and smoking pot, and sneaking behind dunes to kiss and fondle.

But one night—this was at the end of August—Nell took one of those pitchers of gin and tonics and brought it to that lifeguard who worked Friday nights in the kitchen. She stood by the screen door until he finally looked up from the stack of dirty dishes he was washing. Then she held up the pitcher and cocked her head. She wore her bikini top, a white macramé thing, and red shorts. He hesitated, but then he grinned at her, put the wet towel down, and slipped out the door.

They had been flirting all summer, of course. Everyone had flirted with him. But Nell wanted him. Bored with those same boys, their endless boasting, their cold, slippery tongues in her mouth and their hands grabbing at her, Nell wanted this boy. The one no one knew. The star swimmer from the public school. All of the girls whispered about him, things that made him seem even more mysterious and exotic. He had no father. Or his father was an electrician or a plumber or in jail. His mother was a waitress, or worse. That summer night, Nell could think of nothing more exciting.

"Waiter, I do not like my food too spicy," Nell recited with the class. "Driver, please take me to the Peninsula Hotel."

They drank that pitcher of gin and tonics that night, and she listened to him talk about swimming. Nell never could have imagined that there was that much to say about swimming, but he talked about speed and depth, the butterfly and the backstroke. She grew dizzy from his words and the gin and then finally, finally, his lips on hers. And then his hands untying her top and his mouth on her breasts. This was the summer before her senior year and she was still, technically, a virgin. That night, as soon as he untied that white bikini, she knew she would make love with the lifeguard, mostly because he was so different from all those other boys doing these very same things with her friends behind the dunes.

"Please make up my room now," Nell recited. "Please bring me fresh towels."

She heard that he made the Olympic swim team. She heard he went to Brown on a full scholarship. Even now, she felt a thrill remembering that night, how he tasted like chlorine, how he looked right at her when he entered her that first time.

Nell watched Theo slouched in front of the class. He was bored, she could see that. His hair needed cutting, he needed a shave. There was nothing desirable about him, and for that very reason she could only think about kissing him again.

"I am lost," Nell recited, her voice clear and loud. "Could you please help me?"

The class tittered. The exercise had ended and she was the only one still reciting.

Theo grinned at her. "I would be happy to help you," he said in rapid Thai. "Perhaps after class I could buy you a drink."

Nell snuck a glance at the class. No one had understood him except her.

"I accept," she said, happy to have studied so hard.

"I HAVE THE strangest feeling," Nell told Theo that night in the bar. "I think my husband doesn't want to adopt. I think he suggested it because he thought I wouldn't actually do it. I'm not even sure he wants a baby at all."

"How come?"

Nell rolled her eyes. "He wants to sail around the world."

"Maybe he'll take me with him," Theo muttered.

"When this last round of drugs didn't work, he almost seemed relieved. Our fertility specialist said it was time for in vitro and Benjamin said, 'The buck stops here.'"

Theo laughed. "He actually said, 'The buck stops here'?"

"Harry Truman said it—"

"I know Harry Truman said it. I'm not a total philistine."

"Sorry," Nell said. She patted his hand, then let hers rest on it.

"I just didn't think actual people said things like that," Theo said.

"Is it just me," Nell said, "or are you sitting there thinking about kissing me?"

"Oh, I've been thinking about that pretty much since last time," he said.

"So?"

He laughed again. "So, you have a husband who wants to sail around the world, I have a wife who wants to save the world, you want to get in vitro, and I—"

"And you?"

He shook his head. "Sophie is always wanting to know what I'm thinking. Always. It's like she wants a portal into my brain. But there are things I can't tell her."

Nell smiled. "Like how much you want to kiss me."

Theo paused. "Yeah. Like that."

Even later, when they were half drunk and making out in the rain on the sidewalk, Nell couldn't help but think she had disappointed him somehow.

"How romantic is this?" she whispered to him.

The rain was light and warm, like movie set rain. His hands slipped into her shirt, unbuttoning just enough for him to move them over her breasts, dip inside her bra. Somehow, she wanted to shake that feeling that she'd let him down.

"Let's get a hotel," she whispered. "On me."

His hands paused.

"What day can you do it?" she asked him.

Now his hands slid up and down her ribs, across her flat stomach.

"You remind me so much of someone," he said.

"Tell me."

"My big love. The one who got away."

Was that his secret? That he still loved someone else? Nell thought of his wife. Chubby and bland and kind-faced.

"What day?" she whispered. She slid her own hand down until she found him, hard.

"Friday."

"Friday," Nell said.

Later, in her king-size bed with the Frette sheets and her husband asleep beside her, Nell tasted, ever so slightly, chlorine.

EMILY

Emily tried. She took Chloe for ice cream sundaes and long walks around the pond. She remembered her friends' names, that Courtney played tennis and Cate rode horses. She even remembered the names of her teachers and the quirks they had. "Does Mrs. Jellison still have those creepy fingernails?" she'd ask Chloe. "Did Mr. Frank get in trouble for swearing so much?"

She tried. But still Chloe stood mostly with her skinny arms wrapped around her chest like she was freezing. Still she slunk into corners to call her mother and report on everything Emily doesn't do or doesn't remember. Emily would hear the girl whispering and she would look out the window onto her beautiful garden and think of Providence.

In her apartment, all of the windows had looked out onto other houses. Except the bedroom window that faced the street. Her cat slept on the windowsill. Joni Mitchell sang all day from the stereo. And Emily was happy. No skinny kid whispered about how tight Emily's pants were or how late she slept or any of it.

Today, Emily sipped her coffee and watched *Morning Joe*, trying to figure out what she would do with Chloe, her adversary, her stepdaughter. Maya liked to point out that Chloe's mother, Rachel, was the enemy. "Fourteen-year-olds don't have it in them," Maya said. "That mother causes all the trouble." Dr. Bundy said Emily tried too hard. "So what if she doesn't like you?" Dr. Bundy always said after Emily described all the small irritations that added up to Chloe. Michael blamed Emily. "You're the adult here. Make it work," he snapped just last night.

Chloe sat, her back straight, at the table across from Emily. She was already completely dressed, right down to shoes and headband, as if she was expecting to go somewhere. Emily knew Chloe disapproved of sitting around in pajamas all morning. She'd heard her whispering to her mother about that enough times. But Emily liked to ease into the day, to pad around the house barefoot, wrapped in her robe, drinking coffee.

Chloe frowned at her, as if she'd read Emily's mind.

"So," Emily said, "Daddy won't be home until tonight. What should we girls do?"

Chloe shrugged and chewed her fake granola very slowly. Her mother, Rachel, was on some kind of a health kick and Chloe arrived with lists of foods. Wheat bread, not white. This granola. "It's full of sugar," Emily had said, waving the box at Michael. "And five bucks a box. This isn't healthy." She didn't add that she'd read on the anorexia websites that eating healthier was another smoke screen on the disease. Mention Chloe's eating problem and there would be a fight. "Can't you ever let up on her?" Michael would say.

"I know," Emily said. "How about we get manicures?"

Chloe actually brightened. "Really?"

The manicures had been Maya's idea, and once again Emily marveled at how her friend always thought of the right things to do.

"Why not?" Emily said.

"When can we go?"

Emily glanced at the clock. "Now, if you want."

"Well," Chloe said, "you'll have to get dressed first."

"Right," Emily said.

"I mean, it's almost ten o'clock," Chloe said. She stared at Emily innocently.

"It's nine-thirty," Emily said.

"That's almost ten. We just did estimates in math."

Well, good for you, Emily thought, cringing at her own childish behavior. She would have to ask Dr. Bundy why Chloe always brought out the worst in her. With a sigh, she stood and refilled her coffee cup.

"Did you know that caffeine can cause miscarriages?" Chloe said.

Emily inhaled sharply. "Which class did you learn that in?" She wondered if Chloe knew about those lost babies. Surely the child wasn't that cruel.

"Sex education," Chloe said.

"They teach you about miscarriages? They should be teaching you about birth control."

"They teach us that too," Chloe said. She ate another spoonful of cereal with those same slow, careful chews.

The anorexia website said that some girls even chew their food a certain amount of times. Emily watched Chloe's tight jaw move up and down. Was she counting each one?

"My mother gave up coffee when she was pregnant with me," Chloe said.

Sex education, my ass, Emily thought. Rachel knew about the babies and blamed Emily. I gave up coffee, she wanted to scream. And cigarettes and wine and even sex. Afraid she might say those very things, or worse, Emily headed out of the kitchen.

At the door, she stopped. "That cereal," she said. "It isn't healthy, you know. It's full of sugar."

Chloe stopped chewing and narrowed her eyes.

"I mean, I can get you the real stuff at Whole Foods. I just bought you that because it was on your mother's list."

Her cheeks flushed from her own pettiness, Emily rushed upstairs. This was what Chloe brought out in her. The absolute worst behavior. She turned the shower on hot and stepped inside.

"I am a thirty-eight-year-old woman acting like a fourteen-year-old," she said out loud.

She stayed in the shower until her skin was pink and her fingertips wrinkled. Emily hated manicures. Her nails were brittle and uneven, her hands large. Michael knew that. But would he see what she had done to make Chloe happy?

Back downstairs, dressed now, Emily followed Chloe's hushed voice down the long hallway. In the guest bathroom at the end of the hall, its door closed, Chloe whispered to her mother.

"Then she said the granola was unhealthy, and I'm like, yeah, right, *granola* is bad for you. Why don't you go smoke another cigarette?"

Emily pressed her face against the cool door. It was painted a color called Revolutionary War Blue, a color Emily had chosen from a seemingly endless array of paint chips. Back then, she'd been so hopeful. Hopeful that Chloe would fall in love with her, that the baby she was carrying then would be healthy and beautiful. Now, the name seemed appropriate to how it all turned out. Revolutionary War Blue.

Chloe sighed. "We're going for *manicures.* Can you believe it?"

Emily walked back down the hallway quickly. She did not want to hear anymore. She had heard enough.

MICHAEL STOOD AT the oversized Weber gas grill, with its warming tray and multiple levels and the rack from which barbecue tools of every imaginable kind hung, and beamed at Emily and Chloe.

"You both look beautiful," he said.

He turned the chicken over, then dug his iPhone from his pocket. "Hold up those lovely hands, ladies," he said, and snapped their picture.

His happiness over this simple thing made Emily feel so tender toward him that she went to him and kissed his cheek. The manicures had actually been fun. And afterward they'd gone for tea at that funny little place around the corner. Maybe she just had to ease up. On Chloe. On herself.

"Frankly Scarlet," she said.

Michael raised his eyebrows.

"The color," she said, wiggling her red fingernails at him. "And Chloe's is I'm Fondue of You."

He grinned. "There's a job," he said. "Naming nail polish colors." He slipped an arm around Emily's waist, as easy as anything.

Chloe said, "Have you ever heard of the Addams Family?"

Emily and Michael both broke into the theme song, right up until the part where they snapped their fingers.

"O-kay," Chloe said. "Anyway, there's a whole line of nail polish named after them, but it's all shades of black."

"Is that what you were showing me today?" Emily said.

"That was Morticia," Chloe laughed.

"Well, I am very glad you two chose Frankly Scarlet and I'm Fond of You instead," Michael said.

"Fon*due* of you, Daddy!"

Emily snuggled closer to him. The apricot glaze on the chicken smelled sweet. The flowers behind them did too. For a moment, everything seemed right. But then Emily made the mistake of glancing at Chloe, who was busily text messaging, her phone on her lap, a frown on her face.

Emily remembered what Dr. Bundy had told her about how children of divorce feel torn between conflicting loyalties. Just watch, Dr. Bundy had said, just when you think you've won her over, she'll report to her mother. Was that it? Was Chloe guilty for the few hours of fun they'd shared?

Michael was humming now. He basted the chicken, unaware. Emily used to try to talk about these things with him, but somehow she always ended up the bad guy. I'm the evil stepmother, she'd say to Maya.

Abruptly, Chloe got up and went in the house, her head bent, her face hidden by a curtain of hair.

Emily closed her eyes and imagined a baby waiting for them. Soon, she thought. Soon.

MAYA

The Red Thread Adoption Agency was well known for many things: Maya's responsibility, the quality of the babies, the guides it hired in China, the Western doctors who accompanied all of the families to China, and Maya's personal touches. In particular, families liked that she took time to visit each of them separately.

Once the documents had been sent to China, a red envelope arrived in the mail with a handwritten invitation from Maya inside. These invitations were personalized. A family with three hockey player sons might receive an invitation for pizza with Maya after she attended one of the games. A couple that lived near the beach might have an invitation for a seafood dinner.

Maya invited Nell and Benjamin Walker-Adams to dinner at Al Forno. It was one of the most famous restaurants in Providence, and although Maya preferred the coziness of New Rivers or the French flair at Chez Pascal, she suspected the Walker-Adamses liked to be seen where they thought people were watching.

When Benjamin Walker-Adams called, Maya assumed it was to accept the invitation and make a date.

But as soon as niceties were out of the way, he said, "I'd like to meet with you privately. Without Nell."

Maya waited.

"Is that against the rules?" he said finally.

"No, not at all. It's not unusual for someone to want something that he perhaps feels uncomfortable saying in front of his wife."

"Do you sail, Ms. Lange?" Benjamin asked.

Maya hadn't been on a sailboat—or any boat—since she left Hawaii. There, she and Adam had a tomato red sea kayak and a small sailboat named *Nene*. They used to sail around the harbor, with the skyscrapers of Honolulu watching them and Diamond Head standing guard. She packed picnics: cold lemon chicken and curried rice salad and pineapple cut into fat chunks. Later, she'd put plastic containers of Cheerios and mashed bananas in the basket.

"I don't sail," Maya said.

"That's what I do when I want to clear my head. I get on my boat and I go. Ever since I was a kid, that's what I did when I wanted to escape, or to think. My family has a house in Maine, and we always kept sailboats there, and when my mother couldn't find me, she'd say, 'Ben has taken off on one of the boats again.'"

"I don't sail," Maya said again. On the *Nene*, they would spot giant sea turtles, stingrays, even dolphins.

Benjamin sighed. "I got that," he said. "I don't know why I'm avoiding the subject like this. What I want to say, what I want to talk about, is that I don't think I want to do this. The adoption." He sighed again. "That's the first time I've said it out loud."

"This happens all the time," Maya told him. It was true. During the course of the process, people often changed their minds. Sometimes many times. "I always tell my families to just let the process happen. You can always say no."

Benjamin laughed. "You've met my wife. Do you really think that's a possibility?"

"She is determined," Maya said.

"We lived together for three years, perfectly happy. Then one day she comes into my study, and I'm completely focused on a case, and she says, out of the blue, 'Fish or cut bait, Ben. Marry me or get the hell out.' Six months later I'm in the south of France on my honeymoon."

"I used to have a little sailboat," Maya said, surprising herself. "And on the spur of the moment I would sometimes just take off on her. *Nene*. That was her name."

"What? I thought—"

"I understand how it feels to catch good wind. It's almost like flying."

Now it was Benjamin who waited.

"But you always have to turn around and go back to shore, don't you?"

"I don't feel like I'm ready for this. The responsibility. Financially. Emotionally. All of it."

"There are some things," Maya said, "that if we waited for the perfect conditions, we would never do them."

"Right," Benjamin said.

He would wait it out, Maya thought when they hung up. He would panic and sail and worry. But in the end, he would not back out.

Samantha opened the door. "Mei is on the phone from China."

"I used to have a sailboat. *Nene*. I loved that little boat," Maya said.

"I can't picture you doing that," Samantha said. "Sailing."

Something large and painful welled up in Maya. Why had she told Samantha that? What was she thinking?

Samantha was staring at her oddly, her eyes wide behind her pink cat glasses.

"It was a long time ago," Maya said dismissively.

"Uh-huh."

"Why are you just standing there?"

"The phone call?" Samantha said.

Maya stood and motioned Samantha out. "I'll call her back."

She closed the door firmly so that Samantha would know to stay away. Without thinking, Maya retrieved the phone number she'd scribbled off the computer and dialed it again.

But she got his voice mail again. Of course Adam wouldn't be at his desk this early. She had made the same mistake last time.

Maya began to pack papers into her suitcase. She would work at home, she decided.

She paused. She sat back down in her chair and Googled the University of California, Santa Barbara. Then she found the number for their Marine Biology Department and dialed it.

"Marine Biology," the young woman who answered said.

Maya could hear her chewing gum. She imagined a blond surfer girl, freckled and suntanned.

"Dr. Adam Xavier," Maya said, her throat dry.

"Oh, man, he's on sabbatical."

"Sabbatical?" Maya said, trying to hide the overwhelming disappointment she felt.

"Yeah. They're in Naples. Good jellyfish in the Bay of Naples." Then the girl added, "He's my advisor. He's awesome."

All of the information washed over Maya, but what stung was the word *they,* as in his entire little perfect family: Adam, wife, and baby Rain.

"Yes," Maya managed.

"Do you want his personal email address? That's the one he checks."

"Yes," Maya said, more emphatically than she would have liked.

This girl, this surfing marine biologist gum-chewer was offering her the safety of email. No sadness revealed. No words caught in her throat.

The girl was lazily saying the email address, but even so Maya had to ask her to repeat it.

Then she hung up, and hit Compose, and wrote:

> *Dear Adam, I know it has been a long time, and that perhaps I am the last person you want to hear from, but I would very much like to talk to you. Hope you are well. Maya*

Without even rereading it, Maya hit Send. She could almost see her words flying across the Atlantic Ocean, drifting down to a computer somewhere in Naples, Italy, reaching Adam.

THEO

I am a man about to have an affair, Theo thought as he walked across the lobby of the Hotel Providence and then rode the elevator to the fourth floor where Nell Walker-Adams waited for him.

He repeated it again, out loud this time, as if trying it on, like a new suit. He didn't feel guilty. Not at all. And that bothered him. Sophie's face floated into his mind. Why did her openness, her immense understanding and kindness, annoy him so much?

As always, thinking about Sophie and the accompanying irritation that brought with it, made him think about Heather. Heather. Soul mate. Love of his life. She did not irritate him. Even now, after the terrible breakup all those years ago and the disappointments between them, despite everything, when Theo thought about Heather his whole body warmed.

He could almost feel her, the sharpness of her hips and elbows, the callused feet he used to rub aloe vera on. Heather smelled like sweat and Love's Baby Soft, a cheap drugstore scent she sprayed on herself lavishly. She used cherry-flavored Chap Stick instead of lipstick so her lips were always a little waxy and tasted slightly medicinal. Heather's hair, long and straight and blond, was usually pinned up carelessly or held tight in a little bun at the back of her neck. She wore long jersey skirts in jewel tones, and scoop-necked tops or T-shirts, always in black or white or gray. Theo loved these things about her. The combination of carelessness and discipline, her long dancer's legs and neck and cheap drugstore products.

By the time he got off the elevator, Theo had to pause. He had to stand in the hallway with all of those closed doors and clear his mind of Heather. Sometimes, she just overtook him again, the way she had during freshman orientation when he'd first glimpsed her looking bored and lovely in an emerald skirt that draped around her so elegantly that he thought he might faint. But he went and sat next to her, and smiled at her and wrote on his notebook so that she could see: *Will you marry me?* Heather wrote back, right under it: *No.* And then he wrote: *Wait and see.* They were together from then on. Every New Year's Eve, he asked her out for the next three hundred and sixty-five nights, and she always said yes, until . . . Theo inhaled.

"I am a man about to have an affair," he said out loud.

A door opened and a man in a suit came out, lugging an oversized suitcase. He nodded to Theo. Then he glanced back at him, to see if Theo had gone somewhere or if he was just standing in the hallway of the fourth floor. Before the guy called Security, Theo made his way to Room 424.

For some reason all Theo could think about when Nell opened the door was Anne Bancroft in *The Graduate* with her sexy black lingerie and Dustin Hoffman gawking at her, not believing his good luck. Nell was dressed in a black pencil skirt and a white button-down shirt, black stockings and very nice high heels. Nothing at all like Anne Bancroft, but still Theo couldn't shake the image.

"I'm here for an affair," he said.

But Nell didn't get the reference to *The Graduate*. She just frowned at him and offered him a martini, the glass big and sweating.

"I was starting to think you weren't coming," Nell said.

Theo sipped the drink, which was very strong. He usually stuck to beer or wine.

"That you had a crisis of conscience," Nell continued.

"Oddly," Theo said, "quite the opposite."

It felt strange standing here in a hotel room making small talk when the point was to have sex. So Theo gulped down his drink and reached for Nell, pulling her toward him roughly.

"Did you have a crisis of conscience?" he whispered to her as he unbuttoned that damn white shirt of hers.

"My husband is sailing today. That cleared any lingering doubts," she said.

Theo slid his hand up her thigh and discovered that those black stockings were held up by a garter belt, not unlike what Anne Bancroft might wear.

"Is he sailing around the world?" Theo managed.

"Who cares?" Nell said, dropping to her knees and unzipping his pants.

LATER, THEO FOUND himself climbing the stairs to his apartment, half drunk from all those martinis and the sky already growing dark. He should have been home hours ago. Or called

Sophie. But how could he do that when he and Nell had spent the entire afternoon together in that hotel room? What could he have said? What would he say when he opened that door and saw Sophie's wounded face, maybe even tears?

Without an excuse or a plan, Theo opened the door.

The apartment was empty and dark. Relieved, he stepped inside. He would have time to shower, to think. He would surprise Sophie and make dinner, the stir-fry he did that she liked so much. He would use Thai curry sauce, and his wife would think he was being romantic instead of guilty. Theo flipped on the lights as he moved through the living room. With each step, he felt more lighthearted. Maybe he even had time to run out and get a bottle of wine before Sophie came home.

In the kitchen, he took out the wok and began placing vegetables on the counter. Red peppers. Onions. Snap peas.

"What are you doing?"

His wife's voice startled him enough to make him jump slightly.

"You were here?" Theo said. "In the dark?"

Sophie was frowning at him, and studying him too carefully. "I was here," she said. "Where were you?"

"Going over lesson plans with—"

"Downtown?"

Theo considered the possibilities. Even if she had seen him downtown, she had not seen him with Nell. "Yeah," he said. "At Tazza," he added, grateful that he knew the name of the café there.

"You had your cell phone turned off," she said.

"I did?" Theo shrugged. He held up a pepper. "Guess what I'm making for dinner?"

"All afternoon," she said, "I couldn't reach you."

Theo concentrated on the vegetables, on chopping them into even-sized squares. "Sorry," he said.

"So you were at Tazza going over lesson plans?"

Theo thought of Nell. Her long legs and arms. Her perfume. "Why the Inquisition?" he said. He opened the freezer to see if they had any chicken. They didn't. Vegetarian stir-fry, then.

Sophie didn't answer him. But she didn't stop staring at him either.

"You got a FedEx package," she said finally.

Theo glanced at the basket where they put all the mail. On top sat an envelope—Priority Mail, not FedEx, he noticed. The handwriting looked familiar. He put down the knife and picked up the envelope.

"What is it?" Sophie was asking.

"From an old college friend," Theo said.

He put the envelope out of Sophie's reach and went back to chopping vegetables. There was only one reason he could think of for Heather to have written to him, and he wasn't about to tell Sophie what that was.

HE CHOSE Blue State to meet Heather because Sophie never went there. Ever since that envelope had arrived, Sophie had been watching everything he did too closely. Or maybe she had started doing that sooner? At any rate, he couldn't risk Sophie finding out that Heather was in town. He wasn't up for the barrage of questions that would follow. He wasn't up for more lying.

Theo walked into Blue State, his eyes pausing over each person until they settled on a tall woman with blond hair piled messily on top of her head, a garnet-colored wraparound jersey skirt and a black scoop-necked Danskin top.

Theo's first thought was: Oh! Heather got a tattoo. A pink rose climbed up the inside of her leg, from ankle to calf.

Then it sunk in. Heather—his Heather!—was sitting right in front of him.

Theo went to her, and she got up slowly, opening her arms. When they hugged, Theo realized she felt exactly the same as he remembered.

"Wow," he said foolishly after she extricated herself from his arms. He did not want to let her go. "Heather."

That envelope had been full of pictures. He supposed he should say something about them, but he couldn't think straight.

"Wow," Theo said again.

Heather smiled. "Ever the wordsmith," she said, and sat back down.

Theo sat across from her.

Heather was talking about how she was a choreographer, and about the show she was doing in Boston. "But that was all in the letter," she said, shaking her head.

Theo nodded. *Maybe we can meet?* she'd written. *Maybe we can finally talk about this?* But he didn't talk about it. Instead he said, "Sounds exciting. More exciting than teaching businessmen to speak Thai."

"You speak Thai?" she said. She shook her head again, almost sadly, Theo thought. He felt sad too. They were strangers.

Heather started talking again, about San Francisco, where she lived now. And how hard it had been to find him. She was leaving soon, she said. This was the end of the five weeks.

Nod. Nod. Grin.

He willed himself to say something witty or charming or important, but he couldn't come up with one single thing.

"And I thought we needed to talk," Heather was saying. She

bent and opened the large bag at her feet. She always carried enormous bags.

What he hoped was that Heather was not about to pull out pictures of a child. Hadn't the ones she sent been enough? But she did take out even more photographs and she spread them across the table so that it was impossible not to look at them.

"I thought we should talk about Rose. That you deserved to know everything," Heather said. She was holding a few of the pictures out to him.

Theo took them.

"So," Heather said, taking a breath, "as we decided, I gave her up for adoption. I even got to pick the parents. I studied all of these portfolios and I picked this couple in San Francisco. You would like them, Theo. He's a translator and she's an actress."

Theo was staring hard at the photographs on his lap. A little girl who looked just like Heather, but with Theo's bedroom eyes, stared back at him.

"They let me name her," Heather said.

Theo looked down at the pink rose climbing Heather's leg.

"They were with me when she was born. And they send me pictures every year on her birthday and at Christmas. I can even visit her, but it was too painful. I tried once."

"She's beautiful," Theo said.

He could smell that silly Love's Baby Soft wafting from her skin. He remembered how much he had loved her, how they'd had their whole lives ahead of them. Their little apartment with sloped ceilings and a hot plate and a cat they named Twinkle. Her ballet barre stretched across one entire wall and from bed he could watch her there, stretching, the beautiful arches of her feet reaching upward.

When she found out she was pregnant, she was excited. But he wasn't. He didn't want a baby yet. But we'll just get married and have a baby, she'd said. He remembered that look of betrayal on her face when he said no. He didn't want to do that. Not yet. For weeks in that small apartment they'd fought. Until she agreed to give the baby up for adoption. "But then we're over," she'd said. "I will never forgive you."

He should have fought harder for her, for them. He should have kept this beautiful little girl grinning at him.

But instead, he left.

He didn't even stay long enough to be with Heather when the baby was born. He got a message in Bangkok. *It's a girl. Healthy. Don't try to reach me. I just thought you should know.*

"She looks like you," Theo said.

When he finally looked over at Heather, he saw that she was crying.

"They promised me she'd take dance," she said. She lifted a picture from the table. Rose in a white tutu, bowing.

"That's good," he said.

There were so many things he wanted to do: Take Heather in his arms. Fly to San Francisco and take their daughter home. So many things.

"These are for you," Heather was saying. She was getting to her feet, preparing to go. "They're copies. If you want, I can send you more. When I get them."

"Yes," Theo said.

"Are you going to *do* something?" Heather said.

Theo stood too. "You've lived with this. With her—"

"So have you," Heather said. "You just pretended it didn't happen. I think about her every day. All the time."

Theo was aware of someone else standing at the table.

"Shit," he said. "You never come here. What are you doing here?"

Sophie looked like someone he did not know. "I followed you," she said. "I knew you were up to something."

"I'm not up to something," Theo said. He motioned toward Heather, but Sophie was looking at the pictures now.

"You have a child," Sophie said.

"I meant to tell you," he began.

"When? We've been together five years. When were you going to tell me this small detail?"

Theo shook his head. "It was so long ago," he said.

"I don't know what I'm going to do," Sophie said. It was less a threat than a real problem.

"It was so long ago," Theo said again.

"Could you go away?" Sophie was saying to Heather. "Could you leave us alone?"

"I am so sorry," Heather said.

Theo grabbed her arm, but she shook his hand off her.

He walked her to the door, wanting somehow to keep her there. But she wasn't his. She would send pictures as she received them, she promised. Theo watched her walk away. He knew nothing about her. Was she married? Did she have other children? She had told him nothing.

Sophie burst out the door and he followed her. "You had a baby with the love of your life," she said, "and you can erase what that means by saying it was a long time ago? You abandoned her. You lied to me—"

"When did I lie? I didn't lie."

"Haven't you ever heard of a lie of omission?"

"I didn't tell you. I'm sorry," Theo said.

"I'm the one who's sorry!" Sophie screamed at him. "Sorry I ever laid on eyes on you. Sorry—" She didn't finish. Her face crumpled and she began to sob.

Theo moved toward her to comfort her.

But Sophie looked at him, her eyes wild.

"Don't," she said.

Theo watched her as she collected herself, taking deep breaths, her face growing more resolute. He watched her turn from him and walk slowly away.

"Sophie!" he called after her. "Sophie!"

She kept walking down Thayer Street, even though he was confident she heard him.

9
MAYA

Maya dreamed of Italy, a country she had never visited. She fell from Mount Vesuvius to a sparkling Bay of Naples below. She tumbled down stone steps, steep hills, hotel balconies. But in the morning, she walked steadily down Wickenden Street to her office. She put on a pot of coffee. She opened the blinds and let the September sun in. With the coffee ready—too strong and almost bitter, the way she liked it—Maya sat at her computer and scanned her inbox.

When she saw his name, all of her dreams, the falling from dizzying unstoppable heights, came to her so strongly that even sitting down, she had the feeling of plunging. If she deleted this email, then she could return to the safety of silence she'd maintained these years. What would reading this email from her ex-husband do except open old wounds?

True, she had found him. He was happily living his life with a new wife, a new daughter. Even thinking this forced Maya to grab onto the edge of her desk and hold on too tightly. It was her daughter's face that appeared as she thought this. *Their* daughter's face.

Maya clutched the desk and squeezed her eyes shut, but that sense of falling did not go away. She heard Samantha arrive, the front door slam shut. That woman did not know how to close a door. She just let it go so that it always slammed loudly. The phone rang and Samantha's voice filled the office. When Maya opened her eyes, the lights on the telephone flashed. People on hold. People leaving messages. All of them wanting babies.

An email from Jack popped up, and Maya clicked on it.

Just checking in, it said. *And thinking about you.*

An email from Nell Walker-Adams was below it with the subject line: PLEASE CHECK OUR PLACE IN THE QUEUE!

"Your husband is going to leave you and sail around the world!" Maya shouted at the computer.

She took a deep breath. She scrolled past Nell Walker-Adams and all of the inquiries about the adoption process until she landed on Adam's. Maya exhaled and opened the email.

Her eyes scanned the screen, but she couldn't take it all in. He was surprised to hear from her. His wife was named Carly. They had a baby.

Is it forgiveness you want? Adam wrote at the end. *Aren't we past that?*

Forgiveness.

That hadn't occurred to her. How could he forgive the unforgivable? She had killed their daughter. Their beautiful daughter. She had left him without looking back. Maya had no idea how he had moved from that rainy lanai in Honolulu to a new family, the Bay of Naples, a life.

Forgiveness? Maya typed. *No. Not that. But maybe closure?*

She sent it, even though she hated the word *closure*. Even though she knew that in matters of grief, there was no such thing.

Almost immediately, a reply appeared from Adam. It was midafternoon in Italy. Maya tried to imagine him in an office somewhere, the bay glittering outside his window, a picture of his wife and daughter smiling back at him.

I'll be back in Santa Barbara the first of June. If it would help you to meet, then I am willing to do that.

Maya flipped open her date book to June. The June orientation was on the fourth.

I can be in California on June 5, she wrote.

Then she added, *Thank you.*

Maya stared at the screen, waiting for his answer.

Other emails dropped in. Nell Walker-Adams sent a second one, the subject line more emphatic this time: WHAT IS OUR PLACE IN THE QUEUE???

Was he calling his wife? Asking her if it was all right to talk to Maya? Was he changing his mind?

Ten minutes. Twenty. Samantha's voice.

Until finally an answer.

Someone came in the office. Sorry about that! Send me your travel plans and we will work out a time and place to meet.

Maya read it twice before sending back a simple thank-you.

In black ink she wrote CALIFORNIA across the week of June 5.

Then she stood, expecting the floor to sway beneath her. But oddly, it did not. She let go of the edge of the desk and stood in her noisy office. Faxes arrived. Those telephones kept ringing.

Maya opened the bottom desk drawer. From under her senseless knitting, the yards of neat pink rows, she took out a document that was ready to send to China. She placed it in the FedEx box with the others. Emily and Michael's. Sophie and Theo's. Nell and Benjamin's. Susannah and Carter's. Charlie and Brooke's.

It was September 24. The day all of these documents would

go to China. Now, the families had nothing more to do but wait. Maya lifted the box and carried it out to Samantha.

"They're all set?" Samantha said. Her lipstick was a strange orange that clashed badly with her skin. A rhinestone brooch glittered off her tangerine sweater.

"All set," Maya said.

Instead of going back into her office, Maya watched as Samantha stamped the date on each envelope.

Samantha glanced at Maya, frowning. "Something wrong?" she asked, the stamp smeared with red ink poised over a large white envelope.

Maya shook her head. "Just wondering. Who will change her mind? Who will find happiness?"

"Uh-huh," Samantha said. She waited for Maya to continue, but when she didn't, Samantha returned to stamping.

"Where are those babies now?" Maya said softly. "All those beautiful babies."

Samantha paused again. She chewed her orange bottom lip. The phone rang and she answered it. "The Red Thread Adoption Agency," Samantha said.

Maya watched the final envelope get its red stamp: *September 24.* Documents to China.

Hunan, China

CHEN CHEN

"It is bad luck," her mother-in-law said.

Her round face loomed too close to Chen Chen's, so close she could smell the pickled cabbage on the old woman's face. To wrinkle her nose would show disrespect, so Chen Chen tried to keep her expression blank. She breathed through her mouth instead of her nose, the way she did when the stink from the tire factory filled the air and made her gag.

Chen Chen lay as still as possible. This showed calm to her mother-in-law, but it also made her more comfortable. Until a few days ago, her pregnancy had been as smooth as polished jade. No morning sickness, even when the tire factory worked overtime and Changsha's air grew dense with smoke and stench. Her friend Ming who worked beside her there threw up into a small paper bag, her face pale, her eyes sunk back into their sockets.

But Chen Chen remained robust. She craved the spiciest food her mother-in-law could cook, then doused it with extra chiles and hot sauce. Her complexion was clear; neighbors whispered that she had the healthy glow of a woman carrying a son. At night, she reached for her husband with an almost desperate desire, climbing on him and riding him with an abandon she had not felt in the four years of their marriage. "Who is this crazy woman?" he would whisper afterward, stroking her sweaty hair, both of them stunned by this newfound passion.

"Pregnancy agrees with Chen Chen," her mother-in-law announced at every opportunity, gloating as she said it. "Yes," her husband would say, unable to meet Chen Chen's eyes. Her newly awakened libido embarrassed and stunned him.

Before she got pregnant, Chen Chen was pleased with their methodical, quiet lovemaking. She liked the familiarity of it, the way her husband moved his hands across her body the same way he moved his pencil down a line of figures. He was an accountant for the tire factory, carrying large black books everywhere he went, peering through his round wire-rimmed glasses at columns and numbers. That was how they made love: he peered at her, moved from mouth to neck to breasts with his long graceful fingers. Then, as if he were adding up the totals, one fingers tapped at her, checking that she was ready. He climbed on top then, and finished the calculations. Somehow, that had pleased Chen

Chen, making her husband happy that way, having all the numbers add up just right.

Almost immediately, she craved something she could not name. It was as if she wanted to swallow him up. No. As if she needed to. Her hunger for everything was enormous: food and heat, certain music played loud, fresh air, and sex. Chen Chen gobbled and sweat and danced and inhaled and made love. Her mother-in-law told her that anything she craved must be hers. If she craved string beans in spicy sauce and did not get it, her son would be too skinny and dull. If she craved loud music and did not hear it, her son would be noisy and distracted.

When her husband complained one night that their sex life was frightening him, the way her eyes rolled back during her newly discovered orgasms, the way she clutched at him, leaving small bruises, Chen Chen had narrowed her eyes. "If you do not give me what I crave, our son will be a homosexual." Her husband revered his mother more than anything, a trait Chen Chen despised. But now she used this to her advantage. Her husband sighed, and let her once again straddle him. "How many more months of this before we can return to normal?" he whispered afterward. Chen Chen patted his hand. She didn't have the heart to tell him that she couldn't imagine returning to her life as a sexual ledger book. Check. Check. Check.

But last week, something changed. Until then, Chen Chen's stomach had been a beautiful bump, hard and round like a ball. "A boy," her mother-in-law told her, "is always carried like this. All up front." She'd smiled and tapped Chen Chen lightly on her stomach. Her mother-in-law's familiarity disturbed Chen Chen. She was always touching her stomach now that she was pregnant, and poking at her ankles, her cheeks, her arms.

On Tuesday, though, as she walked home from work chewing a pork dumpling, Chen Chen realized she was short of breath. Worse, she was full. Not just so full that she had to put the dumpling in her pocket, but full in a way that made her organs feel crowded. It was difficult to walk. Chen Chen waddled slightly, her hips thrust out oddly and her legs bowed.

That night at dinner, she refused her mother-in-law's beef with five peppers, the long-roasted pork, the hot broccoli. Instead, she sipped some soup. But that seemed to crowd her even more. Her mother-in-law frowned at her. "What is wrong with you?" she asked. Before the pregnancy, she always spoke to Chen Chen in a dismissive tone, as if she were a fly buzzing around the house. That tone returned now.

Chen Chen shrugged. She too was puzzled by this change. "I am full," she said.

Beside her, her husband chewed his food noisily. For the first time, she noticed that he had grown a small potbelly of his own.

"Third trimester," her mother-in-law said. "This is when the baby grows big."

Even the words crushed Chen Chen. She felt a foot or hand in her ribs, another pressing beneath her belly button. Squirming uncomfortably, she pushed gently on her belly as if to readjust the baby.

"This is the golden time," her mother-in-law said. She smiled broadly. "Even if you do not feel hungry, you must eat and make your son strong."

"But if I eat when I am not hungry, won't my baby be fat?" Chen Chen said.

"Why?"

"You told me that I need to satisfy my cravings. If I want string beans and don't get them—"

For the first time all evening her husband seemed to notice she was there. "Stop this talk!" he said. He held his chopsticks midair. "My mother says to eat. We want our son to be strong."

"I'm just pointing out the contradiction," Chen Chen said. She tried to make her voice gentle, contrite. But her mother-in-law glared at her.

"A few sips of soup are enough for mother," she said. "Not enough for baby."

So Chen Chen ate. Each bite seemed to lie in her chest, unable to move past the baby. By the end of the meal, she folded her arms across her belly, realizing that it extended much farther than it had just a few days earlier. She was getting huge.

As if her mother-in-law noticed this too, she caressed Chen Chen's stomach. "Nice big baby," she said. "Maybe you're a little bit wrong on dates. Maybe this baby coming a little bit sooner."

Chen Chen nodded even though she knew exactly when this baby was conceived. Her husband, overworked, had the flu, a thick cough and high fever. On the morning he woke recovered, he had touched Chen Chen like a starved man, his hands yanking on her breasts and his fingers roughly poking at her. He finished faster than usual, and Chen Chen remembered how sallow his skin looked in the early morning light, how sharp his cheekbones appeared hovering above her. With his eyes squeezed shut and his back arched, her husband had looked like a skinny stranger.

When Chen Chen realized she was pregnant, she had worried at first. Their lovemaking was so predictable, something she could count on. The one time it had changed ever so slightly, after ten days of no contact, her husband hacking and feverish beside her, she got pregnant. Could this possibly be a good sign?

"I am sure you are right," Chen Chen told her mother-in-law. "I must be closer than I thought."

The older woman patted her hand. "Rest. You will need it to give birth. That is hard work, let me tell you."

Chen Chen stood awkwardly. Walking was definitely difficult, she decided.

Later, when her husband came to bed, the heat from his body still made her hungry for sex. Lying on her back, she marveled at the size of her belly now. What had been a round, small bulge now rose majestically. Chen Chen rubbed it, enjoying the way it felt beneath her hands.

She rolled toward her husband, her hands reaching for him.

"My mother cautioned me," he said. "We must be careful of the baby now."

"Uh-huh," Chen Chen said as she climbed on top of him.

"We can't do this," he was saying.

Chen Chen began to move as she had these past six months, sitting upright on her husband, leaning back ever so slightly. But tonight she felt there was too much in there. She was so full. Too full. Her orgasm came, but almost painfully. Somehow unsatisfied, she grunted and rolled off him. Her husband grabbed her wrist.

"I am the husband," he said harshly. "I will say when I am finished."

He pressed her down on the bed, but when he tried to mount her, her stomach was in the way. Chen Chen tried to help him, but it was impossible for him to enter her. His breathing grew heavier. His need for her excited her. She tried to remember when he had wanted her this much, but she couldn't think of another time.

Now he was rolling her over, but she couldn't lie on her stomach. Instinctively, Chen Chen got to her knees. Her husband, panting like a dog, entered her from behind. His movements were frenzied, and this new position and his excitement made Chen Chen also grow excited. They were moving against each other in a way she had never imagined, his hands clutching at her full, heavy breasts, his moans growing louder, until they climaxed, her husband right before her, then Chen Chen.

What was it about this pregnancy, she would later wonder, that brought them to this sexual awakening after these six years together? After this night, her husband seemed to come alive. He turned Chen Chen this way and that, he entered her from every direction. He kissed and sucked and stroked. Her belly, stretched big, both kept them apart and brought them together. After dinner, they could not wait to get to bed. "So tired," Chen Chen would say, yawning. "The baby so close." When her husband joined her moments later, he whispered, "My mother said not to do this." Then he would begin again.

They had glorious intimate moments on these nights, Chen Chen and her husband, filled with sex. Until the morning when she found it almost impossible to get out of bed.

"Too full," she told him. "Or something."

They both stared down at her naked belly. It stretched oddly, to the left and to the right, but also straight out in front.

Chen Chen touched the foot under her ribs, the foot in her side. She could see another foot pushing out, and another lower, kicking her groin.

"I'd better get my mother," he said.

Chen Chen nodded. She slipped a pale blue nightgown over her head, but still kept her hands on her stomach, counting.

When her mother-in-law came in, she yanked the blanket down and the nightgown up brusquely. Her cool hands pressed Chen Chen's stomach too hard.

Finally, she said, "This is bad luck."

And all the pleasure Chen Chen had found these past months left her, just like that.

"HOW CAN THIS BE?" *Chen Chen's mother-in-law said later that day.*

She sat on a small chair near the bed, sipping tea and frowning. Her face, surprisingly young-looking, was wrinkled in worry, giving her a dried-apple appearance.

With help from her husband, Chen Chen had gotten out of bed and dressed that morning. She had made her slow, awkward way to work. But once she was there, it seemed as if a damp, thick gauze had been dropped over her. Her movements grew dull, her brain remained cloudy. Struggling to be more alert, Chen Chen tried to focus her thoughts on lively things: the crowded streets and busy markets of the city, the lovemaking she and her husband had enjoyed this past week, the intense pleasures of food and spice.

But all of it seemed to belong to another person, another time. These pleasures blurred, overtaken by a sense of fullness. Like a watermelon,

Chen Chen thought as she peered over her enormous stomach. Like a water lily about to burst into bloom.

By afternoon, her ankles and feet grew too swollen to stand. A company doctor came to Chen Chen and pressed on them, the woman's finger disappearing into Chen Chen's too-pink flesh as if she were testing dough.

The doctor shook her head. "No more work until this baby comes."

She scribbled on a pad, she wrote in Chen Chen's file. "Go home until baby comes."

She told Chen Chen to drink a particular tea throughout the day and to have bed rest.

"It must be a problem in your family," her mother-in-law was saying now. "This never happened in our family."

Chen Chen stared at the sunlight coming through the small bedroom window. She realized she had never been in bed in the afternoon in her life, and it felt strange and wrong.

"I think your family hid this from us," her mother-in-law said.

The mention of her family brought Chen Chen inexplicably to tears. She thought of her own mother, smaller and gentler than her husband's. Once, as a child, Chen Chen got very ill. Her fever stayed high for days, and her mother got into bed with her and held her, forcing her to drink tea and placing cool cloths on her head.

"Perhaps we could call for my mother," Chen Chen said.

"I already did. She must explain this." Her mother-in-law stared in disgust at Chen Chen's stomach. "Twins are always bad luck for a family. Always."

Chen Chen's mother arrived the next day. She brought a basket filled with Chen Chen's favorite foods, the delicate squash blossoms she liked so much, the pork buns made slightly sweet with hoisin sauce. Unlike her mother-in-law, Chen Chen's mother was not upset. She grinned at her daughter, pleased, and placed both of her small hands on Chen Chen's enormous belly.

"Such abundance!" she said softly. "My daughter, you are beautiful."

For an instant, Chen Chen imagined going home. She imagined leaving here with her mother, taking her babies to her own small town, and eating sweetened pork buns by the river.

"It's bad luck," Chen Chen said.

Her mother chewed her bottom lip, a habit that now endeared her even more to Chen Chen. Her mother always had chapped lips from this habit.

"You need to not think of luck right now. Childbirth is a very difficult thing. You need good thoughts and great strength to get these babies born." She offered a dish of food to Chen Chen. "Eat and stay strong. After the babies are here, we can talk."

Relieved, Chen Chen ate the squash blossoms, the pork buns, the pickled plums and fried rice with tiny shrimp. Outside the bedroom, the voices of the two mothers rose and fell. They were arguing, Chen Chen knew. But her mother had come to protect her and her children, to feed her and keep her strong. Safe now, her mother's food filling her, Chen Chen slept.

FROM HER BED, *Chen Chen listened. She heard the voices of the mothers arguing in the kitchen. They argued about how much garlic to add to a dish, how much pepper. They argued about whether it was good luck to sweep dirt out the door, whether it was bad luck to place an empty teacup upside down.*

They argued too about the babies.

"Your fault," Chen Chen's mother would say. "This could be considered a breach of contract. We could throw your daughter and her bad-luck babies out if we wanted."

"My job," her mother replied in an even tone, "is to help Chen Chen give birth to healthy babies. To give her strength."

"Those babies will bring us bad luck!" her mother-in-law insisted.

Chen Chen's mother screeched, high-pitched and continuous. Although she couldn't see her, Chen Chen pictured her mother with her hands over both ears, her tongue wagging, her eyes squeezed shut. She screeched until the other mother stopped talking. Then Chen Chen listened to the angry silence.

Her stomach rose and stretched, like the clay she used to play with as a child. It grew whorls, giant swirling fingerprints on her skin. The shape was no longer round, but oblong at the sides, pointed in the middle.

When her husband came in to change his clothes, he hardly looked at her. But she looked at him. His own stomach kept growing too. His little potbelly now swelled and hung over his pants. His shirt buttons pulled across it. She was pregnant with twins, but her husband was fat, Chen Chen realized. Like a penguin, she thought.

"Don't you even speak to your wife anymore?" she asked him one morning. This was a month after her mother had arrived.

Without looking at her, he said softly, "You don't even resemble my wife. Your face is as round as a cabbage."

Hurt, Chen Chen said, "But soon I will have our babies, and then we can be together. Remember the things we did? Remember how it felt to come from behind me?"

His head jerked toward her angrily. "Ssshhh!" he said. "Our mothers are in the next room."

"Remember when you pulled me onto your lap and—"

"Pigs!" her husband said, his voice harsh. He stood in just trousers, barefoot, his own fat stomach jiggling slightly as he spoke. "We were animals and we have brought this bad luck on my family."

"No," Chen Chen said. "We were humans. Finally, we were alive."

She had to gasp for air as she spoke. The babies took up so much room now that her lungs were compressed and she became short of breath easily.

"You disgust me," her husband said so quietly she thought perhaps she heard him wrong. "You put a spell on me and turned me into an animal. Weren't you born in the Year of the Pig?"

Heartburn caused painful heat to rise in her, to fill her chest and throat. She wanted to say something to him, something about love and desire. But what were the words to express these things?

In the kitchen, the mothers argued.

"Don't we have enough bad luck?" her mother-in-law shouted. "Now you place your teacup upside down, trapping our luck?"

"You are fat," Chen Chen said to her husband.

His face clouded.

"You have grown fat and unattractive," she said. Then she added matter-of-factly, "I hate you."

His mouth opened and closed a few times, like a dying fish. Then he put on his shirt, slowly buttoning each tiny button. He picked up his ledgers and walked out of the room.

"I don't hate you," Chen Chen said to the empty door. "I love you. You woke me up."

"You are cooking too much food," she heard her husband say to the mothers. "Do you want us all to grow as fat as my wife?"

"Your wife is having babies!" Chen Chen's mother said. "She is growing with life!"

"She is bringing us bad luck!" her mother-in-law shouted.

Chen Chen closed her eyes. She put her hands over her ears. She began to screech, loud and without stopping.

CHEN CHEN WOKE with one thought: Get up and move around.

Her heart raced and she could not catch her breath.

Get up and move around! her mind told her.

She put her hands on the mattress and forced momentum so that she could roll to one side. Hadn't her mother told her to sleep on her left side so that she could pump more blood to her babies? But her mother-in-law had said sleeping on her side would flatten their heads. So here was Chen Chen on her back, trying to roll over like a turtle turned upside down on its shell. After several exhausting tries, she managed to get on her side.

Get up! a voice in her head said. Move around!

One leg stretched off the bed, her foot searching for the floor. When she felt it beneath her, Chen Chen hoisted her huge self upward. Two feet on the floor now, her breath coming in rapid pants.

Someone was moaning. The moaning filled the stuffy air. But Chen Chen could only think about moving. She held on to the wall for support, and circled the small room, over and over. Those moans were terrifying, so loud and filled with such pain.

Squat! her mind told her.

Chen Chen dropped to a squat and moved awkwardly to the middle of the room, where she could do nothing but bounce slightly. The metallic smell of blood enveloped her. Perhaps her mother-in-law had killed her mother. Perhaps her husband had killed them both.

The moaning!

Now there came a commotion, rushing footsteps, panicked voices. Above her appeared the mothers and her husband. The mothers looked worried, but her husband only looked confused and sleepy. His hair stuck up funny and his fat stomach peeked out between his pajama bottom and his T-shirt.

"Chen Chen," her mother was saying in a rushed but gentle voice. "Daughter, the babies are coming. The pain will pass. Squeeze my hand, Chen Chen."

That was when she understood the moans were coming from her. She tried to do some calculations. Her husband had had the flu. He was sick for ten days. Then he had taken her in his accountant-like way, checking off all the body parts, impregnating her. That was in February. There had been frost on the window. It was only September, Chen Chen thought. Too soon.

"It is autumn," she managed to say.

The mothers smiled at each other.

"The babies are coming. She is making no sense," they said.

Just when she thought it could not get worse, everything changed and Chen Chen wanted to move again. To sit. To stand. Her mother's hand on her shoulders felt like mosquitoes biting her, and Chen Chen swatted it away.

She said to her husband, who kneeled beside her, "I said I hate you. Remember?"

He glanced at the mothers, embarrassed. But they only grinned back at him.

"The babies are coming. Women say crazy things right before," they told him.

He nodded at Chen Chen. "I remember."

Chen Chen clutched her mother's arm. "I need something," she said frantically.

She tried to get up, but the mothers urged her back to a squat.

"Push," her mother whispered. "Push."

Chen Chen pushed.

She pushed forever.

At one point she said to her husband, "I love you, you know."

The mothers laughed at this.

"Push," her mother said.

Her mother-in-law caught the first baby. She grimaced and cut the umbilical cord, slapped its face until it opened its mouth and howled.

Chen Chen stood, surprising everyone, even herself. "Give him to me," she said, holding her arms out.

"This one is a girl," her mother said. "You are so lucky, daughter. The next one will be a boy and you will have two healthy children."

Even in her exhaustion, Chen Chen understood. The law of her province stated that if your first child was a girl, then you could have another. A boy.

She smiled and took the baby, now swaddled in a clean checked cloth.

Her husband beamed at Chen Chen and their daughter.

But before she could say anything, her body took over again.

"Oh," she said. "Something is happening."

She dropped to her hands and knees and began to crawl, as if she could escape the pains that shook her.

"Oh," she said again.

The mothers gripped her shoulders and forced her to squat again. They urged her to push.

What if this never ends? Chen Chen thought at one point. As soon as she thought it, she felt the baby leave her.

Her mother-in-law pushed her mother out of the way and grabbed the baby. Chen Chen saw the disappointment on her face.

"Here is our bad luck," her mother-in-law said. She spat on the floor to keep that bad luck away from her. Then she handed the second daughter to Chen Chen's mother. "Do what you must," she said.

The second daughter did not seem quite right, Chen Chen thought later as she held them both in her arms in bed. The first one had a steady gaze, good color in her cheeks, a loud cry. The second daughter was much smaller, her arms and legs like little twigs. She had a swath of dark hair, right down the middle of her head. She hardly cried at all. Rather, she took Chen Chen's breast when it was offered and sucked in a slow, steady motion.

Everyone entered the room cautiously, avoiding Chen Chen's gaze. Until the third day, when her mother came to her and sat beside her on the bed. One baby slept across her lap, the other rested beside her. Her mother brought her aloe for her cracked nipples. And tea for strength.

"The second one," her mother said, choosing her words carefully, "is small and slow."

Chen Chen said, "She eats steadily. Soon she will catch up."

"So quiet!" her mother said. "Babies should be loud and robust. That means they have healthy lungs."

Something filled Chen Chen's throat, forcing her to gulp. "Perhaps she is simply content."

"She is not as beautiful as her sister," her mother said, her gaze steady on Chen Chen's face. "Do you understand?"

"I think she is beautiful," Chen Chen managed to say before the tears came.

"Your husband's mother is terrible. I don't trust what she will do to you. To the baby. I cannot stay any longer to protect you. Your father and your brother and his wife are waiting for me to return. Your brother's wife is pregnant too, and I need to care for her."

Chen Chen continued to cry.

"The second one is more undesirable, Chen Chen. Of the two of them, she is the one to get rid of."

Chen Chen looked at her mother with wild eyes.

"No! No!" her mother said quickly. "I will take her myself. On the way home, I will stop in Loudi. It is a small city about three hours from here. I will be sure she goes to the right place. A place that will care for her."

Beside her, the baby stirred.

"I have heard," her mother said, lowering her voice, "that people come from all over, from Spain and America and Holland, and they take these babies home. They give them a good life. Good educations. Perhaps this child will go to a fancy American school. The University of Harvard. Anything is possible. You have one perfect daughter. One inferior daughter. So simple to fix."

Chen Chen could not answer. She could not stop crying. Something was happening to her heart, she thought. It was breaking into dozens of pieces, pieces that would go to Loudi, to America, to the University of Harvard.

She picked up her second daughter and held her close.

"Mei Mei," she whispered.

It was the name she would always call her, even long after the baby was taken from her arms.

Mei Mei. Little sister.

WAITING

Deep doubts, deep wisdom;

small doubts, little wisdom.

10

MAYA

The winding roads that snaked beside farms and the ocean in Westport, Massachusetts, had no signs that Maya could find. Her GPS had lost its satellite reception, and Emily couldn't find their location on the map she had unfolded in her lap.

"Let's forget the Referral Waiting lunch and just find a restaurant somewhere," Emily grumbled.

"Good idea," Maya said. "I'm sure there's lots of restaurants around here."

Emily sighed. "I love being the only married person coming to this alone."

"I know," Maya said. "But I am a very good date."

In the distance, Maya spotted a sliver of blue ocean ahead of them.

"I'm pointing the car toward that," she said. "Brooke told me the house was right on the beach."

It was mid-October, and Westport, like the rest of southern New England, was in the full throes of autumn. The leaves had all turned to orange and yellow and red. Rolling farmland was dotted with neat bales of hay and pumpkin patches full of pumpkins still clinging to green vines.

"Pretty out here," Maya said.

"Why would a famous baseball player live out the middle of nowhere?" Emily said, unwilling to change her bad mood.

"Shit," Maya said as she drove around a hairpin turn and lost sight of the ocean.

"No GPS. No cell phone signal. It's not even on the map," Emily said. "Maybe we're in one of those towns like in *The Twilight Zone*? And there's no way out once we enter."

The ocean appeared again, suddenly close. At the corner, right before she would have to drive directly into the water, Maya saw a street sign.

"Atlantic Avenue," she read. "Hallelujah."

"Tell me again that it's perfectly appropriate for Michael to be at Chloe's school production of *Oliver!* in which she has only an ensemble part, one line in the song 'Who Will Buy?' instead of being here with me to get to better know the very people who are going to travel halfway around the world with us to finally get our baby," Emily said in one long breath.

"You will see these people plenty of times before you are on that plane to China," Maya said. "Chloe only gets to be in her school production of *Oliver!* today."

"Couldn't she have just called him up this morning, sung 'Ripe strawberries, ripe!' and let him come with me where I believe he belongs?"

Three small weathered bungalows stood in a line, just as Brooke had described. Behind the houses, rolling lawns and a tangle of cat-o'-nine-tails and beach roses. As Maya neared, she saw the well-beaten path to the beach through that tangle. Beyond, rocks and beach and the Atlantic Ocean. She could see why Charlie—why anyone—would live way out here. But Emily was in no mood to hear that.

"Hypothetically," Emily said, "I need minor surgery and Chloe has one line in *The Music Man*. Does he take me to the hospital?"

"Emily," Maya said, shaking her head.

"Our baby has one line in her preschool play and Chloe has a lacrosse game—"

"I'm not doing this," Maya said. "We are at the party and we're going to have fun."

"I'm being ridiculous?" Emily said.

"No," Maya said. She touched her friend's hand. "But let's just do this for now and worry about all the hypothetical stuff later."

"Every girl needs a practical friend," Emily said. "Someone with her head on straight. Does anything ever ruffle your feathers?"

Maya reached in the backseat for the pumpkin pie she'd made.

"Nothing does, right?" Emily said. She peered at Maya closely.

"You have no idea," Maya said.

The two women got out of the car and made their way across the grass to the front door.

"Let me guess whose car that one is," Emily whispered as they passed a shiny silver Mercedes.

"Well, he's related to John Adams," Maya told her.

"John Adams drove a Mercedes like that?" Emily said.

"You are going to behave," Maya said. "We are going to get our babies with these people and you want them to think you're nice, don't you?"

"Are you coming?" Emily said, surprised. "When we go to China?"

"Shhhh," Maya said.

The door had opened and Brooke was coming toward them.

"What a gorgeous place," Emily said to her.

"Perfect for kids, isn't it?" Brooke said, taking the pie from Maya and leading them inside.

The first thing Maya noticed, after the jaw-dropping view, was that Sophie, who was usually so open and smiley, looked pale and serious. She stood by the picture window that showed off that view, her arms folded across her chest. Maya thought she might have lost weight too. Her dress, a loose Indian print thing, seemed to swim on her. The husband, Theo, didn't appear to be here.

"Sophie is solo too," Maya whispered to Emily. "See? It's not so strange."

After greeting everyone, Maya walked over to Sophie.

"Is Theo here?" she asked.

Sophie shook her head, but didn't offer an explanation.

"How are you?" Maya said.

Sophie gave a small smile. "Okay. I've been feeling out of sorts lately. Nothing serious."

"You know," Maya said, "the waiting can get to people. Is Theo having a hard time with it?"

Sophie's eyes filled with tears. "We're having a hard time. With everything."

"I can't even begin to tell you how many calls I get from frustrated or anxious couples who are waiting for their referrals. But before you know it, I'll be calling you to say that you have a baby."

"I just hope we'll be ready when that happens."

"Sophie," Maya said, touching her arm, "I'm sorry. I didn't mean to upset you."

"It's not you," Sophie said, wiping her cheeks with the back of her hands. "Everything upsets me these days."

"A lot of people have second thoughts," Maya said gently. "You and Theo have such great plans for a family. Is he backpedaling a bit?"

Sophie laughed. "Well, you could say that there are some second thoughts in our household."

Nell sidled up to them. Even in simple black pants and a white button-down shirt, with black ballet flats and a red headband, she managed to look sophisticated, glamorous.

"You didn't answer my last email," Nell said.

"That's because I've already told you that your DTC group has a long way to go still." Maya turned to include Sophie in the conversation. "We just placed nineteen babies in the December 9 DTC group."

"It's like waiting to give birth," Sophie said. "You have to wait then too."

Nell lowered her voice. "Benjamin wants to go to Sardinia in June to race. But what if he's over there and we get our referral?"

"Please don't put your life on hold," Maya said.

She saw Benjamin standing with Charlie. Charlie was telling a story, his hands moving wildly, Benjamin's eyes gleaming with interest.

"Baseball tales," Brooke said. She held a tray of hors d'oeuvres out for them.

Sophie looked at the food, the dates wrapped in bacon and the little triangles of spinach and feta. "No thanks," she said, turning away.

"I just want something concrete," Nell said. "To work with."

"That's not how this goes," Maya told her. She tried to keep her voice calm, but she heard the edge creep into it. "We just have to wait."

"That's easy for you to say," Nell said. "But this baby is everything to me. Everything."

Out the window stretched a rolling lawn, beach grass, ocean. Maya took in the view to steady herself. Carter was out there with a little girl, playing catch. The girl was awkward, throwing too short or missing the ball when it came to her. So this was Clara, Maya thought. She remembered how embarrassed Susannah got whenever she mentioned her daughter.

"I just want a target date. Winter? Spring?" Nell continued.

"Tell your husband to go to Sardinia," Maya said, and she walked away.

Before she could get to the table where Brooke had laid out a buffet, Susannah cornered her.

"I need to ask you something," Susannah said. "It's important."

"Of course," Maya said.

But Susannah didn't say anything. Instead, her gaze settled outside where Carter and Clara were playing.

"I'm glad you brought your daughter today," Maya said gently.

Still watching them, Susannah said, "Would a pregnancy stop the adoption? I mean, is there a rule about that?"

Maya put her hand on Susannah's arm. "Are you pregnant?"

"I don't know yet. Maybe. Probably. I've been afraid to take the test." Now she looked at Maya and Maya saw that she was crying. "I want that little girl in China who's waiting for me. I want her so bad that it hurts."

"If you're pregnant, that doesn't change anything. We don't even know yet when travel will be. You might already have the new baby by then."

Susannah nodded.

"Some families decide not to go ahead with the adoption if—"

"No!" Susannah said. "I want that baby desperately."

"Then you will have her," Maya said.

Susannah's eyes settled again on her husband and daughter. It wasn't Maya's place to point out prenatal testing, the options around genetic issues.

"Come," Maya said. "Let's get some food. If you are pregnant, you need to eat."

"Right," Susannah said without conviction.

As they made their way to the table, Maya realized that Sophie had been standing nearby, listening. For some reason, it felt like she'd been eavesdropping on them. Silly to think that, Maya knew. But why hadn't Sophie just joined their conversation? Maybe she saw that Susannah was upset and wanted to stay out of it. Still.

Maya watched Susannah place slices of ham on her plate, spoon some potato salad and green bean casserole. It was the kind made with cream of mushroom soup and those canned fried onions. Sophie took just the casserole, a huge pile of it. They talked briefly, and Susannah suddenly looked relieved. Her face softened and she nodded emphatically before the two women went to sit together in two chairs in the corner. Maybe Sophie was helping her after all.

When Maya began to fill her own plate—ham, potato salad, sweet potatoes with little marshmallows on top, no thank you to that casserole—Carter and Clara came in.

"You're a good catcher," Maya said to the girl.

Clara grinned up at her. "I play baseball!" she said.

"You know a famous baseball player lives right in this house?" Maya told her.

"Oh!" Clara said. Suddenly she reached onto Maya's plate and grabbed the marshmallows off the sweet potatoes.

"No, Clara," Carter said. "You can't touch other people's food."

Then he said to Maya, "I'm sorry. We're working on her impulse control."

"It's okay. I didn't want them anyway."

"See?" Clara said. Her eyes shone behind her pale blue glasses. "She wants me to eat her marshmallows."

"Remember, sweetie?" Carter said. "You don't talk with food in your mouth." He smiled at Maya.

He handed Clara a plate of food and led her to a seat.

"You're good with her," Maya told him when he came back for his own lunch.

"I love her," Carter said matter-of-factly. "Susannah has had a hard time, though."

He took a breath, exhaled. "We could definitely have another baby with it," he said. "That's why we decided to adopt. Susannah has been adamant about not having any more children ourselves."

Puzzled, Maya tried to think of a response. Carter spotted Susannah and Sophie across the room.

"Would you excuse me?" he said.

Before Maya could answer, he walked away, leaving his food on the table.

Maya watched him approach his wife. He had no idea she might be pregnant, Maya realized. How many of these families would actually be on that plane to China? she wondered.

Sophie was filling her plate again with more green bean casserole. She saw Maya watching her and she laughed. "I can't stop eating this stuff. Maybe it reminds me of being a little kid. My mother made everything with Campbell's soup."

"My mother too," Maya said.

"I might make it myself tomorrow," Sophie said. "Theo will think I've lost my mind."

"Excuse me," Nell said loudly.

She stood in the middle of the room and motioned to everyone to be quiet. Maya had to marvel at her ability to get attention, to control a room.

"Thank you," Nell said. "I thought since we're all here, maybe Maya could give us some information. A target date, perhaps, when we might get our referrals."

"What a good idea," Susannah said.

Maya cleared her throat. They were all looking at her, expectant, hopeful.

"I wish I could do that," she said, "but as I've told Nell already, I'm waiting too. For them to send the referrals, I mean. We're dealing with the country of China, not with one orphanage or one orphanage director. I just placed children with a group whose DTC was December. So unfortunately there are many groups ahead of you. I always send emails when I get referrals, so that you can see how the queue is moving."

"December," Nell said. "If I do some quick math, that means we'll get our referrals next summer, then?"

Emily groaned. "That's an eternity from now."

"It does sound far away," Maya said, "I know. But sometimes referrals speed up."

"That means sometimes they slow down, then?" Sophie asked.

"Sometimes they slow down."

"So basically, Maya, you're telling us you don't know anything," Nell said.

"Actually," Maya said, "I know that you are all very lucky. I know that your lives will be changed for the better. I know that you will get beautiful healthy babies. I just don't know when. I wish I did."

"If I was pregnant, I would be waiting like this too," Brooke said. "So I think we should just do the things any expectant parents would be doing. Paint the room and buy onesies and read baby books."

"I knit her a sweater," Susannah said.

"That's wonderful," Maya said.

"Just find out when we're getting our babies," Nell said. "That's enough for me."

Maya doubted anything was ever enough for Nell. But she smiled and assured her that she was on top of it. In every group, there was one person that Maya thought didn't deserve one of these precious babies. But then she knew that having children, and losing them, wasn't about deserving. After all, who was she to judge any of them? To make such decisions? She took a small spoonful of that casserole and tasted it. No. She was right. Even though Sophie was on her fourth helping, it was awful.

11

The Families

EMILY

Despite the fact that Maya had told Emily that June was only a possible time when she might get her referral, that Nell had forced Maya to say something specific, that this was out of her hands, Emily still couldn't let go of the idea: I will have my baby next summer. They would go to the beach. They would sit in the garden in the warm summer sun. At night, with the tiki torches lit and the sky abundant with stars, she would point out the constellations to her daughter. That is Orion. The Seven Sisters. The Big Dipper.

Despite her better judgment, she went online and ordered a toddler-size bathing suit, yellow with fat red flowers and a ruffle around the hem. She should know better. With her first pregnancy, Emily had bought tiny Converse high-tops and a hat that looked like an eggplant. That baby should have been born in the spring. When she had the miscarriage, those small items seemed to mock her pain.

Still, the next time, she ordered furniture for the nursery: a crib that could convert to a bed and a changing table that became a bureau. It was practical, and solid with its dark wood and striped sheets. She had to cancel the order before it even shipped. The last time, she'd painted the baby's room midnight blue, and stenciled stars and planets across the walls and ceiling. All of these happy gestures ultimately made her sadder.

But this time she knew there was a baby at the other end. In June, she would be outside with her baby. Daisy, she would tell her daughter. Hollyhock. Petunia.

"You're going to be mad at me when June comes and goes and there's still no referral," Maya told her.

It was a cold, rainy Saturday afternoon and the two women were sitting in Emily's kitchen eating black bean soup and warm bread. Michael was away on business, and Emily was enjoying her time alone making baby plans.

"I won't be mad at you," Emily said. "I'll be mad at China."

"No. This happens all the time. You'll be mad at me. September 1, my phone will be ringing all day. Nell will yell me. You'll yell at me."

"All right," Emily said. "Maybe I'll be mad at you, but I won't yell."

"We'll see," Maya said.

Emily opened the package that had just arrived from Hanna Andersson and pulled out the yellow bathing suit.

"I shouldn't have," she said.

"I think stockpiling clothes is a good thing," Maya said.

"Michael told me not to do anything. In the past, I got so disappointed. So sad."

"This will be different," Maya said. "It will."

Emily traced the ruffle that ran along the bathing suit hem.

"Susannah knit a sweater. Maybe I should do something like that."

"Do you know how to knit?" Maya asked her.

Emily shook her head. "You?"

She thought Maya considered a moment too long before she answered.

"Not really," she said.

"Did I tell you that Jack is on this trip with Michael?" Emily said, studying Maya's face for a reaction.

Maya shrugged.

"Well, he is," Emily said. "Last night apparently, he picked up a woman in the hotel bar. Michael said she was cute, southern."

"Good for him," Maya said.

"Are you two in touch?"

"We email each other." Just yesterday he had sent her one that said: *I am remembering how you felt next to me in bed.*

"I don't understand. If you like him, why don't you go out with him again?"

"Did I ever tell you about Adam?" Before Emily could ask, Maya said, "My ex-husband."

Emily shook her head.

"He's a marine biologist. A specialist on jellyfish. Handsome, but in a scruffy way. Shaggy hair. Sometimes he didn't shave and walked around with five o'clock shadow. All of his shirts used to have frayed cuffs." As she talked, Maya tore her napkin into tiny squares. "He never wears socks. It's funny the things you remember about a person. Drinks his coffee black with one sugar. Likes peanut butter and Nutella sandwiches. At least he used to."

"And?" Emily said.

Maya scooped all of the little squares into a pile. "And I broke his heart," Maya said.

"It was such a long time ago," Emily said. "How long are you going to punish yourself for falling out of love with the guy?"

Maya looked at her, surprised. "Did I say I fell out of love with him?"

SUNDAY NIGHT, the rain still fell hard. Emily lay in bed naked with Michael after making love, listening to it beat on the roof. It was perhaps her favorite sound. She smiled to herself. Somehow, the weekend alone, the time with Maya, the arrival of the yellow bathing suit, the promise of summer, all of it made her feel happier than she had felt in months, since the last miscarriage.

Michael played with her hair, oddly in rhythm with the rain.

"I think Maya is still in love with her ex-husband," Emily said.

"I always forget she was even married," Michael said, his voice thick with sleep.

"It was a long time ago," Emily said.

"Poor Jack. He's crazy about her. Maybe I should tell him."

"The funny thing is, I told her she should go see the ex-husband and apologize for breaking his heart and she said: I'm going to see him after Memorial Day. Never even mentioned it." Emily had felt slightly wounded when Maya told her that. She was so secretive sometimes that Emily was always surprised when she learned anything.

"Do you think they'll get back together?" Michael asked.

"That's even weirder. He's remarried." That had been another surprise. Why pine for someone who's moved on? Why not go out with Jack?

"I think I'll stay out of it, then," Michael said. "Too complicated."

"Guess what I did on Friday?" Emily said.

"What did you do on Friday?"

"I signed up for a knitting class. I'm going to make a sweater for Isabelle."

"Who?"

"Isabelle. That's the name I'm trying out for the baby. What do you think?"

Last night, alone in bed, Emily had dared to read the baby name book she'd bought when she was first pregnant. She had tried not to look at the names highlighted in yellow that she had liked back then. Instead, she got a pink highlighter and started over.

"Too common," Michael said.

"Okay. How about Daisy?"

"Can we do this another time? When I'm awake?"

Don't be disappointed, Emily told herself. He is excited about this baby. He's just tired.

"Okay," she said again. "So I signed up for knitting classes so I can knit a sweater for Daisy."

"Did I tell you that Chloe started knitting?" Michael said. "They have an after-school class and she started a couple of weeks ago and she already knit a scarf."

"Scarves are easy. That's what Susannah said and she's been knitting forever."

"Maybe she can help you," Michael said, and Emily knew he meant Chloe, not Susannah.

"Well," she said, "I'm taking a class."

"She picked it up fast."

Emily felt her body stiffen. She lifted her head from his chest and settled on her side of the bed. Chloe somehow managed to ruin everything. If you let her, Dr. Bundy would say. Emily took a breath, then another, the way she did in yoga. Cleansing breaths.

"Do you like the name Daisy?" she asked again. She could take control of this conversation again. She could get Chloe out of it.

Michael chuckled. "Not really."

"Tell me a name you like," she whispered, her hand finding his beneath the covers and holding it.

Michael didn't answer. His own breathing told her he had fallen asleep.

"You're going to love our baby as much as you love Chloe, right?" she whispered.

He squeezed her hand, but whether it was an answer or just an acknowledgment that he'd heard her, she wasn't sure.

MICHAEL

Michael watched Chloe pick at her food. Maybe Emily was right. Maybe Chloe did have something going on with her eating. He couldn't bring himself to say the word *anorexia*.

"That looks good," he said, aware of how foolish he sounded.

Chloe shrugged and moved the salad around on her plate. She always ordered a chicken Caesar salad. Emily had pointed that out to him and she was right. He wished he didn't know this.

"So what do you want to do next? Maybe go shopping for that luggage I promised you?" Rachel had said that Chloe was sick of always having to be with him and Emily. She needs alone time with you, she'd said, and so here he was, alone with Chloe at the Providence Place mall eating at the Cheesecake Factory, which was loud and crowded and making his head pound.

"I already told you," Chloe said, "I don't want luggage."

"We got all of these papers about traveling to China and there's a weight restriction going in, but not coming out. So Emily thought we could each take an empty suitcase so that we'd have room for souvenirs."

"Isn't Emily smart?" Chloe said. She was lining up all the chicken on one side of the plate.

"Chloe," Michael said.

"I'm not going to China," Chloe said, picking through the salad for more chicken.

The three miniature hamburgers Michael had eaten rolled around in his stomach. "I want you to come more than anything," he said.

Chloe finally looked at him. "If I don't come, what will you do?"

"I'll be hurt, Chloe," he said. "Don't do this."

"You'll be hurt?" she said. "Do you know how it feels to have your parents sit you down and tell you they're getting divorced? Do you? It hurts like hell."

"Chloe," Michael said.

"And then your father tells you he's fallen in love with someone who isn't your mother? Who isn't anybody at all?"

"That's what happens sometimes. Your mother could—"

"And then he says he wants a new baby? Like you're not good enough?"

"That's ridiculous!" Michael said, jumping to his feet.

"Feelings aren't ridiculous!" Chloe shouted at him.

The noisy restaurant grew quiet.

Chloe pushed her way out of the booth and walked through the crowd. Even though Michael followed right away, he lost sight of her. When he reached the exit, she was not there. The mall stretched before him, but he could not spot Chloe.

"I LOST HER," Michael told Rachel. He pressed his cell phone close, like a shield.

"Good move," she said. "She's with me."

"I think you need to help me out, Rachel."

Rachel laughed. "I'm not the one who didn't want to be married anymore. I'm not the one who loved you, but wasn't in love with you."

"Okay," he said.

"I'm not the one so desperate for another child that I'm going halfway around the world."

"I'm not desperate," Michael said. "I'm married to another woman and we want a family." Then he added, "I'm not the one who can't move on with my life."

"Oh, you've moved on," Rachel said. "That's for sure."

"Maybe we could focus on Chloe instead of me?"

"Fine. She called me in tears and I came to get her. We're almost home."

"Rachel, you have to talk to her about coming to China," he said.

"I have to, huh?"

Michael shook his head. "And you have to talk to her about her eating."

"What?"

Michael swallowed hard. "I'm worried about how thin she is. I'm worried about how little she eats."

"You are unbelievable," Rachel said.

He would call Chloe's guidance counselor and talk to her about the eating problem. He would buy that luggage himself.

"I'm hanging up," he said.

"Goodbye, Michael," Rachel said.

Quickly, he pressed the number for home on his phone.

"Hey," Emily said, "you guys having fun?"

"You home?" Michael asked her.

"Yes."

"Stay there," he said. "I'm on my way."

SUSANNAH

Susannah stood naked in front of the full-length mirror that hung on the back of the bedroom door. Yes, she decided, cupping her breasts in her hands, they were larger and tender. She turned to the side and smoothed her stomach. Definitely a bump. Her mouth went dry. If she just took a pregnancy test, she could stop all this. She could decide what to do.

For the hundredth time, Susannah did fast calculations. That night on the sofa was in August and here it was the beginning of November. Ten weeks. She studied her body again. Was this the body of a woman almost three months pregnant? Susannah took a breath, trying to suck in her stomach. Yes, she thought again. It was. So far she had avoided mentioning it to Carter. She knew he would be excited, that he would not even think the only things that Susannah could think. Another baby of theirs could be like Clara. Or worse. Fragile X syndrome had a wide spectrum of potential problems. But Carter wouldn't worry about that. He would say: This baby might be just fine.

That baby in China was just fine. A sure thing. Back before they'd decided to adopt, Carter had argued that there was no sure thing. Do you think an adopted baby will be perfect? he'd asked her. Susannah didn't want perfect. She wanted average. She wanted a child without disabilities.

The door opened and instinctively Susannah crossed her arms to cover her breasts.

Carter stood, his hand on the doorknob, his eyes traveling the length of her body. She was a tall, straight woman. Hipless, small-breasted. When she was pregnant with Clara, she didn't even show until her sixth month. Now, standing naked like this, with Carter studying her, Susannah knew that he could tell instantly. They had not made love since that night, and she had been grateful that their sex life had diminished enough that it wasn't even expected of her anymore.

Carter didn't speak. Instead, a sound came from him. Almost like a growl, Susannah thought, and he came toward her, unbuttoning his shirt, unbuckling his belt. When he reached her, he'd already unzipped his pants.

"Oh," he said softly, almost as if she wasn't even there.

He pushed her down to the rug. Briefly, Susannah worried about ruining the good oriental. Her grandparents had bought it in Tehran back in the twenties. It was hand-stitched in soft colors, with a pattern of birds. But when Carter entered her, she forgot about the rug. She found herself excited, even though it was more like he was taking her rather than really being with her, claiming something that was his.

He finished quickly, then rolled off her and onto his back.

When his breath grew even, he said, "Why didn't you tell me?"

Again, Susannah's mouth went dry. "The first month I spotted, so I thought maybe I wasn't." She couldn't bring herself to say the word *pregnant*. "But then I missed in October and so I'm not really sure what's going on."

"I'm going to get a home pregnancy test."

A wave of nausea spread across Susannah and she swallowed hard. "I want the baby in China."

"Fine. But this is our baby too."

"You're better with children like Clara. You don't understand what it's like for me to watch her. To feel the way I do."

For the first time, Carter looked at her. "What kind of mother are you? What kind of person?"

"I know," Susannah said. She wondered if she might throw up, right on her grandmother's Persian rug. Unsteadily, she got to her feet. "Please don't hate me," she said.

"God," Carter said, "I wish I could hate you. That would be easier somehow. But I love you."

Yes, she was going to throw up. The bathroom seemed an eternity away. Clutching her stomach, she closed her eyes and bent over. But instead of vomiting, she felt something warm trickle down her legs. She opened her eyes and saw a beautiful stream of blood. Such relief came over her that she had to sit.

"Look," she said, trying not to sound happy.

Carter nodded. "Well then," he said.

She could hear the disappointment in his voice, but she didn't care.

Carter pointed. "The rug," he said.

Susannah touched the dark red that stained the pale pink and powder blue birds beneath her.

"It's okay," she said. "It's fine."

NELL

Downstairs in her in-law's townhouse on Louisburg Square in Boston, Nell could hear the violins of a Vivaldi piece, the clank of pans and dishes from the kitchen where the servants cooked and prepped Thanksgiving dinner, and the low chatter of all the Adamses: her mother-in-law Lizzie with a voice full of vodka and strangled with a triple strand of pearls; her father-in-law John's drone; her sister-in-law Liza and her husband and three bratty children; her brother-in-law Trip and his snobby wife and their three bratty children; and her own husband Benjamin with his endless sailing adventure stories.

At this moment, she hated every one of them, including Vivaldi and the stupid gaggle of pugs her in-laws owned. Was a group of pugs a gaggle?

Nell was room-spinning drunk. She had come upstairs to throw up, but instead lay on her in-laws' creepy bed with the heavy maroon-fringed canopy, enjoying her drunkenness. As a teenager, Nell had always liked the spins. She realized she liked them now too.

The bed smelled of her mother-in-law's perfume. The smell made her queasier. She held up her BlackBerry and squinted at it hard. It took three tries before she could find the right number and manage to press the buttons to call it.

When Theo answered, Nell said, "I am so drunk."

He laughed. "I can tell."

"So," she said, "how long does a girl have to wait for the boy she had sex with to call?"

"Nell," he said in a voice that meant, Let's not do this.

But she didn't care. Two months earlier they'd spent the afternoon together in a hotel having fantastic sex. And he never called her or anything.

"I feel the way I did back in high school when I gave a boy a blow job and then he never asked me out again."

"I don't need to know that," Theo said gently.

"Oops," Nell giggled. She hadn't meant to say that out loud.

"I've wanted to see you," Theo said. "I have. But the shit really hit the fan here."

"What?" Nell said, sitting upright so fast she fell immediately back down. "Sonia knows about us?"

"Sophie," Theo said. "Why don't we talk later? When you feel better."

"No, no," Nell said. She wanted to stay on the phone with him. "Tell me."

"I came home that day and my old girlfriend was there with Sophie and . . ." Theo paused. "It is such a mess."

"The one you love so much? The one who got away?"

"Yes," he said. "And I've been sleeping on the sofa ever since. It's such a mess," he said again.

"Well, Happy Thanksgiving," Nell said. "And I want to see you again when you straighten everything out."

Theo laughed. "You aren't making any sense," he said. "Get some sleep."

Then he hung up. Nell lay there, trying to figure out what to do next.

The bedroom door opened and Benjamin walked in. "What are you doing?" he asked.

He loomed over her. "Stop looming over me," she possibly said.

"Oh dear," he said. "Want a pot?"

She narrowed her eyes at him. "I do not," she said. "I'm not going to be sick."

"Cloris is serving hors d'oeuvres," he said.

"Benjamin," Nell said, and she was clutching at his pant legs now, "do you think I'm good in bed?"

He tried to step away from her, but she held on tight. "Of course."

"I'm so drunk," she said.

"I know."

He stroked her hair, which Nell thought was very kind.

"Do you want to make love?" she said. She was crying suddenly. She couldn't explain it, why she felt so sad.

"Why? Are you ovulating?"

"I don't know." Snot was running down her face and she didn't even care. "I just want to do it, you know?"

"Later. Okay?" he said.

Nell nodded and wiped her nose on one of the decorative pillows.

"I just want a baby," she said.

"I know," Benjamin said.

He slipped off her shoes and covered her with the silk comforter they'd brought back from a trip to China. How ironic, she thought right before she passed out. I am covered by silk from China.

BROOKE

Every year, Brooke and Charlie did the same exact things to celebrate Christmas. They got a palm tree from Four Corners Farm and strung white blinking lights on it. They filled glass bowls with seashells they collected together from Elephant Rock Beach on Christmas Eve. They hung their stockings and each filled the other's without getting caught. Then, on Christmas morning, they ate eggnog French toast and drank milk punch and sat together opening presents and made love under a blanket on the cold cold beach.

But on this Christmas morning, when Brooke came into the living room, she found piles of presents, all wrapped in pink foil paper with silver snowflakes and topped with enormous pink bows. A rocking horse stood in one corner. A Johnny Jumper hung from the doorway that led out to the deck. The seashells had been moved to who knew where and the tabletop held a bassinet instead, white wicker with pink and white gingham lining.

A third stocking had been hung over the mantel. A tiny striped one, with silver bells dangling from the cuff.

"Ho ho ho," Charlie boomed. He came in with two cups of his famous milk punch, frothy, the tops dusted with fresh ground nutmeg.

"What's all this?" Brooke said.

"Baby's first Christmas," he said, sipping his drink. "I confess, I've done a lot of tasting already, darling. It's just that I woke up filled with such . . . such joy. That's the word. Joy. In fact, I was thinking of that for her middle name. Frankie Joy. Or maybe Billie Joy? What do you think?"

"I don't know," Brooke said. She tried to understand her confusion. Wasn't this what she had wanted? Charlie on board? Then why did she feel so upset? Why wasn't she delighted?

"Too clichéd, maybe? Like every adopted baby needs to have the name Joy or Hope in it?"

"It's not that. It's just . . ." She looked outside. "What the hell?"

Charlie grinned at her. "Finally! You noticed. I spent all night putting it together."

It was a wooden swing set with a slide and a jungle gym.

"Good thing you never go in the garage," Charlie was saying. "I had the boxes in there for weeks."

Brooke pushed past the Johnny Jumper and stepped outside. The winter sun shone bright and silvery. She stumbled across the deck, down the stairs to the yard.

One of the dogs followed her. He ran around in circles, barking at the curly slide.

"Charlie?" Brooke called. She needed to say something to him, to tell him it was too much. "Charlie?"

Inside the pocket of her red fleece bathrobe, one of his Christmas presents sat nestled in its small box. A double-heart-shaped picture frame, made of Italian mosaic tiles. Brooke had put her picture in one of the hearts and a black question mark in the other. The present seemed foolish now somehow. She had meant it to show him that there was room in his heart for both of them, her and the baby.

Exhausted, Brooke sat on one of the swings. It creaked noisily, then settled in place with a thunk. This should be a happy day. She knew that. But the feeling in her chest was nothing at all like happiness. It was the way she felt when back in college she and Charlie would be at a fraternity party and she'd catch sight of him talking to another girl. Or the feeling she used to get when she'd wait outside the locker room for him after a game and she'd watch women crowd around him. It was ridiculous to feel jealous of a baby. Of *their* baby. It was the opposite of what Brooke had feared. All this time she had worried that Charlie couldn't share her with a baby when in fact it was she who couldn't share him.

One of the dogs ran up from the beach, wet and cold, straight into the sandbox.

"Charlie?" she called again. Maybe they could stop it right now. Before they got their referral, before they saw that little pretty face. Fear ran through Brooke. All these years she had thought she wanted a baby, but now she saw that all she needed was Charlie. His love was enough for her. More than enough. It was everything.

Betsy, their third dog, came running from the beach too, with something hanging from her mouth. She went directly to Brooke and deposited a dead seagull, stiff with matted feathers, at her feet.

"Thanks, girl," Brooke said. Why had she thought that they needed more than this: their house on the beach, their dogs, each other?

Brooke swung harder, pushing off with her feet. She hadn't been on a swing since she was a little girl. She pumped her legs so that the swing rose higher and higher. When she was little, she used to think she could make the swing take off and fly. Wouldn't that be something? she thought. To fly away?

"Charlie?" Brooke said, even though she knew he couldn't hear her. All this time she had believed that it was Charlie who didn't have room in his heart for someone else. Now she saw she had been wrong. She was the one whose heart could not open enough for two. She wasn't sure why, but she knew it with certainty.

"Brooke!" Charlie said. He stood in front of the swing, and each time she pumped her legs and rose higher, she lost sight of him. "I love you!" he said.

He came into view, briefly. Brooke pumped her legs hard, and she rose up and up, until she could clearly see what lay before her.

SOPHIE

Sophie stood at the bedroom window and watched the first snowflakes of what threatened to be a nor'easter fall. *The* bedroom. Not *our* bedroom. Since that terrible day when Heather showed up in her ridiculous dancer clothes and pictures of a six-year-old girl in a tutu, Theo had been sleeping on the futon. He no longer even bothered to fold it back into its frame. Instead, he left it open and unmade.

He was there now. Usually they bundled up and ran outside during snowstorms. For some reason, the memory embarrassed her now. The snowball fights and snow angels and tiny Buddhas they built out of snow. The appearance of Heather and those photographs made Sophie embarrassed about her entire marriage.

The flakes were small and falling fast. Sophie used to know what made a snowstorm a blizzard; she grew up in Colorado. Wind speed. Size of flakes. Amount of accumulation per hour. And? Something else that she could not remember. Her brain these days felt all cloudy and thick.

A couple passed beneath the window, dressed in puffy bright-colored coats, holding hands. Sophie had to turn away at the sight of them. She sat on the bed and opened the drawer in the night table beside it. Rose smiled up at her. When the first envelope of photographs arrived from San Francisco, Sophie opened it and took one for herself. In it, Rose was dressed as a fairy of some kind for Halloween. Her face sparkled with silver glitter, stiff blue wings rose behind her. But it was her eyes that broke Sophie's heart. They were Theo's eyes. Same droopy lids and long lashes. Bedroom eyes. No matter how hard Sophie might try to talk herself out of the truth of this child, those eyes let her know that Rose was indeed her husband's daughter.

A soft knock on the door, and then Theo's voice. "Sophie? It's snowing."

When she didn't answer, he knocked again.

"I know," she said, closing the drawer.

"Want to take a walk?"

She did want to take a walk. She wanted to go out there and catch snowflakes with her tongue and put her mittened hand in her husband's. She wanted the snow to erase everything that had happened the past few months.

"No," Sophie said.

He didn't answer for a bit and Sophie thought he had walked away.

Then he said, "Can I come in?"

Sophie thought of her mother, who taught high school English. She would say, *You can, but you may not.*

"Okay," she said.

The door opened, and Theo stood dressed to go outside: his big olive green parka and lace-up snow boots and funny three-pointed hat.

"Come on," he said.

Sophie shook her head.

Theo clomped over to her and sat beside her on the bed. *The* bed, Sophie thought, not *our* bed.

"You have to forgive me," he said. "You have to."

She tried to find the words that could capture his betrayal. But there were none. "Theo?" Sophie said instead.

"Please, Sophie. I've messed up bad. I have. It's childish, the way I act when I feel pressured or boxed in. But you have to believe that I'm sorry. More than sorry. I'll make it all up to you. If you let me."

She put a finger over his lips to silence him.

"Theo," she said again. "I'm pregnant."

Even then, when he opened his mouth, she kept her finger there.

"Ssshhh," she said.

Her husband wrapped her in his arms, his parka crinkling under her cheek. She had promised herself that when she told him, she would not cry. But here she was, crying. Hard.

"But this is good," he was saying. "This is amazing."

"I am so mad at you," Sophie managed.

"I know."

"No. You have no idea."

Theo took her by the shoulders and looked right at her. He was grinning.

"Wow," he said. Then he laughed and brought her back into a hug.

"Wow," he whispered into her hair.

All of the things she had practiced for this moment melted away. Instead, she let her husband hold her like that and promise her things. Sophie unzipped his jacket and slipped herself inside. His sweater smelled like mothballs and smoke and the smell made her stomach roil. But she stayed there anyway.

12

MAYA

"They don't buy the cow if the milk is free," Maya's mother said, shaking her head.

Day five of Maya's visit home—if you could call her parents' new condo with the pale blue wall-to-wall carpeting and framed prints of museum posters home—and her mother had succeeded in using every cliché known to man. Time to fly back East, Maya thought. Her mother had just run out of things to say to her.

"Go ahead," her mother said, "roll your eyes. But I know that divorced women have a stigma about them." She lowered her voice. "They're easy. Fast. Mark my words."

"Not to worry," Maya said. "I'm dateless and therefore celibate."

"Spare me the details of your love life," her mother said, holding up both hands as if to stop traffic.

Maya sighed. Did her mother ever listen to her?

From where she sat at the counter, Maya could see into the small living room. On the sidebar there, her parents had some kind of digital picture frame that flashed photographs of them on their various trips. Her father in scuba gear. Her mother with a margarita. Both of them standing next to a pygmy in front of a reed hut.

"Panama," her mother said, pointing to the picture. "San Blas Islands. They are the second-shortest people in the world, after Pygmies."

Before Maya could comment, the picture switched and suddenly she was staring at her own image on her wedding day. There she was in her knee-length vintage dress, a wreath of tropical flowers in her hair, her head thrown back slightly, a wide smile on her face. Beside her, gazing at her with so much love it broke her heart to see it like this, stood Adam.

"Surprise!" her mother said. "Your father took all of our old photographs and put them on CDs with a special machine he bought from the *SkyMall* magazine. You know the one in airplane seat pockets? We've found so many interesting items in there."

Maya's wedding picture was replaced by an underwater shot of a coral reef and colorful fish swimming.

Relieved, Maya relaxed a bit.

The underwater scene switched and a photograph of her father eating what looked like a giant beetle took its place.

"We're waiting for this gadget that turns old record albums into CDs," her mother said.

The next picture flashed on, and Maya's breath caught. Looking back at her was her daughter, grinning under a sun hat printed with happy daisies.

Her mother saw the terror on Maya's face and followed her gaze.

"Maya. Maya, I'm sorry. I didn't think it would upset you. Time heals," her mother said. "Doesn't it?"

Maya stared at her baby. Her happy, breathing baby. No, she thought, it doesn't. But before she could answer, her daughter was gone, replaced with a colorful sunset.

That night Maya dreamed that she fell into the giant saltwater aquarium that made up one wall of her parents' guest room. She tumbled past the bright blue fish, past the fat yellow ones and tiny neon ones, until she landed at the sandy bottom. She woke, panting. In her dream, she had been trying to climb out of the tank, its slippery walls sending her falling again and again.

Maya watched the fish swim endlessly. The tank reminded her of the kind in a doctor's office. They were intended to calm the patients, but Maya felt anything but calm. She wished she could leave now for her flight back to Providence, but that would mean calling a taxi—if taxis even came out to this desolate condominium complex in Florida where her parents had retired. It would mean sitting for six hours in the airport, reading women's magazines and dreading the long night that awaited her back home. New Year's Eve. It had been a toss-up deciding which was worse: being alone at home or enduring another night with her parents.

At dinner, her father had announced that they were moving to Costa Rica. "Time for a little excitement before it's too late," he'd said.

"Remember the Pettys?" her mother had asked. Maya didn't, but that didn't really matter. "They moved there and they love it. Absolutely love it."

The good news, Maya supposed, was that she would see her parents even less once they moved to Costa Rica.

She closed her eyes, but in her mind she saw her daughter. That daisy hat. Maya had bought it at a street fair when she was pregnant. That day, she could only imagine the baby who would wear it. What if it's a boy? Adam had asked her. He'll look funny in this hat, then, she'd said. And they had laughed, because they were so happy and could not imagine anything happening to the baby who would wear that hat.

Reluctantly, Maya got up. She tiptoed across the powder blue carpeting, down the stairs, into the kitchen. She turned on the coffeemaker and sat watching the coffee drip into the glass carafe. If she could bear it, she would take her coffee down to the beach that sat at the end of a weathered wooden path. But she was a coward. The beach reminded her of Hawaii, Hawaii reminded her of her old life, her old life broke her heart.

Instead, Maya sat at the glass-topped table. She sipped her weak Maxwell House coffee and waited for the morning to finally arrive so she could go home.

MAYA KNEW IT was a cliché to sit alone on New Year's Eve, eat takeout Chinese food, and watch television. But here she was, doing just that. Maybe she was more her mother's daughter than she liked to admit.

She worked her way through a complete order of fried dumplings, and was starting in on her crispy beef when her doorbell rang. Emily and Michael had gone to Vermont for the weekend, and Emily was her only friend who would think to show up on her doorstep with a bottle of champagne and some silver party hats. Maya decided that even if she found missionaries at her door, she would listen to their spiel.

She did not find missionaries, though, only Jack standing there, with a bottle of champagne and two party hats.

"Happy New Year?" he said.

Maya wondered if she'd ever been so relieved to see someone. She resisted the strong urge to hug him good and hard.

"I have Chinese food," she said.

"I hoped you would," Jack said.

"Do we have to wear the hats?"

"They're just symbolic."

Maya stepped aside to let him in.

"I CAN'T DO THIS," she said on their third day together.

"So you keep saying," Jack said.

She did keep saying it. That first night, New Year's Eve, when they didn't get to the Chinese food until well after midnight because they went straight to the bedroom. Again the next morning when she woke up to the smell of Cajun food and found him in the kitchen making beans and rice. "It brings good luck for the new year," he explained. "I can't do this," she said later that day as they sat frowning over a jigsaw puzzle of the Taj Mahal together. He knew she meant be in a relationship, not finish the puzzle. She said it again that night, after they made love. And again the next morning as he made shrimp and grits. And she said it now, as they walked through the snowy city on this gray afternoon.

"Maya," Jack said gently, "you are doing it."

"But I don't want to," she said.

"Ah. That's different."

Their boots fell heavily on the packed snow.

Last night he had asked her where her daughter was buried. Her name.

Maya couldn't answer either question. These were things she did not say out loud.

"I've worn out my welcome?" he said. His words lingered in the air between them.

"Yes," she said.

"You'll miss my cooking."

"I will," she managed to say.

"You can keep sending me away," he said, "but I will keep coming back."

He took her hand in his. She was wearing lumpy Ecuadoran gloves that her parents had given her for Christmas, along with a Peruvian sweater, Laotian socks, and a quilt with appliquéd sea creatures from Honduras. He was wearing big suede gloves lined with fleece. Maya was not a small woman, but Jack was a very big man, and her hand felt fragile in his, even with the layers of wool and suede and fleece between them.

He held her hand the whole way back to her house. He got in his car and drove away. Maya watched him go, then she went inside and threw away all the leftovers. When she was done, she scoured the pots and dishes they'd left behind. She washed the sheets and towels. She vacuumed the floors. She cleaned until she finally believed she had erased every trace of these last three days.

Hunan, China

MING

On the same day, both of Ming's dreams came true. The first arrived in the form of a letter. The envelope, a large manila one, was covered with postage stamps and large red block letters in English. When it arrived, she did not open it right away. Instead, Ming propped it on the kitchen table against the pots of herbs her husband planted. Fragrant basil and cilantro leaves. Gnarled gingerroot. Something Ming could not identify, a brown stalk in dry dirt.

Ming ate her rice and the spicy pork with three peppers that her husband had made her before he left for work this morning. Her husband was called Buddy because of his time in America as an exchange student twelve years ago. Buddy meant friend. But it also meant America. Buddy made the spicy pork with three peppers, then he came into the bedroom and he kissed her goodbye: first on the lips, then on her belly.

"Goodbye in there," he said, his mouth pressed to her stomach. "If you decide to come out today, wait until I come home."

Ming chewed her food, enjoying the perfect combination of crunchy and soft, hot and sweet. She stared at the envelope. Her friend Yi had told her that good news from Brown University came in a large envelope. "Small envelope, small news," she'd said. "Big envelope, big news."

Inside that big envelope, then, was her letter of acceptance to the Ph.D. program in American literature at Brown University.

Inside that envelope, was her dream.

Inside her belly was her second dream. She and Buddy had waited for a baby. First, he got his promotion in the Economics Department at the university in Changsha. Then Ming finished her master's degree. Then Buddy went for further studies at the London School of Economics. When he returned, Ming applied to Brown University in Providence, Rhode Island, in the United States. Providence, Rhode Island, was a speck on the map. So tiny it seemed to dangle off North America, into the Atlantic Ocean.

While they waited for news, Buddy said: "Time for a baby."

Buddy was impetuous. Ming more thoughtful. She thought: Nine months until I hear from Brown University. Nine months to make a baby. Her friend told her the number nine was good luck for people born in the Year of the Monkey. Both Buddy and Ming were Monkeys.

"Time for a baby," she whispered to Buddy that night in bed.

Two weeks later, Ming was walking across the campus to her office and without warning she was lying flat on her back on the sidewalk looking up at the green leaves and blue sky.

A woman with a panicked face screeched at her: "You fainted! Bad blood! Sickness!"

Ming lay looking up at the puffy white clouds floating past and the sunlight that came through the green leaves and she smiled. Baby, she thought.

Now she sat at her kitchen table eating spicy pork with three peppers and staring at the big envelope from America. She thought of that tiny speck dangling into the Atlantic Ocean. On the website, Brown University was full of smiling students, brick buildings, autumn leaves. Ming imagined herself walking across the campus with her baby in a sling. She would be smiling too. She would have books by Ernest Hemingway and Willa Cather and F. Scott Fitzgerald in her backpack. She would have stories in her head and happiness in her heart.

Ming put down her chopsticks and picked up her cell phone.

Big envelope, *she texted her husband.*

The people in the apartment upstairs walked loudly all day. Above her, they pounded across the floor, back and forth.

Hooray! *Buddy texted back to her.* Celebration tonight.

Ming took her bowl to the sink and squirted dishwashing detergent on it. The people above her pounded and pounded. But even all that noise could not change her high spirits.

She set the bowl to dry. She walked across the small kitchen and picked up the large envelope. Sliding a chopstick under the flap, she opened the envelope and took all of the papers from it. Before she could sit back down to read them, something inside her made a small pop, like the first fireworks of New Year's. Immediately, Ming felt the warm liquid flow out of her.

Come home now, *she texted to her husband.*

The first pain rippled across her lower back. She sat down, and waited for her second dream to be born.

MING AND BUDDY WERE from the same village. Their mothers traveled four hours by train together to meet their granddaughter.

"She is so ugly!" Ming's mother said with delight. This ensured that the ancestors wouldn't want her.

"She is stupid," Buddy's mother said, grinning.

Ming met Buddy's eyes and tried not to laugh. Their families still clung to superstition and old wives' tales. Her mother had brought her elephant garlic to eat raw; this would keep the baby healthy. His mother had brought a shard of jade to be placed in the baby's crib; this would ward off evil spirits.

When Ming stood to make tea, her mother shrieked. "Bad for your blood to walk around so soon!"

That night in bed, with their daughter nestled between them, Ming whispered, "When are they going home?"

Buddy stifled a laugh. "Bad luck!" he said. "Mothers must stay and drive new parents crazy!"

Ming reached across the baby and found his hand.

"We are so lucky," she said, closing her eyes. Sleep was approaching fast.

"Ssshhh," Buddy said. "Don't tempt fate."

Her last thought before sleep came was that Buddy sounded serious when he said that.

AT THE BUS STATION, *her mother took Ming by the arm and led her away from the crowd gathered to board the bus north.*

"I know you have good education, Ming. I know I'm a silly old woman," her mother said, holding on tight to Ming's arm.

"I don't think that—" Ming began.

"But sometimes we need to pay attention to omens."

Ming smiled at her mother. "I know," she said.

Her mother's face was smooth and round, but when she talked, creases appeared like the wrinkles in the apple dolls they used to make together when Ming was a little girl. She would make those someday with her own daughter. The thought filled her with hope, and with love for her own mother.

"The astrologer at home sees disruption in your chart," her mother said.

The good feelings that had surged through Ming just a moment ago turned cold.

"Don't be foolish," she snapped. She stroked the tuft of black hair that stood upright on her daughter's sleeping head.

"Perhaps the disruption is this Brown University? You taking Geng away for so many years?" her mother offered, peering up at her taller daughter.

Oh! Ming thought. I get it now. This is her way of making me feel guilty for going to America. Her way of trying to get me to stay here.

"Perhaps," Ming said, nodding.

"Perhaps it is something more," her mother added.

She stared hard at Ming, in a way that made her uncomfortable.

"Buddy prepared you a delicious snack for the long ride," Ming said, taking her mother by the elbow and steering her back into the crowd. "Fried pork dumplings. Your favorite."

"He's a good son-in-law," her mother said without enthusiasm. "A good man."

Ming tried to get Buddy's attention, but his mother had it all. She was fussing with his shirt, smoothing his hair, jabbering nonstop. Finally, the bus arrived in a noisy squeal of brakes and a blast of black smelly smoke. Buddy made sure the mothers had their dumplings, their small bags. He helped them push through the waiting crowd and onto the bus, where he selected the best seats for them, two together so they could gossip the whole way home.

Ming stood outside. She could see Buddy settling them in, then fighting his way off the bus. Ming's mother pressed her face against the window and peered out until her gaze fell on her daughter and granddaughter. Ming waved to her. Her mother lifted one small hand and waved back.

The bus came alive with more smoke and a long, protracted wail of brakes.

Ming kept waving. The bus backed up in such a way that her mother appeared right above her. Ming stared up at her and saw that her mother was crying, her hands both open, palms pressed against the window like a plea.

THE BABY WAS CALLED *Geng, which meant bright and shining to their mothers but to Ming it meant to have guts. Her daughter would be fearless. She would be brave. She would be daring. In America, Ming decided, the baby would be called Willa. That meant all of those things to Ming. Brave. Fearless. Daring. Gutsy.*

She would write her dissertation on Willa Cather, a gutsy woman herself. Perhaps Ming and Geng would travel to Nebraska. They would be like pioneers themselves in this strange land. The two of them, side by side on this enormous adventure. Ming unfolded the Rand McNally map of the United States that Buddy had given her. It spread across the kitchen table, covering it with its thin blue lines of highways and mountain peaks and red stars marking capital cities.

With her finger, Ming traced the route from Providence, Rhode Island, to Red Cloud, Nebraska. Her finger gobbled up towns and states as it marked a certain path West. She uncapped a yellow highlighter and retraced the route in permanent ink, a bright yellow route shining halfway across the country. She traced another to New Hampshire, where Willa Cather was buried. So many journeys ahead of them.

Geng was five months old, a baby so beautiful that old ladies on the busy streets of the city of Chengsha and in the crowded markets by the river had to touch her. Her mouth was a perfect rosebud, pink and plump. Her hair shone black in the spring sunlight. She smiled readily. She lifted her arms and opened and closed her fingers when she wanted to be picked up.

Even though they would not leave for three more months, Ming began to make stacks of books to be shipped. She collected baby clothes to bring, warm sweaters hand-knit by the old ladies at the university, and blankets for the cold New England winters. She made endless notes on things to pack, things to see, things to do.

Sitting across from her husband, the baby sucking happily on her breast, the table full of long beans in garlic sauce and sizzling chicken, Ming listened as Buddy talked. He waved his chopsticks in the air to make his point about the world economy, office politics, the importance of this and that. Ming watched him and listened to him and loved him, but in her mind she was already leaving. She could picture the Atlantic Ocean from paintings she saw by Winslow Homer. It was rough and gray with waves crashing over rocks. She could picture the autumn leaves and smiling students at Brown University. She could see miles and miles of books in the John D. Rockefeller Library, stretching endlessly before her.

The baby sucked and gurgled. Buddy talked. Ming dreamed her new dreams.

THE DAY THE TICKETS *to Providence arrived, Ming dressed extra nice to go to the United Airlines office and pick them up. She wore her slim black skirt and a red silk blouse and the jade earrings Buddy had given her for her birthday last year.*

"You don't have a date, do you?" Buddy asked her when she walked into the kitchen.

"Yes, I do," Ming said, smiling at him. "A date with United Airlines."

Buddy chopped scallions and put them into a neat pile. "A formidable competitor," he said.

They had done it before, separating like this to study abroad. During the three years that Buddy was at the London School of Economics, Ming had only visited him twice. Now, she and the baby would be the ones in the distant place, and Buddy would make his way to them once a year. When Ming thought of being alone in this strange place called Providence, she felt a mix of excitement and loneliness. Buddy had written down odd things she might encounter there, but the list made her nervous: SUVs, canned vegetables, large dogs.

Buddy began to julienne red peppers. "I am making a celebration dinner," he told Ming. "We will celebrate the arrival of your tickets."

Ming stood behind him and wrapped her arms around him. Buddy smelled like ginger and mint soap. She breathed deep, filling herself with Buddy.

"I'm going to miss you," she murmured into his back.

He paused. "Me too," he said. He didn't turn around. He just went back to slicing the peppers.

Ming moved from him and began to pack Geng's diaper bag.

"Don't wake her," Buddy said. "Go and get your tickets. I'll be here."

Ming hesitated. She always took Geng with her, tucked snugly in the sling. Ever since she'd had the baby, she did not feel quite right without her daughter resting against her chest.

"Go," Buddy said. "She'll be fine." Then he laughed. "You'll be fine," he added.

"All right," Ming said, trying to sound convinced. She took a sliver of pepper and Buddy slapped her hand playfully.

"Not yet," he said.

She leaned in and kissed him softly on the mouth.

"Mmmm," Buddy moaned. He kissed her back, harder and with intention.

"Not yet," Ming said.

At the door, she stood and watched him for a moment.

"Go," he said, without looking up.

And so she went.

THE WITNESSES SAID *the car just jumped the curb. It did not zigzag down the street, or veer erratically off course. One moment, it was driving along with all the other cars. The next it was on the curb. When it hit the crowd walking on the sidewalk, the sounds were unforgettable. One witness said bodies flew in the air. One said she would never forget the screams.*

For Buddy, these statements were all he had to make sense of losing Ming. He told anyone who would listen each detail. She stole a sliced pepper. She kissed him goodbye. She was just three blocks from home. The car showed no sign of danger. It just jumped the curb. Bodies flew everywhere. One woman would never forget the screams.

After he said this, he told how when he heard the knock on the door, he thought Ming had forgotten her keys. He opened the door and found two policemen standing there with serious looks on their faces. One had a mustache. One had small drops of blood on his cheek. From shaving or from the accident, Buddy did not know. But he did worry over this detail. The one with the mustache asked him if he was Ming's husband. That was when he knew.

"She was on her way to the United Airlines ticket office," he always said to whoever was listening to his story. "You know the one? The main one? Her ticket to America was there."

His mother wanted him to move back to Loudi with the baby. But where would he teach economics in such a small place? His mother-in-law wanted the baby. "I told her there would be disruption," she said.

Disruption did not seem a big enough word for what had happened. Catastrophe. Cataclysm. No, even those were too small. Ming was dead. And Buddy did not know what to do.

FOR WEEKS, *Buddy woke feeling as if he had not slept. Rather, the night just went on and on in a tumble of darkness and sweaty sheets until eventually morning came. Then he rose from the bed, fed the baby, and tried to think of what to do next. But this morning, as he watched Geng eating her mashed bananas, an idea came to him.*

Outside, a cold rain fell, smearing the windows and casting a gray tone over everything. Buddy imagined the cocoon of his office, the polished wooden desk and silver lamp with its high-intensity bulb. He imagined the hum of the fluorescent lights in the outer office, the astringent smell of cabbage that lingered in the air. In the apartment, Ming's fingerprints covered everything. But in his office, he would be safe from grief.

Buddy lifted the baby from her high chair.

"You are supposed to be in America," he whispered to her.

Even the baby wore Ming's fingerprints. Her blue pants, her socks covered with blue flowers, the red jacket he buttoned on her now, everything said Ming. It was too much. Was he really meant to endure this pain, day after day, hour after hour?

With his daughter pressed close to him, Buddy left the apartment, balancing umbrella, diaper bag, baby. The rain fell hard. By the time he arrived at the bus depot he was wet and chilled. He took a cloth from the bag and dried his face and hands. The baby watched him solemnly.

When the bus arrived, Buddy boarded, choosing a seat by the window so that he could rest his head against it. The baby slept, snoring slightly. Buddy closed his eyes and listened to the rain and the traffic. For the first time since that careless driver jumped that curb and killed his wife, he slept.

TO KILL TIME until nightfall, Buddy went to a restaurant. The waiters all wore the red uniforms of Mao's Red Army. A large picture of Mao hung on the wall. But the food was good, spicy and plentiful. A waitress took a liking to the baby, and offered to play with her while Buddy ate. He handed his daughter to her without emotion. This is how you give your child to someone else to care for her, he thought. He was surprised how easy it was, how light he felt when the young woman took the baby from him and walked away.

Diagonally across the street sat a low, squat building, undistinguished in every way. From the restaurant, Buddy could see into its courtyard, where even in the rain a small group of children played with a ball. The children were laughing and squealing.

"Excuse me," Buddy said to the woman playing with the baby. "I need to run a simple errand. May I leave her with you for a moment?"

The woman did not hesitate. She was singing a song that required counting the baby's fingers and so she held the baby's hand in her own, ready to continue.

"That's fine," she said. "We're having fun here."

"I see that," Buddy said. The baby was smiling her toothless smile. She seemed happy.

He took his umbrella and stepped out into the rainy street. Not far from here was his mother's house. He didn't even consider going there, however. His daughter was not going to live in that backward village with no opportunity. He and Ming had worked hard to get educations, to make a good life for themselves and their child. He couldn't betray his wife.

At the entrance to the courtyard, Buddy paused.

One of the children, a boy with strange crossed eyes, called to him. "What do you want?"

"What is this place?" Buddy asked.

The children looked at each other, and then they looked down at the ground. The ball sat in a puddle.

"Do you all live here?" Buddy asked.

A girl of about six with a twisted arm said, "We are the ones no one wants."

"Why?" the cross-eyed boy said. "Are you looking for a baby? There are hundreds inside."

"Not hundreds," another boy said. "But dozens."

He seemed like a fine boy, older than the others but without any obvious defects. Buddy wondered why no one would want him.

"What happens to those babies?" Buddy asked.

The cross-eyed boy said, "Some of the littlest ones die. The damaged ones stay. But the lucky ones, they go to paradise."

"Paradise?" Buddy said.

A little girl with thick black braids stepped forward. She was pale and skinny. "America," she whispered.

"Or Spain or Sweden or—" the cross-eyed boy began.

A door flew open and a gray-haired woman in a yellow business suit stepped out.

"Hush!" she told the children. "Inside now." She narrowed her eyes at Buddy. "Get out!" she said. "Get out or I'll call the police."

Buddy nodded, but he did not leave. He watched the children file inside. They walked in a very orderly fashion. None of them even glanced his way.

BACK AT THE RESTAURANT, Buddy ordered tea. The waiters sat at the table across from him and took kale from cardboard boxes. They stripped the tough outer leaves from the kale and rinsed the tender part left behind in a plastic dish of water. Buddy watched them for a while, then he watched the building across the street.

It was growing dark. The rain slowed to a drizzle. The woman in the yellow pantsuit came out of the building and walked in small fast steps to a gray car. She had a briefcase in one hand and an umbrella in the other. When she drove away, Buddy asked for the bill. He paid it, and gave some change to the young woman who had played with the baby.

The baby was asleep now.

"My daughter has a long ride back to Changsha," he said to one of the waiters. "May I take this box to use as a little bed for her?"

The waiter shrugged. "It will just get thrown away. Take it if you want."

Buddy took the cloth from the diaper bag and placed it on the bottom of the box. He gently laid his daughter on top of it, then placed the pale green blanket his wife kept in the bag over her. When he lifted the box, he was surprised at how light it felt.

With great purpose, Buddy walked out of the restaurant and across the street. He entered the courtyard. The blue ball still sat neglected in a puddle. No sounds came from the building.

Buddy placed the box at the doorstep. He gazed down at his sleeping daughter. She looked so much like Ming that his heart tightened with pain and he had to look away.

He pressed the button by the side of the door. Even from outside, he could hear the loud buzzing. He pressed again, and then a third time. When he thought he heard footsteps approaching, Buddy walked away, fast. He stood across the street, in the shadows, waiting.

The door opened, and a woman in purple sweatpants and a gray sweatshirt that said GAP across it, peered out. She looked to her right, and then to her left. He could not see the expression on her face, whether she was angry or disappointed or perhaps even joyful at the sight of the baby asleep in the box that moments earlier had held kale.

The woman bent and lifted the box. She seemed to look inside. Perhaps she cooed to the baby. Perhaps she pressed her warm hand to the baby's cheek, the way a mother might. Perhaps she whispered tender words to her. Buddy could not know what happened in that moment before the woman stepped back inside with his daughter and closed the door.

REFERRALS

Many dreams can occur over a long night.

13

MAYA

Panicked, Maya had called Emily before her flight to California and told her where she was headed. Now, lying on the bed in her hotel, she called Emily again. Maya wanted nothing more than to be in her office at the Red Thread, faxing information to China, working on getting families their babies.

"I am so anxious," Maya said. "You need to talk me down."

"Do you want to know what Dr. Bundy would say?" Emily asked. She didn't wait for Maya to answer. "Dr. Bundy would say that flying across the country to see your ex-husband would of course make you anxious."

"Thanks," Maya said. "That's really helpful."

"Dr. Bundy would ask you what your expectations are for this meeting," Emily said.

"Well," Maya said, "we're meeting at a taco place. So I guess tacos? Cervezas?"

"You," Emily said, "are in denial."

"I know," Maya said.

When she hung up, she stared at the ceiling for a while more, wondering what her expectations were. Somehow, she could not move forward without seeing Adam. But what if seeing him actually moved her backwards? Maya thought of these past several months and how her heart had started to open itself ever so slowly. After New Year's, Jack had steadily emailed her until she invited him to Providence again. And now they had almost settled into a routine of weekends together. But every time he left, she thought about how she could not fall in love with him. In some ways, Maya decided, backwards did not really sound so bad. It meant back to her workaholic life. Back to long days in the office where placing those babies was the only thing she thought about. Back to falling into bed at night alone, with just a glass of wine and a book beside her. Back to a safe place.

Maya sat up. Something settled in her. If Adam blamed her for the death of their daughter and for ruining his life, for ruining everything, then she could go back to her old life. And maybe that was what she had come across the country for. *Thank you, Dr. Bundy,* Maya thought. Then she got up and began to get ready to meet Adam.

THE TACO PLACE was a dive, a low-slung turquoise building with a sagging roof and peeling paint.

"Best tacos in Santa Barbara," Adam had told her when they set up the meeting yesterday.

Of course now Maya remembered how Adam loved to find offbeat places that surprised with great food. They had driven for miles to the North Shore for coconut shrimp, or tracked down a truck parked on some far-flung beach because he'd heard they made the best coconut shrimp. Adam loved to dress up and pay too much for the chef's tasting menu at Alan Wong's, but he also loved this: a dive that happened to serve unforgettable tacos.

Walking across the parking lot, Maya could almost smell the ginger Adam grated into his homemade teriyaki sauce, the garlic he studded into pork loins, the pineapple-infused vodka he made by cutting fresh pineapple into good vodka and letting it marinate for two weeks. Adam fed her. All she could make was a decent roast chicken. The memory of that smell combined with the pungent ones coming from the restaurant made Maya feel off-kilter. Her heel hit the gravel awkwardly and she tripped, tumbling onto the hard asphalt, skinning her knees and the palms of her hands.

Loud Mexican music blared. Why had she opted for shoes with heels instead of flip-flops? she thought as Adam appeared above her, shaking his head.

"I watched you go down," he said, bending to help her to her feet. "But I couldn't get here fast enough."

Maya felt blood trickle down her leg. She was standing in a parking lot with Adam, bloodied and stinging. She could not think of what to say.

He had her by the elbow and was leading her toward the restaurant door.

"Let's get you cleaned you up," he said.

Hot tears sprang to Maya's eyes. She turned her head so Adam wouldn't see.

Inside, he disappeared briefly. Maya watched him get napkins and two beers from a cooler. He was taking care of her, the way he had a million years ago when they were married. Maya wished she could stop the flood of memories, but she was powerless here in this brightly lit restaurant with the loud music and the blood oozing down her leg.

Adam handed her a bottle of beer, took a sip from the other one, then kneeled at her feet.

"Ouch," he said as he gently wiped the blood. He dabbed at her knees, pausing only to take another swallow of beer.

He had proposed this way, on his knee on a deserted beach at sunset. Maya had cried then too, at how much she loved this corny romantic guy. Now, she heard him actually singing along in Spanish to the song playing. Without thinking, she reached out and touched his hair. Still too long and sun-streaked, wavy and out of control. She used to try to tame it with her fingers.

Adam jerked away from her touch and looked up at her, startled.

"I think you'll live," he said, getting to his feet.

Other than some silver strands in that hair of his, and more lines around his eyes, Adam looked exactly as she remembered. His legs were tanned and muscled beneath khaki cargo shorts. His UC Santa Barbara T-shirt hung untucked over his flat stomach and still-broad shoulders. He used to be a swimmer and a surfer, and Maya guessed he still did those things.

"You look good," she said. She'd been staring at him long enough to owe an explanation.

"You too," he said stiffly.

"Number seventy-four," the cashier called, and Adam said, with relief, "That's us."

Us. The word made Maya shiver. For the first time she noticed the large gold wedding band shining on his finger as he walked back toward her with a tray of food.

"Tell me about your wife," Maya said after Adam explained all the taco fillings he'd ordered.

Adam nodded as if to say, Fair question. "She's a librarian," he said, smiling. "Carly."

Carly was a young person's name, Maya thought. She'd placed

three babies who got named Carly. His wife must be young and beautiful. A good wife. A good mother.

Maya nodded now. She hated Carly.

"One day I went to the library in Honolulu, the downtown branch, and they were having a story hour," Adam was saying.

Carly was a children's librarian, Maya thought, hating her more. She pictured a Laura Ashley dress, clogs, glasses.

"And I stupidly stopped and watched these beautiful little kids listening to the story, and all of a sudden, I'm crying all over the place, thinking about how my daughter never got the chance to sit in a library on colorful mats and have a story read to her. And she never would get that chance. And all of the things she would never get to do kind of jumped up and hit me in the head, and I sat right down in the middle of the library and cried. Carly came over to me, she was in the stacks doing research, and without saying a word she put her arms around me and held me while I cried."

Maya was nodding like an idiot, like she understood this story and was glad for it. Carly the Research Librarian. Carly the Angel.

Adam looked right at Maya. "She saved my life," he said.

"Wow," Maya said stupidly. "I can see that." She thought: *I ruined it and Carly saved it.*

As if he read her mind, Adam said, "You ruined it and Carly saved it."

Maya swallowed hard. The taco tasted like dirt. "Yes," she said. "Yes."

"I am a person who sticks things out," Adam said softly. "I wanted to stick it out, even after."

"I know." She dared to look right at her husband's face. Ex-husband, she reminded herself. "I couldn't stay." Her mouth and throat were so dry she thought she might not manage to eke out the words. "It was my fault. I couldn't face you every day knowing what I did."

Adam put his hand on hers. "I never blamed you," he said.

Maya shook her head. "You didn't have to. I blame myself."

"Don't," he said.

Maya tilted her head toward his until their foreheads touched lightly. Tenderly, he lifted her hand and kissed it.

"You have a good life now, right?" Maya asked him.

"Yes." He didn't let go of her hand. "I think of her every day."

Maya nodded.

"I guess that will never go away. But there's a kind of comfort in that. No matter how far from her I am, she's still with me. I keep her picture in my wallet, you know. The one where she's wearing the lei the office secretary made for her first birthday. And she has chocolate frosting on her face and she looks so happy."

"She was happy," Maya whispered.

"She was," Adam said. "Happy and beautiful and loved."

They sat silently for a while, her hand still resting in his. Then Adam said, "Would you come for dinner tonight? Meet Carly and Rain?"

"Oh, I don't think so," Maya said.

"I would like for them to meet you. For you to see my life now."

It seemed a small thing to ask, Maya thought. "All right," she said. "I'd like that."

"WITH THE NEW WIFE?" Emily said when Maya called her after she got back to the hotel. "Oh, this is terrible."

Maya had heard enough stories about the few times Emily had to be with Michael's ex-wife to know that it was never easy.

"I feel like I need to do it, for him and for me."

"Why?"

"Emily?" Maya said. "I want to tell you something."

"Okay," Emily said.

"Adam and I . . ." she began. She closed her eyes to ward off the light-headedness that swooped in. "We had a baby. A daughter," she added.

"What?" Emily said.

"And something terrible happened to her." The tears she had been hoping for all afternoon came now. "I did something terrible to her."

"No," Emily was saying, "no you didn't."

"It was an accident," Maya said. "But she died."

"You don't have to do this," Emily said.

Maya wasn't sure if she meant she didn't have to tell her what happened, or that she didn't have to go to dinner.

"Come home," Emily said.

"I feel like if he wants me to come to dinner, then I need to do it. I owe him so much."

Emily was silent. "I think," she said finally, "you only owe yourself forgiveness."

"Ah," Maya said, "just the easy stuff."

SHE BROUGHT FLOWERS, an oversized bouquet of beautiful gerber daisies in vivid reds and pinks. She brought wine, white and red, both too expensive. These small gestures did not calm Maya, but she at least wanted to appear like a gracious person, like someone who did not kill babies or walk away from grieving husbands.

But as she stood at the door of Adam's house, her extravagance seemed foolish. Flowers and wine did not erase what they all knew. As she waited for someone to open the door, Maya wished there were a bush or shed to drop the gifts into. The house was all weathered wood and glass, low-slung and open. No hiding places here. Maya sighed and pressed the doorbell again. She hoped she was hearing wrong and it didn't chime "Ode to Joy."

When the door did open, Maya was surprised that Carly had come instead of Adam.

"Look at all this!" Carly said, making Maya feel even more foolish for the too-large bouquet and ridiculously expensive wines.

Carly had straight blond hair, long with bangs, and black square glasses that Maya would have called librarian glasses, if Carly weren't a librarian. She was pretty, in an urban way that Maya hadn't expected: the cool glasses and the black leggings and ballet flats. One arm was lined with Bakelite bracelets. She was more Sheryl Crow than Laura Ingalls Wilder, Maya thought. Her eyes paused a moment on Carly's stomach. When she looked up, Carly was nodding at her.

"I know," she said, stepping aside so Maya could come in. "We're due in October."

We're. Maya cringed. "Wow," she managed. "Congratulations."

Outside the wall of windows, the Pacific Ocean crashed noisily against the beach. Adam stood, holding a platter of steaks, poised to go outside. A little girl, blond like her mother, naked except for a diaper, held on to his leg with one hand and a droopy stuffed pig in the other.

"That's Rain," Carly said.

Afraid she might fall, Maya sat on the nearest chair. Everything inside was blue and white and green, as if the ocean were inside too. Maya closed her eyes for an instant. When she opened them again, Carly was standing in front of her with a glass of wine.

"White okay?" Carly asked.

Maya took it from her and set it on the coffee table—a monstrous thing with a glass top. Beneath it was sand and starfish, shells and sea glass.

"Adam made this," Carly was saying, pointing to a platter of roasted tomatoes sprinkled with rosemary and garlic and feta cheese.

Maya put some on crostini and took a bite. "Delicious," she said.

Carly watched her chew.

To Maya, the crostini crunched too loudly. Uncomfortable, she tried to eat it quickly.

"Thank you for coming," Carly said. "I needed to see you for myself."

Finally, Maya could swallow. "Not what you expected me to look like?" Maya said.

"I've seen pictures, of course," Carly said.

"So why did you need me to come here?"

Carly shook her head. "I don't know. I needed to look in your eyes. Isn't that strange?"

Maya took a sip of wine, unsure what to say next.

"My cousin died when she was a baby. My aunt never really got over it," Carly said.

"You don't get over it," Maya managed to say.

"Do you sleep at night?" Carly said.

"It was an accident," Maya heard herself say.

"I know," Carly said, gently. "But still."

"I am known as a solid person," Maya said. "Both feet planted on the ground. Trustworthy."

Carly narrowed her eyes. "That's what I thought," she said.

SOMEHOW, TIME PASSED. The steaks cooked. The salad was tossed and dressed. Maya said nice things to the little girl. Dinner was served. For Maya, it was like she was watching a foreign movie. Nothing seemed familiar, the subtitles were too blurry.

In her pocket, her cell phone vibrated. Probably Emily, calling to offer support.

Maya ignored it and listened to Adam catch her up in his career. The phone vibrated again. Emily wouldn't be so persistent. She would know Maya was still at dinner, unable to talk.

The little girl stared at Maya with solemn eyes. She ate slices of avocado with a plastic fork shaped like an airplane.

Maya's phone vibrated again.

"Can you excuse me?" she said. "My phone keeps going off and I just want to make sure everything's okay."

She didn't wait for an answer. Turning slightly away from them, Maya pulled her phone from her pocket and looked at the missed calls. They were all from Samantha, at the office.

"Work," she said, holding the phone out as evidence.

The little girl frowned at her.

Maya got up and walked over by the windows. The sun was low in the sky now. The water had calmed.

Samantha's voice message came on.

"Maya. Hi, it's me. I hope your vacation's going good. You're not going to believe this, but we just got a batch of referrals. DTC September 24. All the babies are from Hunan. What cuties!"

Maya took a breath. Held it. Outside, the sky was streaked lavender and violet.

"Maya," Samantha continued, "should I wait until you get back before I call them?"

Rain had come over to where Maya stood, and now she peered up at her. Something in her face made Maya feel like she might fall right out this window, to the ocean below.

"Lady?" Rain said. "Lady?"

It was the eyes, Maya realized. They were just like Adam's. They were just like her own daughter's.

"Should I call them now?" Samantha was saying, and the little girl who was not hers kept asking, "Lady? Lady?"

Quickly, Maya dialed Samantha's number,

Maya squeezed her eyes shut so that she did not have to look into Rain's face. She struggled for equilibrium, to keep from falling.

"Wait," she told Samantha. "I'll take the red-eye and be there first thing in the morning."

"So I should—"

"I'm on my way," Maya said.

14

The Families

SOPHIE

Sophie stood in Jack and Jill, a used children's clothing store, and fingered the soft onesies, the feetie pajamas, the blankets decorated with bears and baby bottles. She had waited for so long to be this person, a woman shopping for her baby. But she did not feel the thrill she had imagined she would. Sophie had always believed that if she were a good person, good things would come her way. Instead, here she was, finally pregnant, with a husband she could not trust. Even when she'd told him about the baby and he'd taken her in his arms, Sophie wondered if his emotions were genuine. She had let him back into bed that night too. His careful lovemaking, as if she might break, had irritated rather than pleased her.

Remembering, she turned from the sherbet-colored clothes and headed for the door. Her doctor had estimated that she was just entering her second trimester. Plenty of time to figure out what to do about her marriage. There was plenty of time to buy baby things.

Emily from the adoption group had invited her to her house to knit a baby sweater. Sophie had wanted to go. She'd even bought lemon yellow yarn and large needles, hoping she would remember how to knit. Back in college, she'd knit a sweater for her boyfriend. It had taken her months to finish, and by the time she did he had broken up with her. Carefully, Sophie had unraveled the entire sweater, rolling the yarn back into a fat ball. Her mother had warned her to never knit a sweater for a man who wasn't her husband. "It's bad luck," she'd said. Sophie hadn't listened to her then, or when she'd told her not to marry Theo. "He doesn't look people in the eye," her mother said. "What's he hiding?" Only a five-year-old daughter, Sophie thought as she got into her car. She wished her mother were still alive so she could call her and tell her that she had been right about everything. Sweaters and Theo and Sophie's blind optimism.

Now that the morning sickness had finally passed, Sophie wanted to eat all the time. She unwrapped an Almond Joy and ate it in her parked car. When she finished, she ate another one. The snow on the street had turned gray and dirty. Everything looked sad. Sophie sighed. The elastic waistband on her pants felt tight and itchy. Her craving for chocolate, her expanding waistline, all of the things that should make her happy only made her more aware of how uncertain she felt about everything.

Her mother would not let her wallow in self-pity like this. She'd moved from a farm in Idaho to Colorado when she was only eighteen years old. "No future on that farm," she'd told Sophie matter-of-factly. "The only person you can really rely on is you." Sophie had laughed at her. "I can rely on Theo," she told her mother. "You've never truly given yourself to anyone. You don't know how wonderful it is." Her mother took a long drag on her Marlboro Light and shook her head. "Always keep a part of your heart to yourself, Sophie. Don't give the whole thing away."

But she had. She had given everything to Theo. Sophie fished in her bag for another Almond Joy. Only empty wrappers. In the glove compartment she found two Reese's Cups and she ate them, slowly. She pulled the waistband on her pants below her belly and glanced down. Sophie smiled. That was the belly of a pregnant woman, no doubt about it. She placed her chocolate-smeared hand on her stomach.

"Hello in there," she said softly.

THEO

He had told Nell no, he could not meet her, even just to talk. But here Theo sat, in the backseat of her BMW with her, smoking a joint.

"Do you do this much?" Nell asked him.

"Yes," Theo laughed. "I just wouldn't think you did."

"My fertility doctor gave it to me. She said I needed to relax." Nell leaned across the front seat and pressed the cigarette lighter. She brought it back with her, its tip glowing red. "As if I could relax."

Theo watched her light the joint and inhale. She leaned back and closed her eyes, holding the smoke.

"It has been years," she said without opening her eyes.

Theo wondered if she meant years since she'd gotten high, or since she'd tried to get pregnant. She took another hit, and he began to wonder if she was going to pass the thing to him.

"Vietnam is closed. Guatemala, closed. A woman at work said she could get me an older kid from Hungary or somewhere.

There's Kazakhstan, but not a proven record. Russia is still good."

The car filled with the sweet smell of marijuana. Theo reached over and took the joint from her. "You don't share," he said.

She still didn't open her eyes.

"You look pretty stoned," Theo said. "It makes you look kind of smeared. You're usually too neat."

Nell laughed. "You should see our house. You could eat off the floors."

Her cell phone rang from the front seat but she ignored it. "Brazil. I put in an application for Brazil, but then they closed too."

"Whoa," Theo said, "your doctor gets good pot."

"It's the medicinal stuff," Nell said.

They passed the joint back and forth in silence. In the distance, Nell could see shoppers pushing carts to a big Wal-Mart. Her phone rang again.

"What?" Theo said.

Nell shook her head. "It's too complicated," she said.

Theo shrugged. "If we smoke all of this, we are going to be so wasted."

"I think I already am," Nell said. She thought about all of the countries in the world, all of those babies. And she couldn't get even one.

"Sophie is pregnant," Theo said.

Or that was what Nell thought he said.

"I am definitely stoned," she said.

"No," Theo said. "Well, yes, you are. But you heard me right. Sophie's pregnant."

Nell sat up. Her mouth went dry as sand. When she opened it to talk, her lips smacked together loudly. "That's not fair," she said, hating the way she felt with her sandpapery tongue and her cloudy brain.

"Remember Heather?" Theo said.

"No." As if from somewhere very far away, her phone rang again.

"The woman I love? The love of my life?" Theo was saying. "She showed up with pictures of our baby and Sophie is so pissed at me because I never told her—"

"What are you talking about?" Nell said.

"Heather had a baby. That's why we split up. I thought I told you."

Nell swept her hand through her hair. "I don't believe this," she muttered.

"One day I have nothing, and now I have two children," Theo said.

"Shut up," Nell said, gritting her teeth.

When the damn phone rang again, she answered it. "What?" she demanded.

The voice on the other end began to talk. Nell shook her head, as if that would help her understand better.

"What?" she said again, gently this time. "What?"

When she hung up, she turned to Theo.

"Three," she said.

He smiled a lazy smile at her. "Three?"

"You had nothing, but now you have three kids. That was Samantha from the Red Thread. Our referrals are in."

Theo was saying something, but Nell didn't listen to him. She didn't care if he had three kids or three hundred kids. She had one. One baby. She had everything.

CHARLIE

Charlie could not pinpoint when the idea of a baby stopped scaring him and became, instead, the one thing he wanted. For years—forever, he sometimes thought—all he had wanted was Brooke. All the years she had talked about a baby, Charlie had just let her talk, knowing that he could not do it. He could not take in someone else's child and love it as his own. Even if they had been able to have a baby themselves, Charlie did not think he could be a father. At least, not the kind of father a kid should have. He loved Brooke. Wasn't that enough?

"You just go along with things," Brooke always told him. She didn't mean it as a compliment. She shook her head when she said it. Her mouth went all tight and thin. "You just go along."

He wanted to tell her that was how he survived his childhood. Plates crashed. Fists landed. Shouts and insults flung about. Charlie just went along with things. He ducked. He hid. He went into the backyard on hot Florida nights and hit baseballs until the house grew mercifully quiet.

"I know I do," Charlie agreed. "That is just my way."

When Brooke started taking home brochures full of smiling Asian babies, he read them and nodded and said how cute the babies were.

He sat through the orientation, letting Maya Lange's piercing gaze rest on him. He shook hands with the guy who recognized him. He smiled at Maya's jokes and let Brooke do the talking.

Then there were forms to sign. A social worker looking in their closets and asking them their business.

Charlie went along with it all. But deep down he feared he would not go through with this adoption business. Even when Brooke made him his favorite fish tacos one night, and lit tiki torches in the backyard, and told him statistics: a hundred and fifty thousand abandoned baby girls in China a year, maybe more; a one-child policy that favored boys; how in China, it's the boys who inherit property and money and even ancestors long dead; in some provinces, Brooke told him as she fixed him another taco, adding that coleslaw she made with chipotle peppers and homemade mayo, in some provinces they can have a second child if that first one was a girl. "See, Charlie?" she'd said. "They can try for a boy. But if the second one is a girl too, she gets abandoned." He felt bad about all those baby girls left in boxes and baskets, on roadsides and bridges and doorsteps. But he didn't want one. He didn't want anything except Brooke.

Until something changed.

Standing in what used to be the spare bedroom, his jeans dotted with yellow paint, the smell of fresh paint all around him, the walls the soft yellow of lemonade and sunshine and every other corny yellow thing Charlie could think of, his heart felt enormous and open and about to burst. He stepped back and surveyed his work. The room was beautiful. When the paint dried he would move in the white crib he'd bought, hang the mobile of a fat crescent moon and a cow and a spoon. He would put the rocking chair in the corner, the rug shaped like a daisy in the middle of the floor.

Charlie liked boy names for girls. He always had. It was sassy and sexy and funny to hear the name Johnnie or Frankie or Pete and have a girl answer to it. He thought for sure Brooke would fight him on this. Her own name was so feminine. It was trickling water. It was warm and babbling and gentle. Surely she would want that kind of name for their daughter. He imagined she would put up a fight, insist on Lauren or Lilly. But last night, when he brought it up, Brooke had said sure. Just like that.

"Which one, then?" Charlie asked her. "Pete? Johnnie?"

Brooke took his hand and held on tight. "Johnnie," she said. "Why not?"

Charlie dipped a paintbrush in red paint, and with the greatest care, he wrote above the door of his daughter's room: JOHNNIE.

He stepped back and looked at her name, written in his own handwriting. Seeing it there like that, like an announcement, made it even more real. His daughter Johnnie.

Then Brooke was standing there in the doorway, frowning.

"You are as quiet as a kitten," he said. "I didn't even hear you coming down the hall."

God, he loved her! She had on her old jeans, torn at the knee, and a faded Red Sox T-shirt, and she was the most beautiful woman who ever lived. Charlie took her in his arms, like they were at a high school dance. She put her bare feet on top of his own, and he shuffled the two of them back and forth to music only he could hear playing.

"They called," she whispered.

Charlie kept dancing the two of them across the floor where the daisy rug would sit and the mobile would spin and the rocking chair would rock their baby to sleep.

"We got a baby," she said.

Charlie could not speak. He thought: Johnnie. My daughter.

"We got a baby and, Charlie, I don't want to do it."

He held his wife tighter. "Of course you do."

"No. Ever since Christmas I've known that this is not what I want. I thought I did. But, Charlie, you have to believe me, I don't."

"You're having prebaby jitters. That's all." He didn't like how serious she looked. "Like premarital jitters. Right before you take a big leap into the unknown, you feel like you can't do it. But then you leap and everything is all right. Better than all right."

Brooke stepped away from him and looked him square in the eye. "I never had premarital jitters. I'm not a jittery person. What I want is this. You and me."

"When you look at that little girl's face," Charlie said, stepping closer to her, "you'll feel differently."

Even though he heard his wife saying no, even though he saw her in front of him with her arms folded tight against her chest and shaking her head, Charlie could not believe that she wouldn't come around. Like he had.

EMILY

Emily did not like sports. Sure, she didn't mind rooting for the Patriots or the Sox. But she did not enjoy watching a bunch of kids running around with sticks: on ice or grass or—like this afternoon—on mud. Dr. Bundy had told her that she should make an effort to be more involved in Chloe's life. This might ease the tension. So here Emily stood, shivering and damp, watching Chloe and her team play lacrosse while Chloe's mother shouted at them.

I will not be a mother who stands on the sidelines yelling at my kid, Emily decided.

Thinking things like this made Emily feel better. She had a long list of what she would and wouldn't do. She wouldn't take vacations to Disney World, let her daughter have a cell phone until she was a teenager, play video games, or get her ears pierced. She wouldn't have a daughter like Chloe.

Michael stood halfway between Emily and Rachel, the shouting, overenthusiastic ex-wife. He was neither by Emily's side nor by Rachel's. Instead, he hung between them. Talk about pathetic fallacy, Emily thought. Or just plain pathetic. After all this time, Michael wasn't sure whose side he should be standing on.

The girls ran back and forth across the muddy field, sticks in hand, all of them oddly alike with their blond hair and green kneesocks. Emily sighed.

Seemingly for no reason, the girls stopped and moved off the field.

Halftime, she realized. At last.

"What a game, huh?" Michael said from his place in limbo.

Rachel didn't answer him. She was too busy opening a giant cooler and pulling out juice boxes and orange sections for the team. Snack mom. Cheering mom. Emily shuddered.

"Thanks for coming today," Michael said, taking a step toward her. "It means a lot to Chloe."

Emily wanted to point out how little it meant to Chloe, who was ignoring her completely. But Dr. Bundy would not like such honesty, especially here at this boring lacrosse game. Especially when Emily was supposed to be easing tension, not creating it.

"Well," she said, raising her hands in defeat, "I don't know that much about lacrosse—"

It didn't matter. Michael had already walked away and taken his spot beside Rachel, handing out juice boxes to the girls. Rachel had her hair pulled into a ponytail, and she wore blue shorts with the name of Chloe's school written in white and a green windbreaker, also with the school name on it. She looked ridiculous, Emily thought as she watched Michael talk to his ex-wife. What the hell did he have to say to her that was that exciting? Rachel's head bobbed up and down as he talked, and now Chloe had joined them, and she too was nodding.

Emily's heart lurched. They looked like a family, she realized.

Here she was on the sidelines, literally and figuratively. An outsider. A bystander. A nobody.

"Hey!" she called to Michael.

But he didn't hear her.

Shrugging, Emily dug her hands in her coat pockets and walked to the parking lot. The SUVs were lined up like tanks. She got into Michael's car and pulled out her knitting. She was a terrible knitter, and the sweater she was making for her baby—*her baby, goddamm it*—looked twisted and wrong. Emily had gone to Susannah for help with it. Susannah was an expert knitter, making things with cables and buttonholes. She said things like *seed stitch* and *kitchenette,* things Emily did not understand.

"Let's do it again?" Susannah had said that afternoon, and Emily had said that was a great idea, even though it wasn't.

Still, it was important somehow that she make this sweater for her baby. Maybe she couldn't carry a baby herself. Maybe she didn't understand lacrosse, or have someone to feed orange sections to or a kid's school colors to wear. But she did have a baby waiting for her in China. Every stitch she knit brought that baby closer to her. Susannah had taken out some of the messy rows and redone them. "You're good to go," she'd said when she handed it back to Emily.

Sitting here in the car alone, Emily knew she was good to go. If only. She sighed. If only a million things would change or happen.

And then, the phone rang.

THE SECOND HALF had started. Without Emily there, Michael was by Rachel's side, cheering and shouting just like her.

But Emily didn't care. She walked right in front of them, stood her ground.

"Michael," she said, even though he was frowning at her for blocking his view. She felt like a balloon, about to float into the air.

"Michael," she said again.

Rachel glared at her.

"Samantha from the Red Thread just called." She should take him aside, Emily thought. This wasn't Rachel's news. It was theirs, hers and Michael's.

"Great," he said. "Can you tell me about it after the game?"

Stunned, Emily took a step back, away from him and right onto the playing field where a girl from the other team knocked into her.

Emily almost lost her balance, but managed to regain it quickly. The girl, however, seemed to fly right past her and into yet another girl, this one from Chloe's team. They fell in a tangle of kneesocks and sticks. Parents and coaches came running from every direction.

"I'm so sorry," Emily said.

Chloe was staring at her in angry disbelief.

"What the hell are you doing on the field during a game?" a red-faced father yelled.

"I didn't know," she said. She searched the crowd for Michael, but couldn't find him.

The two girls got unsteadily to their feet, and their teammates cheered.

"My stupid stepmother," Emily heard Chloe saying to someone.

"Get off the field!" an official-looking person was screaming.

Emily finally understood he was screaming at her. "I'm so sorry," she said again.

"Get. Off. The. Field."

"Right, right," she said, scurrying back. "Sorry."

Finally, she found Michael in the crowd as it moved off the field. He had one arm across Chloe's shoulders and his head bent toward Rachel.

A family, Emily thought.

She turned and went back to the car, wondering how this man who could not take sides, who could not stand beside her, would manage now that they, at last, were going to be a family too.

SUSANNAH

Maya looked tanned. That was what Susannah thought as she took a seat across from her at the restaurant, the Rue de l'Espoir. Funny this was where Maya had suggested they meet. Although the name was just French for Hope Street, the street it sat on, the word *hope* itself seemed appropriate.

"Have you been on vacation?" Susannah asked.

"Kind of," Maya said. "Not really." She shook her head. "I was in California for a few days. Business, actually."

Susannah smiled and opened the menu.

They went about the business of ordering, then small talk, until the food arrived. Then Maya said, "You wanted to talk about the referral?"

"I can't do it," Susannah said calmly.

The next day, all of the families were going to the Red Thread offices to see their babies for the first time. They would get three pictures, a health report, and information about what she liked and disliked, her temperment and schedule. They would find out when they would leave for China to bring their babies home.

"Why do you think that?" Maya asked.

Susannah focused on her salad, the figs and goat cheese, the toasted pecans. It was easier than looking at Maya.

"Because I am terrified that I am a terrible mother," Susannah said. She had rehearsed these words on the drive from Newport to Providence so that now they came easily. "I am," she said, moving the mixed greens around on her plate. "I am already a terrible mother."

Maya said, "You've had your share of challenges."

Susannah looked up then.

"I know it isn't easy for you," Maya said.

"But you can't guarantee that this baby is any different."

"I've seen the babies," Maya said. "I've read the reports. They're all healthy, beautiful children. Every one of them."

The two women grew quiet and concentrated on their lunch.

After a while, Susannah said softly, "My mother was wonderful, you know." She had not rehearsed this, and her voice sounded wobbly as she spoke. "We were together constantly, ice skating in Central Park and going to Rumpelmayer's for hot fudge sundaes. When she got sick, my father sent me away. He didn't think I should be around her like that. Once, he took me to the hospital and pointed to her window. He told me she was standing there waving at me, but no matter how hard I looked, I didn't see her there. Then he put me on a train and sent me to my grandmother's in Rhode Island. Until she got better. But she didn't get better."

"I'm sorry," Maya said. "You were how old?"

"Ten when she died. My grandmother lived in one of the mansions on Belleview Avenue, and I wandered around that big house and the grounds like I was lost. I would peek into armoires and beneath shrubs, always looking for something. But I could never say what it was exactly. And I know it sounds foolish to complain when I had everything, in a way. All kinds of lessons and a wonderful education. I was sent off to boarding school when I was fourteen, and it was one of the best schools. Everything was the best," Susannah said. Then she said, "Except Clara."

"You're trying to—" Maya said, but Susannah interrupted her.

"But I feel like it's my fault. Clara. The way she is. The way I am with her."

Maya had remained calm while Susannah talked. Until now. Her face changed, and Susannah saw real pain etched there.

"Guilt," Maya said, "will get you nowhere. Only you can change that. Forgive yourself and start over."

"Could you do it?" Susannah asked. "If you were me?"

Maya paused. "It doesn't matter what I would do."

Susannah studied Maya's face. "What did you do," she asked her, "that you cannot forgive yourself for?"

To Susannah's surprise, Maya began to cry.

"Maya," she said, reaching for Maya's hand across the table. But Maya pulled away.

"I'm here to help you," Maya said. "I'm sorry."

"Perhaps," Susannah said, "you should take your own advice?"

Maya smiled.

"Perhaps," she said. "But for right now, I want to tell you that I saw a picture of a nine-month baby girl who is adorable and healthy and, Susannah? She's yours."

Now it was Susannah's turn to cry. She buried her face in her hands and sobbed all of the tears that she had held inside since she was a girl in a hospital parking lot, waving up at an empty window.

Maya slid into the booth beside her, and rubbed Susannah's back gently, the way a mother soothed a child.

"There, there," Maya said softly. "There, there."

15

MAYA

"They are beautiful, these babies, yes?" Mei asked Maya over the telephone.

Maya agreed. "Yes, they are beautiful."

Mei and Maya had been working together since the Red Thread placed those first babies eight years ago. From her office in Beijing, Mei helped Maya solve problems and intercepted bad news to try to fix it before it reached the United States. To thank her, Maya sent Mei monthly boxes of Gap jeans, size zero; hand lotion; commemorative stamps; Red Sox memorabilia. Whenever Maya was in Beijing, she and Mei went out to dinner. They drank Tsing Tao beer and laughed like old friends.

"They are healthy," Mei said, and again Maya agreed.

"All nine months old," Mei said. "A good age to find your family."

In the outer office, Samantha was preparing everything for the families. She had hung the red paper lanterns and set out platters of steamed dumplings and egg rolls and bamboo skewers of beef and chicken. Maya insisted on each referral session being a celebration, and she always served food and wine to the families.

"Tell me," Mei said, "the parents. All nice?"

It was their ritual conversation. Mei asked the same questions and Maya gave the same answers.

"Very nice," she said.

She thought of this group, of Nell and her Type A personality. Not a woman whom Maya necessarily would call nice, but she did think Nell would give a good home to a child. There would be advantages, sailing lessons and a good private education. If Maya truly believed in the red thread, then the baby who most needed Nell as a mother would be hers. The same could be said of each of these people. Over these months, Maya had seen them at their best, politely listening to her that first night. And she had seen some of them at their worst, during those long months of waiting. Or just yesterday, at lunch with Susannah.

"We did good," Mei was saying.

"We did," Maya said.

Mei laughed softly. "As if we actually had anything to do with it."

What they both knew was that somehow each of these babies was perfect for the family they got. That was the beautiful mystery of it.

"The red thread," Maya said.

Samantha caught her eye through the open office door and pointed to her watch.

"They're due any minute," Maya said.

"Good," Mei said. "Give them their babies."

Maya's breath caught.

"And Maya? If you need anything at all—"

"I know," Maya said. "Thank you."

When she hung up, Maya sat at her desk and took out the

yarn in her bottom drawer. Her knitting stretched perhaps eight feet or more if she unfolded it. Eight feet or more of nothing but neat rows, one after the other, rows that marked all the waiting she had done in that hospital in Honolulu, in this office. Waiting for news, for babies, for her life to somehow start again. These rows were like the *X*'s a prisoner made on a cell wall to count the days. Sometimes, Maya thought she was a prisoner of sorts. A prisoner of her past and her guilt. A prisoner of the accident that changed everything.

She heard voices now, and smiled when she recognized Emily and Michael's. She was glad her friends were here first. Laying the yarn on her desk, Maya smoothed her hair and checked her lipstick before going to greet them.

As soon as Emily saw her, she squealed and jumped with excitement like a schoolgirl.

"She's been like this all day," Michael said. "Help?"

Emily slapped him lightly on the arm. "You've been pretty excited too. Don't pretend for Maya's sake."

"Help yourself to some food or wine," Maya said.

But Emily shook her head. "Please. The baby."

Samantha had fanned out the folders on a table. Each folder had the couple's name written across it. Inside was all the information and pictures of that baby.

Maya took Emily's elbow and led her to the table. She picked up their folder and opened it.

"Your daughter," Maya said, handing Emily the photograph.

Maya read from the orphanage's statement.

"'This baby was found in the park during the Flower Festival by the workers erecting the pavilion. She was about five days old, in good health, and dressed in the cloth of a village to the north.'"

Maya glanced up from the papers and into her friend's face.

"And now she's really mine?" Emily said.

"You will be in China holding her in your arms in about a month," Maya said.

The others started to arrive, and Maya took each of them to the table, opened their folder, and handed them their daughter's photograph.

She noticed things. Sophie was obviously pregnant now, her stomach round beneath a black maternity dress. She had had families who decided not to adopt if they got pregnant. But Sophie had reminded Maya that it was her dream to have many children, adopted ones and biological ones. A little space in between might have been nice, Sophie had said, laughing.

"'This baby,'" Maya read, "'was approximately six months old when she was found on the doorstep of the police station. She was dressed in pajamas. She was quite fat. However, she cried almost inconsolably for many days. However, we can state with confidence that she is now a happy baby. And still fat.'"

She noticed how Nell seemed softer. Her husband, suntanned from sailing in Sardinia, seemed softer too. He took his wife's hand and held it tenderly as Maya read from the orphanage report.

"'This baby was found with a sweet potato tucked beside her. To the very poor in rural Hunan, a sweet potato has great value. It is our opinion that her family are farmers. It is our opinion that they wished us to know she was considered valuable.'"

Samantha served red wine and passed the food while everyone shared the pictures of their babies. Parents for only twenty minutes or so, and already they were bragging. Maya smiled as she watched them.

Two folders still lay on the table. Charlie and Brooke. Susannah and Carter.

Had Charlie decided he could not go through with it after all? Maya wondered. Had guilt and fear won over Susannah?

Then she heard footsteps on the stairs, and the door opened.

Susannah and Carter burst in, but pushing past them was Clara. Her hair neatly braided and she was dressed as if for a party.

"We came for my sister!" she said to Maya.

Maya met Susannah's eyes over her daughter's blond head.

"Well here she is then," Maya said, opening their folder. She handed the photograph directly to Clara.

Susannah kneeled down for her first look at her new daughter.

"She's beautiful," she managed to say before Clara shouted, "But this is a baby, not a sister!"

"Just wait," Carter said.

"'This baby was very small and skinny when found at the orphanage gate. Believed to be about six weeks old, we believe she was breastfed and well cared for.'"

Susannah looked up at Maya. "Then why?"

"So many possible reasons," Maya said. She shrugged helplessly.

"We're naming her Blossom because she's a Powder Puff Girl," Clara said.

Carter laughed. "It's true. Last night we told Clara she could pick out her sister's name and she wants Blossom."

"Better than Elmo or Cookie Monster," Susannah said.

Blossom. Now as they passed around the pictures they shared their daughters' names with each other. Nell and Benjamin chose Jordan. Emily and Michael were naming their baby Beatrice, Sophie and Theo Ella.

That one folder still sat untouched.

When the phone rang, Maya went into her office to answer it. Closing the door against the joyous noise, she picked it up expecting to hear Brooke crying on the other end. But it wasn't Brooke who was crying. It was Charlie.

"She won't do it," he said as soon as he heard Maya's voice. "She's changed her mind."

Maya sat in her chair at her desk. "What happened?"

"She's changed her mind," he said again. "That's all. She won't talk to you. Hell, she won't hardly talk to me."

"Are you sure—"

"She wants nothing to do with it," he said.

"I'm sorry, Charlie," Maya began.

"I painted her room. I painted her name right above the door."

"You know, you can take time with this. Go back in the queue."

"I don't think that's going to happen," Charlie said, his voice cracking. "Wait. She does want to talk to you."

Brooke came on the phone. "Maya. He thinks I've gone crazy, but remember what I was afraid of? That Charlie wouldn't be able to love me and a baby? Well, I was wrong. I'm the one who can't make room. I saw all of the baby things, and how excited he was, and I tried to imagine our life with this third person in it, and I couldn't picture it."

"A lot of people—"

"This isn't about a lot of people. It's about me. And if I go through with it, and I'm right, I won't be able to forgive him for talking me into it. But if we don't do it, we can go back to how we've always been. Just us. And he'll be mad at me for a while, but eventually he'll forgive me. He will."

When she hung up, Maya did not move. She listened to the sounds of laughter, of happiness.

Slowly, she unraveled the knitting on her desk. All that waiting, Maya thought. All for what?

Maya picked up the phone and carefully dialed a number. If no one answered, it was a sign that she should not do this.

But Mei did answer.

"I'm calling for a favor," Maya said.

Mei listened. She told Maya to stay put, to wait for her to call back. While Maya waited, she picked up the needles and yarn and began to knit. One row, then another. She knit without thinking, without hoping. She simply knit until the phone rang again.

Mei's voice on the other end was excited. "It's done," she said. "Congratulations."

Maya rolled up all that yarn, all those years of despair. She almost put it back in the drawer, but she thought better of it and placed it in the garbage. Her waiting was over.

Back in the outer office, Maya opened the last folder.

The baby who looked back at her had a Mohawk of black hair, a rosebud mouth, startled eyes.

She read from the orphanage report.

> This baby was about six months old when found at the orphanage door. A man, perhaps her father, was seen lurking around that day. He was obviously distraught.

Maya held the photograph to her chest. She took a glass of wine and joined the happy group.

"This group is unique in many ways," she said. "One of those ways is that I am going to China with you. I will also bring home a baby."

Emily did not wait for Maya to say more. She pulled her into a hug.

"Brave friend," she whispered.

One by one, the group began to clap. They did not know her story. They didn't have to. Each of them had their own, and Maya had hers.

"And what's this baby's name?" Susannah asked.

Maya lifted her glass in a toast. "To Blossom," she said. "And Jordan, and Ella and Beatrice. And Honor Maile." Maya's voice broke when she said that middle name, a name she had not dared to say out loud in eight years.

"Maile?" Sophie asked.

"It's Hawaiian for the flower used to make leis," Maya said. "I loved a little girl named Maile."

"It's beautiful," Emily said.

Maya clinked her glass against the others, careful not to miss any of them.

"To our daughters," she said.

The others repeated her words. "Our daughters."

CHINA

Follow love and it will flee;

flee love and it will follow you.

16

MAYA

In Maya's attic sat one box that she had not dared to open in eight years. But after the families left the Red Thread, after Maya and Samantha cleaned up, after she locked the office door and walked down Wickenden Street toward home, she stood in her own dark foyer, keys in her hand, the sound of her own breathing the only thing she heard. Maya turned on the light that led upstairs. At the top, she pushed open the attic door and climbed the short, narrow stairs that led up there.

She didn't have to struggle to remember where the box was. Maya knew its exact location. Whenever she came up here to retrieve her winter sweaters, or add receipts or forms to her tax return files, she caught sight of it, neatly tucked into the farthest corner. On some of those days, she averted her eyes as soon as she saw it. Other times, she looked at it head on, daring it to bother her. Of course it always did.

Tonight, Maya would open it.

Without taking off her coat, Maya walked straight to that far corner and slid the box close to her. Such an innocuous thing. Cardboard, pale green with chipped corners and a slight dent on the lid, as if someone had stepped on it. A thin layer of dust covered it, and Maya wiped it off with her palm almost protectively.

When she lifted the lid, the jumble of items inside broke her heart. They reminded her of how hastily she had tossed them inside. How she had stood on a drizzly afternoon in her daughter's room and tried to guess what items in it were the most important. How does a mother choose what to keep to best remember her dead child? The little leopard booties that she never even wore but that Maya had bought her for her two-month birthday? The cotton blanket that smelled slightly of spit-up, so ordinary in its appearance and usefulness? The brown stuffed dog that the baby had grown so attached to, its rubbed ear showing signs of her love?

Maya had been that woman, torn by grief, standing in the middle of the small, happy room, eyeing everything with a wild need. That room came to Maya now, so vividly she shut her eyes against the image. The lavender walls. The lamp that sent images of dancing horses across the ceiling when it was turned on. The violet pillow embroidered with her daughter's name and birthday in white.

"Maile," Maya said out loud, the beautiful name so painful to say.

There it was, that pillow. Maya lifted it from the box and traced the curving script, the elaborate *M* and the flourish of the final *e*.

"Maile," she said again.

It was not easier to say the second time.

Maya placed the pillow on her lap. She took each item from the box and held it in front of her: footie pajamas decorated with pineapples, a fat butterfly that played a tune when a cord was pulled (and how could that tune still play so easily, so clearly, after all this time?), a teething ring marked from her baby's gnawing, a tiny denim jacket, each item bringing back memories that caused her pain.

At the bottom of the box, she found a large envelope. Inside were all the cheerful cards of congratulations. IT'S A GIRL! Beneath them, two sonogram pictures, her daughter's grainy face turned right toward her. *She's a friendly one,* the technician had said. And finally, a handful of pictures.

Here was her younger, hopeful self, hugely pregnant in a bikini on the beach. Here were the first pictures of her baby, eyes shut and still bloody. The three of them, Maya in the hospital bed holding the baby and Adam leaning in beside them, a happy family, stunned at their good luck.

They'd had hundreds of pictures of their daughter, careful recorders of her every grin and milestone. Maya used to put them in albums, old-fashioned ones in which she tucked the corners of photographs into holders. Perhaps these were the ones that she had not yet put in an album. Perhaps in her panic she had grabbed them from a tabletop. The pictures were blurry, as if taken from a distance or by an unsteady hand.

On the bottom of each photograph there was a date. Two days before she died. Maya searched her memory for what they had done that day. But that day was gone, overtaken by the horror that followed it. She should have asked Adam for a picture. Or even one of the albums. But how could she take even those from him too?

Maya placed everything back in the box carefully. When she picked up the pillow from her lap, she lifted it to her nose, as if maybe after all this time she might still catch a whiff, no matter how faint, of her daughter. Maya placed the pillow on top of the other things. She once again traced her daughter's name with her fingertip.

"Maile," she said softly.

She closed the box, making sure the lid was on good and tight.

17

The Families

EMILY

The packing list was long and complicated. Two thousand dollars in clean hundred-dollar bills. Medication for scabies and lice. Baby clothes ranging in sizes from six months to toddler. Baby bottles with the tips of the nipples snipped off. Antibiotics. A diaper bag, diapers, wipes. Antibacterial soap. A list, five pages long, and Emily loved every task, every item, every odd request.

She stood in line at the main branch of her bank and asked for that money with its unbent corners, free of marks or creases.

"I'm on my way to China," she said brightly to the frowning teller. "To adopt my daughter."

Emily told everyone: the pharmacist who measured out powders and liquids. The cheerful saleswoman at babyGap in Garden City.

"For my daughter," Emily said, beaming.

After each item was secured, she put a small checkmark beside it. She would put this list in the scrapbook she had already started for Beatrice. Bea. Even thinking of her daughter's name made

Emily smile. She bought tiny fuzzy slippers, yellow-and-black-striped with small antennas at the toes. She bought bumblebee rain boots and bumblebee barrettes.

"My daughter Beatrice," Emily explained. "We call her Bea."

"Isn't that adorable?" the saleswoman at babyGap said. "You don't hear that name so much."

Emily nodded happily. Her daughter had an extraordinary name. An extraordinarily beautiful unique name.

Check. Check. Check. The pages slowly got completed. The visas arrived in the mail. Emily didn't even mind that Chloe was coming to China with them. *The chance of a lifetime,* Michael had said. And it was. The Great Wall. The Forbidden City. *Beatrice.* Emily ordered a T-shirt, pink, with block letters that said: BIG SISTER. She would give it to Chloe in China. She got one for Beatrice too: LITTLE SISTER. They would wear them together and Emily would take pictures of them, Chloe holding Bea in their matching pink T-shirts.

She bought a new digital camera. Memory cards. A small video camera. Batteries. Check. Check. She called Maya and compared notes on Canon versus Nikon. She called Maya and told her what the woman in babyGap had said. "You don't hear that name so much," Emily said. She sighed. Beatrice.

At the Travel Clinic, she and Michael got tetanus shots, hepatitis B, polio boosters. They sat beneath a map of the world. China sprawled across it. Emily found Hunan Province, its capital of Changsha, the smaller city of Loudi where Beatrice waited for them.

"When is Chloe getting hers?" Emily asked him.

"She missed the appointment," Michael said. "Play rehearsal."

The doctor came in with their inoculation records stamped.

"Have a good trip," he said. He had a Caribbean accent. "A safe trip."

"We're going to get our baby," Emily said. How she loved those words. "Our daughter."

"Well then," the doctor said, "good luck to the three of you."

Emily took the wallet-sized photo of Bea out of her purse. "This is her," she said.

The doctor put on his glasses to inspect the picture. "Beautiful," he said.

"I hope you don't make everyone you pass look at that," Michael said as they walked out of the office.

"Of course not," Emily said.

"Good luck now!" the receptionist called to Emily. "She's a real cutie!"

"Caught," Emily said.

Michael laughed. "Come on, proud mama. I'll buy you dinner."

She was on the last page of the list. There was not much left to do but get on that plane.

"DO YOU THINK I've gone too far?" Emily said.

She stood in the doorway of the den, where Michael sat in the leather club chair, the phone in his lap.

Emily held up a bumblebee Halloween costume. "I know it's months away. I know she will probably grow up to hate everything bee. But I couldn't resist."

Michael forced a smile. "Cute," he said.

Emily looked around. "Why are you sitting here in the dark?" she said, and began to turn on lamps.

"The Internet is a dangerous place for first-time mothers," she said as she moved around the room. "Where else can you buy a Halloween costume in March?"

He didn't answer.

"Michael?" she said, moving toward him. She perched on the arm of the chair, the bee costume in her hand.

He held up the phone. "I just spoke with Rachel," he said.

Emily waited.

She would not let Rachel ruin this for them. For years now, Rachel had managed to mess up Christmas dinners, weekend trips, anniversaries. She had managed to book a flight for Chloe to meet her and her new husband in St. Lucia that left in the middle of Christmas Day so that they spent Christmas at Logan Airport. She had found reasons for them to leave parties early to get Chloe, or miss them altogether. But Rachel would not ruin this.

"Chloe won't come to China," Michael said.

Emily didn't care if Chloe went to China with them as long as she and Michael were on that plane. She studied her husband's face.

"And?" she said, starting to worry.

"Apparently there's no talking her into it. She doesn't want to miss rehearsal—"

"It's school vacation," Emily reminded him.

"Well, there's still rehearsal."

"She doesn't have a big part," Emily said.

His jaw tightened. "She needs to learn all the songs."

She stood. "So what are you saying?"

"If I leave her here to bring back our baby, Rachel suggested Chloe might feel abandoned. Again."

"I don't believe this," Emily said.

"Look, nothing's decided. But since Maya is going too, you would be okay. You'd be together."

"It's our baby!" Emily said.

"I know that. I just feel so torn, Em. No matter what I do it's wrong."

Emily tried to catch her breath. In the packet about what would happen in China, there were more pages of things to do: physical checkups, paperwork, more paperwork, interviews. *We strongly suggest you travel as a pair since one person will likely tend the baby while the other handles the official business.*

"Who's going to handle the official business?" Emily managed. She gulped air as if she were drowning.

"What do you mean?"

"Have you even looked at anything they've sent us?" she cried.

"You're having so much fun doing it all, I just let you handle it."

"This is our baby. And you are going to be on that plane with me next week. Do you hear me?" Of course he did; she was screaming now. But she didn't care.

"Do you?" she shouted.

She didn't wait for him to answer. Instead, she walked out of the room and closed the door good and hard behind her.

"WHO WILL BE your significant other?" Emily asked Maya that night over the phone. "Who will handle the official business?"

"I know our guide," Maya said. "She'll help out."

Emily sighed. "What am I going to do if he doesn't come?"

"He's going to come," Maya said.

SOMEHOW, EMILY FELL ASLEEP. She felt the bed dip as Michael sat beside her.

"I've been on the phone with Chloe and Rachel," he said.

Emily tried to make out his features. She tried to remind herself that she loved him. That Beatrice was theirs.

"I talked to them and I sat there and I thought about everything. About her, and about us. What you've been through with the miscarriages. How happy you've been these past few weeks." He touched her hair. "Your little lists. And the way you tell everybody you see that you're getting your baby."

Emily squeezed her eyes shut, but it didn't stop the tears.

"How could you have for one minute considered not going to China?" Emily said.

"What?" Michael said. "I never said that. How could I not go and get our baby? I just want to figure out how to make this work better."

"What an idiot I am," Emily said

Michael was covering her with kisses and she was laughing and crying at the same time and he was undressing her.

NELL

"I can't believe we are the only ones who upgraded," Nell whispered to Benjamin.

He grunted an answer and kept his face buried in the *Wall Street Journal.*

"I mean, it's something like an eighteen-hour flight," Nell said. "In coach?"

She glanced around the gate area. Odd that everyone was here, but no one sat together except Maya and Emily. It was as if they hadn't had all those brunches and potlucks together, as if they hadn't shared all those nervous emails during these long months of waiting. As if, Nell decided, they were strangers.

There was Theo and Sophie. The sight of the two of them—his hand on her arm, her pregnant belly—made her feel slightly queasy. What in the world had she been thinking? When Theo's hand rested ever so lightly on Sophie's stomach, Nell looked away, a surprising sting of tears in her eyes. Foolishly, she reached for Benjamin's hand and grabbed onto it, too tight.

"What?" he asked her.

Nell tried to think of something to say.

"Hey," Benjamin said, "you're crying." He wiped a tear from her cheek with his thumb.

What an idiot I am, Nell thought. She made herself look over at them again. Sophie had a magazine open, practically resting on her belly, and they were both reading something in it with great interest.

"Is it even safe for her to fly?" Nell said.

Ben followed her gaze. "Don't be jealous," he said, patting her leg. "We are on our way to get our baby."

"I'm not jealous," Nell said.

She almost asked him why some people got two or three children and they had to work so hard for just one? But he had gone back to his newspaper and the gate agent, in her military navy blue uniform, was at the Jetway door, ready to call them on board.

SOMEWHERE OVER THE Pacific Ocean, Nell woke gripped with panic. She looked around the dim cabin. Ben was asleep beside her, stretched out in the first-class seat, the red blanket tucked around him. Someone's computer glowed eerily in the dark. Nell was not afraid to fly. For work, she had logged thousands of miles on this same route to Asia. She had spent hours hunched over her own MacBook, working numbers and spreadsheets, preparing PowerPoint presentations. But tonight, she could not focus on anything as simple as the magazines she had brought to read. Now this. A gripping in her gut, her heart pounding.

Nell nudged Ben, but he didn't wake up. Maybe he had taken an Ambien. Maybe she should take one. She'd read about people doing crazy things, asleep on Ambien. Driving cars and eating raw meat. Nell did not want to do anything she would regret. She realized her foot was tapping like crazy. Was it anticipation? Or terror? In three days, she would be holding a baby. *Her* baby. Finally.

The flight attendant appeared at her side.

"Would you like anything?" she asked. She was so old and overweight that Nell thought she should be sitting down herself. Flight attendants used to be so beautiful, so lovely in their crisp uniforms and perfectly made-up faces. This woman was so rumpled and tired-looking that Nell almost felt sorry for her.

"Maybe some scotch?" Nell said. "Neat?"

The flight attendant smiled wearily and shuffled off in her scuffed loafers. Shouldn't they wear high heels? Nell sighed.

The scotch did calm her a bit. She took out her iPhone and made notes: *Pack diaper bag. Iron red blouse. Get baby.*

She added the items she would put in the diaper bag. Two diapers. The travel case of wipes. A change of clothes. A burp cloth. A sweater. Two empty bottles. A board book. A plush toy.

The red blouse was silk. Red to stimulate the baby. Silk to soothe her.

Nell looked at the third thing. *Get baby.*

Her heart started to race again. Wasn't this what she had wanted for years now? She thought of all the tests, the dye shot into her fallopian tubes, the D&C's, the vaginal sonograms. She thought of the hope that each tablet of Clomid held, how she had gritted her teeth and bent over the bed while Benjamin gave her shots in the ass because those shots, that sting of the needle, held the promise of a baby. She'd had her eggs counted and her ovaries overstimulated and her moods swinging. All of it somehow wrapped up in this moment, this journey toward a baby. And now she couldn't remember why she'd even begun it.

Nell made lists. She made lists and she carefully checked off each accomplishment. Even in grade school she had goals that she carefully wrote in her lined notebook. Win the spelling bee. Read every book for the Read-a-thon. Become champion in jacks, in T-ball, in jump rope. With each item checked off, Nell's accomplishments grew.

Years later, she wrote: *Have a baby.* Months passed, then years. In three days, Nell would be handed a baby girl, and that night, in her bed in a hotel in Changsha, China, she would finally check off that item.

"Benjamin?" Nell said, shaking her husband hard enough to wake him.

He looked at her through half-open eyes, his cowlick poking upward, his breath sour with sleep.

"What happened?" he mumbled.

"Benjamin," she said again.

Nell did not let go of his arm. "What the hell are we doing?"

THEO

Theo stood on top of the Great Wall and stared out. The group had come here by bus—they went everywhere by bus, together. Their guide had pointed in one direction and said that was the easier climb. Then he pointed in this direction and told them it was more difficult. Of course, Nell had babbled to him in Mandarin, made some joke that sent him into a fit of laughter, then she headed off this way without waiting for anyone else.

"Either way," the guide said, "be back at bus at one o'clock. Then we'll all go for lunch."

"Maybe you shouldn't climb it," Theo had told Sophie. Even the easier way had crumbling steps and steep inclines.

"I'm in *China,*" Sophie said. "I'm climbing the Great Wall. You go and do the hard route. I'll take the easy one."

"Okay," he said reluctantly. From where they stood, he could see young children and a couple of women in high heels scampering up the easier path. "But be careful." He'd kissed her and held her close so that he could feel her hard, round belly against him.

Standing here at this high point, the Wall snaking endlessly before him, Theo actually, ridiculously, missed his wife. He would have liked her standing beside him, taking in the view. Sophie had done her research. He knew that. If she was standing next to him, she would be able to tell him how long it took to build it, how many people were buried inside it.

Ever since they got off the shuttle at Logan Airport and she'd slipped her hand into his and said: "Let's go," Theo had believed he was almost forgiven. She'd smiled up at him when she'd said that, and it was the first time her smile looked like Sophie's own instead of some strained, tight version of it. Theo's heart had soared in that moment. He'd walked side by side with his pregnant wife toward the plane that would take them to their daughter. He felt huge and abundant and grateful. He still did.

When Heather was pregnant, her swelling breasts and the small bump of her stomach had repulsed him. For the first time since they'd met, he did not want to touch her. He moved from their bed to the sofa, and then he moved out. But Sophie became beautiful to him. The larger she grew, the more he wanted her.

"You are glorious," he told her last night in the hotel.

The group had eaten at a restaurant famous for its Peking duck, and later, in their room, Sophie had stood before him, lifted her shirt to reveal that beautiful belly, and groaned.

"I am not glorious," she'd said. "I am full of duck." She smiled at him as he kissed that belly. "I am gluttonous," she added.

"Glowing," he'd murmured, inching her black maternity pants off her hips.

Sophie let him lead her awkward naked body to the bed. Afterward, she whispered, "Glad."

"Me too," Theo said, though glad did not say enough.

"Am I really glorious?" Sophie said. "So fat and getting fatter every minute?"

"You are," he said. "Glorious."

That was how they decided to name the baby she was carrying Gloria. Someday he would tell his daughter how she got her name, how her mother was so beautiful when she was carrying her that she looked glorious.

Abundant, Theo thought again as he looked at that narrow Wall. He was a goddamn cornucopia.

"A bhat for your thoughts," Sophie said.

There she was in her black maternity pants and her beautiful stomach, her face flushed and damp, standing on the difficult climb of the Great Wall of China.

"I am thinking about cornucopias," he said.

Sophie narrowed her eyes. "Like at Thanksgiving?"

"Yes," Theo laughed.

Sophie took in the view. She had her back to him when she said, "You slept with Nell Walker-Adams."

Theo's breath caught. He could lie to her so easily. He could change facts and deny everything.

"I can't even describe how I knew," Sophie said. "Just a hunch. The way you avoided looking at her. How late you came home from those classes she took with you. Then that day you told me you were at Tazza doing lesson plans. See, I was at Tazza that day."

If he thought hard, he could make up an explanation even for that. "I'm sorry," he said instead.

"She's not even very pretty," Sophie said, her back still to him.

"I can't explain it," Theo said. Then he tried to explain, how it had only been once, stammering about his fear of children and his nervousness about the adoption and a sense of drowning.

Sophie said nothing. It was as if she wasn't listening at all, but rather that she was deciding something.

When she finally turned around to face him, she said softly, "Someday we'll come back here with Ella and Gloria, and maybe even Rose. We'll come back with our family."

Theo wanted to say thank you. He wanted to drop to his knees with relief and love. But Sophie did not give him a chance. Instead, she began the arduous climb along the difficult path, taking small, careful steps.

SUSANNAH

"Tomorrow at eleven a.m., you will get your babies," the guide said.

They had landed at the airport in Changsha and were headed by bus to their hotel. The guide had the improbable name Elvis, and to live up to it, he wore his hair slicked back into a pompadour.

"We will meet in the hotel lobby at ten-thirty sharp and we will board the bus and we will drive to city hall and get your babies." He grinned at them. "I'm all shook up. How about you?"

Carter laughed beside her. He was such a good sport, the guy who helped the guides count everyone to make sure they were all there. The guy who figured out the checks in restaurants and collected the money. At dinner in Beijing the first night, Carter had stood and made a toast to Maya, thanking her for their babies. The toast was heartwarming and funny and poignant. Perfect. So why had Susannah hated that he'd done it?

She stared out the window, trying to see something of the anonymous city they drove through. It was almost midnight, and she was jet-lagged and irritable. Maya had insisted that they all spend three days in Beijing before flying on to Hunan. It was important, she said, that they see some of China and learn about its history and culture. Bleary-eyed, Susannah had listened to tour guides talk about dynasties and emperors. She'd waited too long in line to catch a glimpse of Mao's body, wandered for hours through the Forbidden City, visited silk factories and porcelain factories and jade factories. Carter had bought souvenirs everywhere. T-shirts and a Mao watch and a jade bracelet and a porcelain dragon for her astrological sign, all for Clara. He'd bought silk comforters, garish things with Chinese designs in jewel tones. "What are we going to do with all of this?" Susannah muttered as he bartered and bantered and shopped.

"Hunan girls are called Spicy Girls," the guide was saying. "Hunan food is very famous for its spiciness, so the girls are Spicy Girls."

Susannah pressed her face against the cool window. She imagined Carter would buy chili peppers and cookbooks here. The bus slowed, and the bright lights of a hotel broke the darkness.

Everyone stood and filed out. Every time the group got on the bus, they took the same seats, as if they'd been assigned to them. When they got off the bus, they were always in the same order, Susannah squeezed between Carter behind her and the ever-glowing pregnant Sophie ahead of her.

When Susannah passed Elvis he touched her shoulder lightly.

"Tomorrow morning at eleven a.m., you will get your baby," he said. "No problem."

Susannah jerked her head around to look at him. Why had he said this to her and not Sophie?

Carter was grinning at the guy. "See you in the lobby," Carter said brightly.

Emily walked past Elvis, and he said nothing.

Susannah stood at the door of the bus watching the rest of the group get off. Elvis smiled and said, "See you in the morning!" and "Get a good night's rest!" But only to her had he made that pointed remark. No problem? Susannah thought. Why would he say that to her?

THE HOTEL ROOM had a crib set up in it. In the bathroom, there was a small plastic baby bathtub. Propped in one corner was a lime green portable stroller. Everything waiting for the baby whom Susannah would get at eleven o'clock the next morning.

Carter whistled in the shower, and Susannah willed him to stop. But he didn't. He kept whistling until he appeared, a towel wrapped around his waist.

"One in the afternoon at home," he said. "Let's call Clara and tell her she'll have her sister in under twelve hours."

Susannah watched him as he sat on the bed and dialed the United States. He had mastered everything here so easily. Long-distance calls and the currency conversion. The lights in the hotel worked on some system involving the room key, and he had that figured out too. Annoyingly, he could even say simple phrases in Mandarin.

"It's Mommy and Daddy!" he was saying into the telephone. "I did buy you more presents," he said. "Oh, I can't tell you. They're surprises. Mommy has something to tell you." He motioned for Susannah to come and take the phone. "Of course you want to talk to Mommy," he said.

"She doesn't," Susannah said flatly. "That's fine."

Still he coaxed and pleaded. "Mommy has such good news for you, honey."

"For Christ's sake, just tell her so we can get to bed," Susannah snapped.

She climbed under the covers and rolled away from where he sat, still talking in that tone of voice that drove Susannah crazy. The crib stood there, empty and forlorn. No problem, Elvis had said. So of course there must be a problem, something he knew that he was trying to prepare her for. When Clara was born, Susannah noticed the nurse frown slightly when she examined her. "Is everything all right?" she'd asked, panicked. The nurse, a doughy-faced woman in pea green scrubs, had smiled at her. "No problem," she'd said.

Finally Carter hung up, and slid naked beside her.

"Clara's excited," he said.

"Mmmm."

"You excited?"

The crib took on an ominous shape in the dark room. Susannah thought: I am terrified.

"Of course," she said.

Just like that, her husband was asleep, breathing the tiniest snores. Susannah told herself everything was all right, or Maya would have come to their room. She would have told them the truth. No problem, Susannah thought. Then she waited out the long night.

18

MAYA

Maya awoke from a dream in which she was falling off the highest part of the Great Wall into an abyss below to the sound of pounding on her door. For a moment, even as she lay in bed struggling to get up and answer it, she felt that stomach-dropping feeling of falling from great heights. When she finally stood, she had to hold the edge of the bed for balance. The banging did not let up, even as she paused to wrap the hotel robe around herself and glance at the clock. 5:40.

A pale, wild-eyed Susannah burst in as soon as Maya opened the door. She'd had this happen before. Women, about to get the baby they have yearned for, fall apart. How many hours had Maya sat in hotel room across China listening to a mother-to-be's fears and anxieties about the baby she was about to hold. Once, it happened right in the corridor as the group walked to the room where their babies waited for them. Maya had to keep everyone there in the hallway for over an hour while she calmed the woman, the babies' restless crying growing louder and louder in the overheated building.

"You have to tell me now," Susannah said. She was thin in her funny pink pajamas decorated with poodles, and trembling. "What's wrong with this baby?"

Maya filled the electric kettle with water and set about making tea for them. She measured the loose tea leaves into the spoon-shaped silver holders and placed them in the small teacups. In no time, the kettle whistled, and Maya was handing a steaming cup of tea to Susannah, who had dropped into one of the gold wingback chairs. She had dark rings of smudged mascara beneath her eyes.

"Is it the same kind of thing? Is she like Clara?" Susannah asked. She held the teacup in both hands but did not drink from it.

"Susannah," Maya said, sipping the floral-tasting tea, "Blossom is fine. She is healthy. She loves music and she smiles whenever she hears it."

"The guide, that Elvis, he said there was no problem," Susannah said.

Fear had no logic. Maya understood this. In the ambulance that raced her and her baby to the hospital in Honolulu, she had thought that if she could just hold her daughter, she could save her life. She had believed that if she promised God things—to give up her work, to feed the poor, to go to church—Maile would live. None of it made sense. Her daughter died from head injuries sustained in a fall from her arms, and no amount of bargains or mother's love could change that.

Maya said, "This baby is fine. And you will love her and be a wonderful mother to her. I know this, Susannah."

When Susannah cried, relief washed over her like the sun coming out.

After she left, still tearful but ready now for what lay ahead, Maya opened the heavy draperies and watched as the sun struggled to break through the haze of pollution and clouds that hung over the city.

In five hours, a woman would call Maya's name and when Maya stepped forward, a baby would be put into her arms. Her own fear rose inside her now. How tightly could she hold a baby in her arms? She did not doubt that she would love her daughter. Maya knew the enormous love a mother felt. But she worried now, watching the city below her come to life, that knowing what children could do to your heart, how could she hold another one? Brave friend, Emily had called her. Maya did not feel brave this morning. Instead, like Susannah—perhaps like each of the women waiting in these hotel rooms—she feared falling in love again.

THE FAMILIES FILLED the empty cribs with soft hand-knit blankets brought from home, and stuffed dogs and bunnies and pigs. They dared to unpack the baby clothes they had so lovingly chosen back when this day seemed impossibly far away, and to place them neatly in a dresser drawer. They placed baby powder and diaper rash cream and No More Tears shampoo on the bathroom counter, and put soft sponges shaped like ducks and monogrammed pink towels beside them. They lined up copies of *Goodnight Moon* and *I Love You Like Crazy Cakes* on the bureau, and lay out toys: toys that played Mozart and toys with wheels and toys that had Big Bird pop out from them. The families prepared the hotel rooms for their babies. Then they prepared themselves. Dressed in their Sunday best, they triple-checked their video camera batteries and their diaper bags. They primped and they checked and they straightened until there was nothing left to do but leave this room and get in the elevator and go to the lobby where the others would be waiting. They would all get on the bus and take their usual seats and drive through these clogged streets into their future.

In her dual role of mother-to-be and head of the Red Thread Adoption Agency, Maya did all of these things and also packed her briefcase with the paperwork for the head of the orphanage and the papers each person would sign when they accepted their baby. If she focused on that role, Maya thought, perhaps she would not shake so much. Perhaps she would gain confidence. Perhaps this would really go well.

The bus was unusually silent. The air was filled with the constant smell of exhaust that permeated the air here and a mix of everyone's perfumes.

"Fifteen-minute ride," Elvis said from his perch at the front of the bus. His pompadour gleamed blue-black. "Then inside city hall to waiting room. Then"—he paused, grinning a wide grin—"then into room where babies are waiting for mommies and daddies."

To Maya, it seemed the entire bus held its breath. She forced herself to breathe.

In front of her, she saw the tops of Nell and Benjamin's heads, bent toward each other.

Benjamin had called Maya the day the referrals came. He was scheduled to leave for Sardinia to sail that very next weekend. "She's healthy, right?" he'd asked Maya. "And adorable?" When she told him yes, she was healthy and adorable, Maya added, "And she's yours."

"And I thought I wanted to sail around the world," he'd said.

Now, Maya heard him say in a calm, soothing voice, "Remember on our first date, all we could talk about was *The Great Gatsby*?

Remember how much we love that book? And we said that very night in the unlikely event that we ended up married we would name our first baby after one of the characters in it?"

"Tell me again," Nell said in a low voice.

"You wore a black cashmere coat. And red lipstick. We went to Casa Romero in Boston and you ate all of my pork. We drank too many margaritas and talked about *The Great Gatsby*. The entire evening, all I could think about was how I could convince you to go out with me again."

"Not true," Nell said, laughing softly.

"Don't be afraid," Benjamin said.

Maya felt all of their fear, though. It rose up from them and mixed with the exhaust and perfume. She had had a baby before, and what she felt now—what they all felt—was no different from the way she felt as she and Adam raced to the hospital to have their baby. Then, as now, fear and love and hope overtook everything else. Until the moment they handed her daughter to her nine hours later. In that moment, everything settled into one thing: a mother's love. There was nothing like it. Nothing. It was made up of all the other emotions, fear and dread and anxiety and hope and joy and faith. Maya wondered if it would be the same when this baby was handed to her. Could she feel it twice? Could she love this baby, this stranger?

The bus pulled in front of a nondescript cinderblock building.

"Let's go, mommies and daddies," Elvis said.

With the pneumatic opening of the door, the atmosphere changed and everyone turned from somber to giddy. In that building, their babies were waiting for them. They rushed from the bus, following Elvis's shiny blue jacket into city hall, up a flight of stairs, and into the waiting room.

Emily and Michael each hooked an arm into Maya's and walked with her.

"Our daughters are going to be friends forever," Emily said.

Michael said, "Think of it, Maya. Slumber parties and tea parties and visits to Santa. Beatrice and Honor side by side."

If her friends were not moving her forward, Maya did not think she would keep going. Because being here with the expectant faces of these people around her and the distant sound of babies crying, Maya realized that she could not do it. She could not risk loving another baby. She could not fall from that great height again.

Emily was spinning a future now in which their daughters became best friends and Maya and Emily grew old together. She was talking about first steps, losing baby teeth, learning to ride bikes. Maya's steps slowed, but Emily and Michael urged her into that room.

She watched Sophie and Theo giggling together and Benjamin taking a video of everyone waiting there and Nell applying lipstick and Carter videotaping Benjamin videotaping.

"I can't," Maya said. She thought she said it out loud, but no one heard her. Emily did not let go of her arm.

The door swung open and Elvis grinned his wide grin and said, "Your babies are ready for you." He stepped aside so that the parents could rush out.

"I can't do this," Maya said.

Someone else took her arm and looked her right in the eye.

"We can do it," Susannah said. "Come with me. We'll go in there together. And we will hold our daughters and we will love them fiercely."

Somehow Maya's feet moved, one in front of the other, down that long corridor, Susannah's hand firmly in her own.

Somehow she walked into the conference room where the aunties—the caretakers from the orphanage—stood erect, each with a baby in her arms.

The orphanage director stood in the middle of the room with a clipboard in her hands. Her face had too much powder on it. There was a smudge of lipstick on her front tooth.

Without any opening remarks, she said, "Mr. and Mrs. Walker-Adams."

Confused, Nell and Benjamin stepped forward. Carter videotaped their every move as one of the aunties handed them their baby.

QUICKLY, EACH NAME was called, and each couple stepped forward. The babies were dressed in double pairs of threadbare footie pajamas. They looked surprised as the auntie put first Jordan, then Blossom and Ella and Beatrice safely in their mothers' arms.

Then she heard her own name called. "Maya Lange."

"I can't," she said.

Emily and Susannah and Sophie and even Nell surrounded her, their babies already settled into their arms.

Maya opened her arms.

An auntie nodded at her. She stepped toward Maya. She held a baby in purple pajamas. The auntie placed that baby in Maya's arms, then stepped away.

Maya held her breath. She looked into her daughter's eyes. Her daughter looked back.

A calm came over Maya, the same feeling she'd had when they'd handed Maile to her nine years earlier in Honolulu.

"Hello daughter," she whispered.

EPILOGUE

On the flight home ten days later, the families moved up and down the aisles of the 747, comparing their babies. Which one cried too much at night. Which one liked to eat shrimp. Which one had already started to stand up. These were their children, and they were proud and proprietary.

In the airport that morning, Maya had paused to say a silent thank-you to the brave women who had dared to leave their daughters in the hope that there would be a life for them somewhere, that they would be loved and nurtured. For Maya in particular, as a mother who had lost a child, she could not begin to express what she felt for the woman she would never know who had lost a daughter too. But through that loss, Maya was finding herself again.

Maya stood among the beaming new parents and their daughters and said, "These mothers gave us a gift, but they will never know how grateful we are."

"I hope they know," Emily said. "I hope that somewhere deep inside them they do know what they've done for us."

Now, Maya sat with her daughter on her lap, and watched the families. All of them, happy.

What she could not see were the families they were leaving behind as China disappeared and the ocean stretched before them. The woman, already pregnant again, staring out a window and wondering where the daughters she'd abandoned were now. Were they safe? she wondered. Were they loved? While Emily rubbed the baby's nose against her own and the baby laughed, a new baby rolled and kicked in its mother's belly. *I am here, Mother,* it seemed to be saying. *Do not look back. Only look forward.* Still, every day of her life, she did look back, and worried over her lost daughters.

Or the young girl, her daughter nestled here on Nell's lap, walking down a dusty road with two sweet potatoes in her basket, staring into an empty field hoping for a glimpse of a young man who had gone to Beijing without her.

Or the mother playing with her daughter, laughing with her, even as she ached for the girl's twin sister. That baby had been weak and small, but in Susannah's arms she looked healthy, her cheeks rosy, her eyes bright. The woman wondered: Did she survive? Somewhere deep inside her did she also ache for her sister and her mother who had loved her?

Or the mother who went every Saturday into Loudi, and walked the streets of the city and the pathways of the park, clutching a photograph of the daughter who was snatched from her but today slept so soundly in Theo's arms. *Have you seen a baby who looks like this?* she asked people she passed and store clerks and street cleaners. They all shrugged and looked away. *A beautiful baby,* she told them. *A happy baby. My baby.*

And Maya could not see the grief-stricken man at his desk

in his office at the university, crying for his dead wife and the daughter he had left at the orphanage doorstep. Crying even as he prayed that his daughter had somehow found her way to America, when at this moment, pressed close to Maya, that daughter was indeed on her way to America.

The plane reached 40,000 feet, high above the clouds. The babies grew sleepy. Maya held her sleeping daughter across her lap. Before she left the White Swan Hotel in Guanzhou this morning, Maya had called Jack. "I understand if you don't want to see me again," she told him. "But Honor and I land at Logan tomorrow night at ten o'clock. I would like you to be there." Unbelievably, Jack had said, "I will be there."

The sun shimmered outside the plane, sending bright light through the windows. In that light, Maya almost saw it, that red thread, tangled and curved, connecting each baby to their mother. She blinked. The red thread glimmered and then slowly disappeared. No matter how knotted or tangled it became, at the end of it was the child you were meant to have.

ACKNOWLEDGMENTS

In 2005, three years after our daughter Grace died, my husband Lorne, our son Sam, and I traveled to Changsha, China, in Hunan Province, to bring home our baby girl, Annabelle. I have many people to thank for helping us on our journey, but first and foremost are Lorne and Sam. Also, my mother Gloria Hood, Aunt June, Aunt Dora and Uncle Chuck, my niece Melissa Hood, my mother-in-law Lorraine Adrain, and my cousins Gina Caycedo and Gloria-Jean Masciarotte, who, in many ways, traveled this path with us. Our adoption was made possible through China Adoption with Love in Brookline, Massachusetts, and I have endless gratitude to its director, Lillian, and our social worker there, Stephanie. Thanks too to Sharon Ingendahl, Amy Green, Mary Sloane, Coral Bourgeois, the Thachers (Sarah, Andrew, and Olivia), Ned and Polly Handy, Helen Schulman, Tracey Minkin, Frances Carpenter, Lisa Van Allsburg, Nancy Compton, and Lisa Van Adlesburg, who all helped us in some way to get to China and welcomed our family home. The comfort given to us by Matt Davies, Faith Pine, and Dan Moseley is appreciated and never forgotten.

The adoption stories in this novel are a work of fiction, all given birth in my imagination. For background about China and its abandoned daughters I read *The Lost Daughters of China* by Karin Evans and *Wanting a Daughter, Needing a Son* by Kay Ann Johnson. In China, we traveled with ten families who also brought home daughters, and I wish to thank them for sharing this time in their life with us. A special thank-you to the Sitrins—Steven, Laura, and Shira—who continue to celebrate with us. Kerrie Hoban and Mary Hector helped me by giving me the space in which to write this book. As always, a thank-you to my extraordinary agent, Gail Hochman, and my wise and generous editor, Jill Bialosky. And to Erin Lovett, Marianne Merola, Joanne Brownstein, Maya Zin, Jody Klein, and Adrienne Davich, who all work tirelessly in my behalf. Finally, in memory of my daughter, Grace. Always.